Undercover in San Diego

Donna Del Oro

Published by eXtasy Books Inc, 2025.

Table of Contents

In lovely, sunny San Diego, FBI agent Jake Bernstein and his girlfriend Meg discover a web of murder, military espionage, and terror.

A WEB OF TERROR AND espionage emerges as the investigation of a murder unfolds. Two seemingly unrelated crimes—a gay female Navy officer is murdered, and a Muslim mother is beaten and almost killed—take place within twenty-four hours of each other. Are both women the targets of hate crimes?

FBI agent Jake Bernstein is recruited to help Naval Crime Investigators uncover the truth about the Navy officer's murder. What he and his girlfriend, Meg Larsen, discover is a plot of evil that strangely intersects with the Muslim woman's case and threatens them all. For even in sunny San Diego, you never know where danger lies.

About the Jake Bernstein FBI Thriller series, NY Times bestselling author Brenda Novak says, "...this intriguing romantic thriller series combines politics, romance, mystery...and captivating action."

Undercover In San Diego
Copyright © 2025 Donna Del Oro
ISBN: 978-1-4874-4328-3
Cover art by Martine Jardin

Published by eXtasy Books Inc

Look for us online at:
www.eXtasybooks.com

Undercover In San Diego
Jake Bernstein FBI Thriller – Book 3

By

Donna Del Oro

Dedication

I dedicate this novel to my family and friends who have encouraged me over the years to tell my stories. I'm truly grateful for your faith and confidence in me!

Acknowledgments:

ONE OF THE TWO MYSTERY subplots in this novel is based on a true crime story of the so-called *Muslim honor killing* that took place in Escondido, California, a couple of years ago. When I read about it in a newspaper, I almost couldn't believe the story. I checked it out to make sure it was true, and it was. It's remarkable and perplexing to me that the news media tend to underplay the Muslim male-on-female violence in this country, but the FBI is all too aware of this growing problem. In the Escondido case, the mother was killed, and her daughter finally overcame her fear and exposed her father, his pals, and their jihadist plot. In court, his defense was his belief in Sharia Law. He's now serving 25-to-life. Sometimes, the truth is stranger than fiction.

The second subplot is based on a declassified CIA report that focused on the number of Chinese nationals who come to this country as foreign students but who actually double as spies for their country. The numbers are astonishing! And the West Coast Navy bases are sometimes targets of this military espionage. The Navy is aware of this and, of course, takes precautions.

Chapter One

SAN DIEGO, CALIFORNIA

Tuesday, January 3

Sarah Daoud's father revved his car's engine. As if in response to her father's impatience, her mother's footsteps clacked on the concrete walkway. Within moments, her parents were gone.

Time to act.

Sarah held her cell phone up to her ear and said two words. "Let's go."

Making sure she had her house key in her right pocket, Sarah opened the front door and ran to the curb just as her friend Marsha pulled up. Sarah chuckled and continued speaking into the phone, which she still held to her ear. "That was fast!"

Marsha—Sarah's best friend since they attended El Cajon High School—broke out laughing as she steered her old Volkswagen Caddy back onto the street. Sarah joined in the laughter but swiftly sobered. She and Marsha were on a secret mission.

Ten minutes later, Sarah's father's car stopped outside the southern entry to San Diego City College. Her mother walked up the steps and disappeared through the double-door entrance. A moment later, her father drove away. Sarah believed he would head to his regular Tuesday meeting with men from his mosque. Her father, patrons from his restaurant, and some longtime friends from Iran met and discussed the Qur'an, then held their evening prayers. Sarah had never thought to question whether that was really what her father did on Tuesday nights. She'd always believed her father, a devout Muslim, would not lie.

Sarah wished she could be devout, but as her father often said disparagingly, she was too American. Her mother, Sarah suspected, was also too American.

This was why Sarah and Marsha were on this stakeout. Spying on her mother's Tuesday night activities had been her father's idea. Sarah felt rotten. Disgusted. Afraid. But she never said no to her father, something her mother, Fatimah Daoud, sometimes did.

Sarah and Marsha kept their attention on the entrance from their spot in the parking lot. After just a few minutes, Sarah's mother rushed down the steps. When Fatimah headed for the parking lot, she and Marsha ducked down. After a few seconds, she dared to peek over the back of her seat.

She gasped when she saw Fatimah whip off her *hijab* and jump into the passenger seat of a black Honda sedan. Sarah couldn't see the driver, and her heart sank and raced with fear.

Her mother had lied to her family.

"Do you want to follow her?" Marsha inched up in her seat, her hand already on the ignition key.

Sarah nodded solemnly. Her eyes filled with hot, bitter tears.

"Maybe she's having dinner with a friend," Marsha said. "My mother does that at least once a week. Usually when Dad plays poker or has buddies over for football."

That was not possible for Fatimah. She worked every day at the family's restaurant in East San Diego and had no time for friends outside their immediate circle, unlike Sarah, who'd been born in America and had made friends at school. Sarah's father controlled every aspect of her mother's life. He had been born and raised in Iran and couldn't accept the American ways. Her mother, born in Egypt, had become more American, too, right under her father's watchful gaze.

Sarah and Marsha followed the black sedan down Main Street, southward to the harbor district. Along the boulevard, restaurants and specialty stores dotted the piers. Along the wharf was a replica of an old seventeenth-century sailing schooner, a few modern charter fishing and sightseeing boats, and the ferries to Coronado Island. An old Navy aircraft carrier took up the largest berth among them and eclipsed all the others by its sheer size.

The Honda turned into the small parking lot directly across the boulevard from a café. Wrenching her neck, Sarah noted the name. *The Amazons.*

"Maybe she's going into that café. Want me to keep circling the block?"

Sarah shook her head. "No, I think I know what's going on. Mama'll stay until just before her class ends, then head back to City College. She'll pretend she was in class the whole time. How jacked is that?" Her emotions spilled over. "Why lie? Who is she meeting? Why is she doing this?"

Marsha pointed to the café. "See that sign for the place next door to the café? The Lido? My older brother told me it's a gay and lesbian club. Y'know, where they come to meet each other, hang out, dance. Gross, huh? The café, he said, is owned by the same women who own the club. Everyone knows about this place. It's, like, famous. Gay tourists go there. Straights go there, too, to check out the gays, I guess." She preened a little as she revealed this information.

"Turn around," Sarah said suddenly. "Drive by that café again."

"Sure."

Marsha took three more lefts to return to the boulevard. She slowed the car to a crawl, ignoring the honks from the car behind her. Sarah craned her neck and stared through the café's front picture window but saw no sign of her mother. Marsha drove by one more time while Sarah bit back tears. Marsha's look of pity made her feel ashamed.

"Let's go," Sarah said. "My little brother might get suspicious. I told him we were going to the store, but we're taking too long."

"I'm sorry," Marsha said. "We won't say anything, okay? I promise not to say a word. To anyone." She made a crossing gesture over her heart, then brightened a little as she sped down the boulevard. Her look of pity morphed into an encouraging smile. "This is kinda fun in a totally scary way. Exciting, too. Totally. Like, it reminds me of the Nancy Drew books I used to read."

Sarah flashed her friend an ironic look. *You don't know how scary this really is.*

NAVY LIEUTENANT SAMANTHA Carlton watched two women enter the café, examples of total contrast. The dark-haired woman, probably in her mid-thirties, was petite and pretty, her long hair smoothly captured by a barrette at the nape. She had the darker complexion of a Latina or Middle Eastern woman.

The older woman was tall, broad-shouldered, husky, and plain of face. If they were a couple, the older woman was the butch, the pretty, younger one the femme. But the way the pretty one ducked her head shyly on her way to the conference room in back, Sam doubted they were together. Samantha thought she recognized the big, plain one—one of Lonnie's Amazonian friends. The pretty one was probably a straight woman coming for free counseling, a service the owners provided for women of all sexual persuasions. Whatever the need, they offered it. Discreetly, free of charge, and always on Tuesday and Thursday evenings. Whether the woman was an abused wife, a single mother facing eviction, or a gay or transgender female in search of identity, Lonnie and her friends would help.

Sam didn't need counseling. In fact, this was her first time at The Amazons on a Tuesday night. She'd usually have dinner in the restaurant on Saturday nights before heading to the club next door that catered to the GLBT crowd to blow off steam and meet girlfriends or, as she preferred to call them, wives for the night.

That had all changed one night three months ago when she met Xing at the club. Gorgeous Xing Lee Chung. A foreign graduate student in electrical engineering at San Diego State University. They had locked gazes over their drinks and shared an instant connection.

Xing had adopted the American name Sheila. The *X* in her name was pronounced like the *sh* sound, so Sheila was a close enough approximation. Sam had found both names charming and Xing's body heavenly to explore. Their personalities had meshed, too—Sam calm and reserved, Xing the outgoing type.

Xing had begun staying overnight a few weeks after that first meeting and was planning to move into Sam's condo on Coronado Island. Maybe things were moving too fast, but hell, they were in love. That's what lesbians did when they fell in love. They tried out domestic life together. Besides, Sam was forty-two, single, a career Navy officer who spent months each year on overseas tours of duty. That she'd met Xing while stateside was a gift from the gods.

Fuck it, she was lonely, lonelier than she'd ever been in her entire life. Excruciatingly lonely. If they worked out together, Xing could apply for a work visa and get on the citizenship track. Maybe they could settle down together...maybe even marry someday.

A bubble of hope rose within her, and she beamed.

Sam downed the rest of her coffee. Xing was late. The thought registered just as her pager buzzed. Damn. She was wanted back at the Naval base. Now what? She was off duty, but the other officers wouldn't bother her if it wasn't serious. Swearing under her breath, Sam picked up her cell phone and punched in Xing's number. The call went straight to voice mail. Sam frowned. What the hell? Xing always kept her phone on.

She couldn't wait any longer. She'd keep calling Xing while she drove back to the Navy base. She sent a brief text...

Where are you?

Leaving a five-dollar bill on the table, she waved to her server and scurried out the front door.

Sam had taken the precaution of parking behind the building, reluctant to have her distinctive car noticed by one of her shipmates. Reserved mostly for staff, the parking lot behind the café was hidden from Harbor Boulevard and afforded more privacy. Lisa and Lonnie, who understood her need for discretion, had given her permission to do so long ago since Naval officers had to be cautious.

The lights on Sam's new Cadillac XTS, courtesy of her wealthy father, flashed when she punched the remote. She pressed the trunk button until it popped open. A little silver-foiled wrapped box, a gift of jewelry for Xing, lay inside the trunk. Extravagant, maybe, but Sam had wanted to surprise her. She gently placed the gift inside her black nylon garment bag, which held her uniform. Her officer's cap and government-issued ankle boots rested in a cardboard box next to her uniform. She'd change in the women's locker room on base before boarding the ship.

Suddenly, heavy footsteps crunched on the gravel-topped parking lot. An alarm went off inside Sam's head, and she stiffened. She opened her mouth to scream.

Too late. Muscular arms seized Sam from behind, and a needle punctured the side of her neck. She fought wildly, using her legs for leverage against the rear bumper of her car. Whoever held her was larger and stronger—*much* larger and stronger—than her five-foot-six, one-hundred-and-thirty-pound frame.

Sam couldn't scream because the attacker's right arm pinned her neck in a suffocating headlock. She clawed at the arms, head, hair, and anything she could reach, even slapped where the attacker's head had been but met only air. She fought with all her might until the drug took effect, making her legs give out and her arms fell limp.

In the moment before she lost consciousness, all her muscles went slack, and her thoughts shrank to pinpoint thoughts of Xing and how happy she'd been with her gorgeous girlfriend.

A split second later, her heart seized in her chest.

Chapter Two

SAN DIEGO

Friday, January 6

Jake rolled over in bed and opened one eye. He touched Meg's shoulder, then ran his fingers down the curve of her back, tracing the cinch of her small waist down to the flair of her naked hips. He smiled and snuggled up behind her, spooning her and molding his groin to the soft cushion of her derriere.

She stirred and sleepily murmured something unintelligible, then whispered, "You're back."

"Yep, took the red-eye from Dulles. Got back as fast as I could. Three days of debriefing at HQ was all I could take. God, I missed you."

He waited for her to return the requisite *I missed you, too.* During the lengthy silence, self-doubt seeped into his psyche, not for the first time since he'd hooked up with Meg Larsen nearly seven months ago. He had no doubts about their physical acts of making love, but he felt unsure about their emotional status. His fault? Probably. But he couldn't understand what he might've done to make her angry or wary.

He sighed. This was what happened when he broke his first rule, *don't get emotionally involved.* He'd broken that rule that first night of lovemaking back in Ireland while he'd been undercover, investigating Meg's grandmother. Falling in love with the old Nazi spy's granddaughter wasn't in his life's plans, but—what do they say?—life happens when you're busy trying to avoid it.

Meg rolled onto her side. Jake pressed his arousal against her side, but she inched away so their naked bodies no longer touched. In the darkness of her bedroom, her features were barely discernible, but the image of her loveliness was forever etched in his brain. He pictured her pursing her lips in disapproval.

"Jake, you said you'd be gone for four days. You were gone a week. What back in DC—what woman—kept you there so long? I want to know, and you've got to tell me. You owe me that much."

So that's it.

He suppressed a smile. Apparently, Meg was as insecure in their relationship as he was. He stroked the planes of her face, from her forehead to her cheekbones to her jawline. The cross-country flight had exhausted him, but he'd been too keyed up to sleep much. All he'd been able to think about was seeing Meg.

He leaned on his elbow to face her. "It took longer than I expected to get everything done. I had to debrief the Counterterrorism Division and then feed the details up the chain of command. All my superiors wanted their own questions answered. Then Quantico wanted a piece of me. I gave a sanitized rundown of the operation to two classes of CTD trainees, then renewed my marksmanship rating while I was there. Got together with my pal Eric to watch some football. Also saw a game with an HQ cop named Manny and his sons. My condo had plumbing problems, so I had to take care of that. I told you all this each time I called you. What's the story, Meg?" He added the last with a slight plea to his voice.

She flung her arms around his neck and pulled him down on top of her. A little huff escaped her pretty lips. "I'm sorry. Just forget it. I'm being a total ass." She raised her head and kissed him soundly.

"I get it." And he did because he needed the same reassurance from her. He nestled his throbbing groin between her open legs, their hip bones aligned with each other. He braced his weight on his forearms as he rubbed his chest against her breasts. "I got a promotion."

"I'm so proud of you, baby." She gave him a congratulatory kiss. "Are you getting a SAC position?"

Meg was picking up the FBI's verbal shorthand faster than he realized. Special Agent in Charge usually ran a field office or task force.

She smiled. "Wouldn't it be great if you took over the San Diego field office?"

"Not so fast. Those field office SAC jobs are seniority-based to some extent. I applied, but now I've got to wait for a vacancy to come up, which doesn't happen often. San Diego is a plum venue. I have to wait 'til the SAC retires or...dies, God forbid. But I got my SAC."

"What's your new title...I mean, your new mission?"

"In a month or two, I take over a CT task force." He felt her physically deflate. Being in charge of a counterterrorism task force meant being based in DC.

Meg stiffened a little. "When exactly do you start?"

"I report back to HQ February first. Heading a CT task force is a big step up from the analyst-in-the-field assignment."

"Really?"

"Yes, really. My boss, Terry, says I'm on the fast track to an assistant deputy director assignment. Course, I've come close to being killed several times to make it this far. I guess I've been lucky. All in all, not too shabby."

Thanks to one successful field investigation and one highly important undercover assignment a few months earlier in Silicon Valley. He and four other agents, working undercover in five cities, exposed a massive terrorist plot to blow up football stadiums and kill thousands. His nearly getting killed in November had played a vital role in his new promotion. The FBI liked that kind of dedication to the job.

Meg pulled his head down to nuzzle his face. "I know, and I'm proud of you, your skills, and your courage. You're a patriot in every sense of the word."

Jake heard the *but* in her voice.

Meg continued, "But, Jake, three weeks from now? That's so soon. Listen, I've got some insider info about the San Diego office."

"What do you mean?"

Meg's hair smelled like lavender and roses. A heady feeling began to flood his brain, threatening to misfire all his synapses. Rational thought began to wane.

"I dropped by to offer my services as a Special Support Group volunteer. Like Linda Brown does up in San Jose. They turned me down. Said I stood out too much for surveillance work."

"Sorry to hear that."

The FBI sometimes hired civilian specialists for their Special Support Groups, but Jake understood why they'd turn her down. Her looks were too striking, too much like a Hollywood starlet. Meg was tall, slim with a graceful bearing, and wore young, stylish clothes. No way could she blend into the background. Older women like Linda Brown made good tails because they were invisible to most men. He didn't have the heart to discourage Meg from trying, though.

"Anyway, I heard their SAC was going to retire or transfer to another office soon. One of the agents, the scuba diver who worked with me on that fake drowning last fall—Chuck's his name—he told me. Maybe next fall. So you might not have to wait long."

Damn. Jake knew Chuck, a former Navy man like himself. Single, good-looking, built like a running back. He had no doubt the guy would move in on Meg once he returned to DC. That is if he returned to DC without Meg.

The fake drowning had been a ruse Jake had pulled off in early November with the indispensable assistance of the FBI's San Diego field office. During that operation, he'd had to prove his loyalty to an Islamic terrorist cell by *killing* his American girlfriend. The fake drowning was a ballsy move, one of those bad ideas that was so over-the-top it had to work. Sure enough, it had. The San Diego agents had saved his ass and his operation, in the process, saving thousands of Americans from certain death. He owed the San Diego team. But not enough to turn Meg over to one of their agents.

"Right, I'll look into it," he said, even knowing getting a SAC position in San Diego was as likely as winning the lottery.

What if Meg refused to go with him to DC in three weeks? Then what? Would they call it quits? Would they attempt to keep their bi-coastal relationship going?

"So...no SSG surveillance training on your already full schedule," he said. "Does that mean you'll have time to take some side trips? Like going back to Catalina Island for some charter fishing?"

"I can't, Jake. My German classes at the university are in full swing. And..."

"And what?" He barely held back his disappointment.

"I agreed to do some tutoring for a few kids at El Cajon High School. Smart kids but under-achievers. They're having trouble with Spanish and French and just need a little extra help. Some of them are children of immigrants."

"What about a weekend?"

"Sure, I'll make time," she replied, her mouth against his ear. The playful swirl of her tongue sent shivers up and around his skull. "Oh, before I forget, Uncle John said to have you call him when you got back."

"Hmm, what's that about?" With growing impatience, he shifted a little and urgently deepened his kisses.

Her reply was a mumbled moan, cut short by a gasp as he thrust into her. "Hmm, later..."

Jake agreed. Any more catch-up news could wait.

BREAKFAST HAD COME too soon for Jake as he sat at Meg's kitchen table in his briefs and t-shirt, watching Meg scurry around him. Apparently determined to make her morning German Literature class at UC San Diego on time, she grabbed a piece of toast and stuffed an orange into her tote bag, which was already bulging with books and notebooks, then leaned over and gave him a smooch. He kissed her back and watched her run for the door.

"See you at five."

"Dinner's on me," he called out. "Italian, French, Chinese, Thai, Mexican?"

"Persian," Meg called back, already closing the front door.

Jake was proud that Meg took her graduate work at the University of California, San Diego seriously. She was on sabbatical from her high school teaching job just north of Dallas and working to add German to her teaching credential, with Spanish and French being her majors. Her sabbatical would end the coming summer, and she was scheduled to return to her high school teaching job in Frisco, Texas. Or resign and teach in San Diego.

Unless another plan intervened.

That possibility hung at the back of his mind. He had until the end of summer to talk Meg into uprooting her life a second time and moving with him to DC. He doubted she would go unless he proposed. The very idea scared him shitless. His record on that field was zero to one. The emotional scars from his first marriage ran deep, though no longer raw and bloody, thanks to Meg. She'd helped him heal. Still, the possible failure of another marriage left him reluctant to take his relationship with Meg to the next level.

Jake drank his black coffee to the dregs and cleaned up breakfast. An hour later, he drove his Ford rental down the hill in the opposite direction from the university campus. He headed toward Torrey Pines Golf Course with his new golf bag in the cargo hold. His badly sprained ankle had healed, though it was tender at times. He'd have to walk the Torrey Pines fairways with caution, wary of reinjuring the ankle on a divot or sprinkler hole. His scapula, or shoulder blade, where Hussein's bullet had torn through the muscle, would probably give him a twinge of pain whenever he swung his club. But these were discomforts he could handle.

Terry wanted Jake fully healed and in combat-ready physical shape for the assignment in DC, so he'd asked for and received longer medical leave. The extra month off was needed physically, and as it happened, it worked to his advantage personally. He needed the time to persuade Meg to follow him east when she finished her classes. The possibility of leaving Meg and paradise behind didn't sit well with him.

On the other hand, mending his body would get boring. In truth, he looked forward to getting back to work. Almost on cue, his cell phone buzzed. He punched the button for the car's hands-free connection.

"Jake, welcome back." Rear Admiral Snider's gruff baritone boomed through the speakers. John Snider, Meg's uncle, commanded a newly commissioned destroyer, the USS Dixie, stationed at the San Diego Naval Air Station, the anchor base for eight military installations. "I have a favor to ask of you."

"Just ask, Admiral. I've got nothing right now on my plate."

"Well, it's a tall order. You may have plans with Meg..."

"No plans for the immediate future. What can I do for you?"

"I'd like you to meet with one of our NCI teams, see if you can help them. Offer another point of view, a fresh pair of eyes."

"A Navy Crime Investigation team? What's the crime?"

"Murder. One of the officers on my ship. I think an objective look is needed."

"What happened to him?"

"Her. Lieutenant Samantha Carlton was found dead in the trunk of her car three days ago. The preliminary tox screen showed nothing, but the lab did an advanced analysis. She'd been poisoned with ketamine. Made her heart stop.

She was forty-one and in excellent physical condition. Also, someone crushed her larynx and windpipe."

"Sounds like a case of overkill." Jake rubbed the underside of his chin from force of habit. The GPS microchip the FBI techs had inserted during his last undercover op was gone, but the tiny scar still irritated him, especially when he shaved. "However, the ketamine doesn't fit. This sounds premeditated, made to look like a crime of passion or rage. That'd be my off-the-cuff assessment. Someone wasn't counting on the advanced tox screen."

"Good, now we're getting somewhere," Admiral Snider said. "The local cops are pushing the NCI team in one direction. Their theory doesn't hold water. They claim it was a hate crime."

"Hate crime? How?"

A heavy sigh came through the car's speaker. "Her car was found behind The Amazons. It's owned by the same group of women who own The Lido, a nightclub next door known for its gay and lesbian clientele. Do you know the place?"

"No, should I?"

"Just thought Meg might've pointed the place out to you. It's across the street from Pier Five, where the bay cruise ships are moored. Anyway, the local police believe that a hate group is on a campaign to drive homosexuals out of the city. They've vandalized some businesses in the area and even gone up to La Jolla and Oceanside and left their calling cards. But this murder would be a first."

"You don't agree with San Diego PD, Admiral?" Jake probed.

"Something smells rotten, if you know what I mean. Also, her military-issued shoes were taken out of her trunk. Lieutenant Carlton always carried her uniform and shoes in her car in case of a sudden call-up to base. The night she was killed, we had an emergency drill. The officers had been told to expect one that week, and it is protocol to carry your uniform and shoes at all times. Stealing her shoes doesn't make sense, though. She was wearing diamond studs and a watch worth thousands, yet the killer left the jewelry and took her shoes? See what I mean?"

"Yeah. What does the NCI team think?"

"Same as I do, Jake. Something smells fishy."

Jake pulled into the parking lot of Torrey Pines and passed under the porte-cochere entrance to the clubhouse, waving off the valets, and drove just beyond the clubhouse, stopping at the curb. He stared out at the rolling emerald green fairways that hosted the likes of Tiger Woods and Ernie Els every year. He kept the engine going.

"When do you need me?" Jake asked, only mildly intrigued by the case. He realized, however, it wouldn't hurt to ingratiate himself with the man. More than just a Navy admiral—and Jake was former Navy—John Snider was Meg's family. He was the father she'd never had.

"In an hour. If you can make it. I can have the NCI team meet you at the crime scene. They can run through their facts with you while doing some second-round interviews. Afterward, they're giving a briefing to the local cops at the station on Coronado Island. Your observations will lend credence to their briefing, whichever way it goes. You're a good investigator. Just use your skills. Can I tell them to expect you?"

Well, so much for working on my golf game. Jake glanced back at the clubhouse and sighed. *The fairways will still be there tomorrow.*

But how could he refuse a Navy admiral after such praise? "Tell the NCI guys I'll be there. Behind The Amazons, across from Pier Five. Got it."

"Thanks, Jake. I owe you."

Good, because he planned to collect when the time came.

Chapter Three

JAKE PULLED INTO THE rear parking lot of The Amazons and noticed the two NCI investigators—male and female in their twenties. Both were slim, fit, and carrying briefcases—dressed in casual khaki shirts and trousers, each sporting one star and a single yellow strip on their epaulets. The young, serious officers were huddled together by the rear bumper of a black Toyota Camry. The male investigator approached him and extended his hand. With his black hair, dark brown eyes, and deep tan, he looked Hispanic.

"Ensign Javier Blanco, Agent Bernstein. This is Ensign Mary Lou Taylor." Javier indicated the African American woman, who stepped forward and also offered her hand. She looked almost frightened, her eyes rimmed in red as though she'd been crying.

Jake blew air through his teeth. No wonder the admiral has asked him to help out. These two Navy investigators looked young and inexperienced, yet here they were, investigating a murder that the commander had already assessed as not a run-of-the-mill hate crime. With the swagger and bluster that local homicide dicks were known for, the cops would mow down any dissenting opinions that came from these two.

Jake shook hands and exchanged pleasantries with the ensigns, filling in his background with the Navy SEALs and with undercover FBI investigations. Ensign Blanco's black hair was cut Marine-butch style, and the mention of SEALs snapped him to attention. Jake asked for a summary briefing while they walked him to the crime scene halfway down the alley. The victim's car had already been towed, but crime scene chalk outlining the vehicle was still visible at the site.

Ensign Taylor read from her notebook in an accent that bore a slight Southern drawl. "Lieutenant Carlton's car was a 2013 Cadillac XTS. It's impounded in the Navy storage yard on base. It was discovered, trunk closed, Wednesday, the morning of January fourth, at exactly oh-six-hundred, when one of the owners of The Amazons—a Lonnie Pezzerella—arrived to open up. She knew the car belonged to Lieutenant Carlton because the woman was a regular at both the café and the nightclub next door. Ms. Pezzerella said she called the Navy base but was told Lieutenant Carlton was AWOL. She reported the lieutenant's car in her back alley and then called the local San Diego Police, who called us on base. They reported that the smell of decomp hadn't set in, but the cops first on the scene had popped the trunk and found the lieutenant's body. We arrived soon afterward."

Ensign Taylor took a moment to compose herself before continuing. "Lieutenant Carlton is—I mean, *was* an exemplary officer. Always on time for duty calls, had an excellent record, and had deployed on eight missions in the Pacific and four missions in the Arabian Sea. She did occasional stints on base. Not a single blemish on her record."

Jake nodded, studying the rear of the buildings that housed the café and the nightclub. There was no alley between the two buildings. Their brick façades were worn, probably dating back over fifty years. The alley behind the joined buildings was immaculate, completely devoid of litter. Even the large trash bins bore clean exteriors. Not a place where homeless or druggies would hang out and feel at home. On either side of the chalk outline were more diagonal lines painted on the gravelly asphalt, where Jake presumed employees parked.

"We examined the body, sir, and..." Ensign Taylor swallowed hard. "Rigor had begun. The Medical Examiner verified the TOD at about nine p.m. The waitress on duty that night in the café knew Lieutenant Carlton and said she left around eight-fifty-five. The lieutenant checked her cell phone, paid for her coffee, and left. She went out the front entrance and must have circled around to the back, where her car was parked. She must've been attacked almost immediately."

Ensign Blanco took over when his partner, finally overcome with emotion, mashed her lips and turned aside. "Sorry, sir. Mary Lou knew Sam fairly well. All of us—well, we are all shocked and torn up. The way she was killed got to us." He straightened his shoulders, gathering himself to his full height of maybe five-ten. Even so, the young man had to look up to meet Jake's eyes. "COD, crushed windpipe. Suffocation. Or so we thought... After the advanced tox came back, we were blown away. Special K, ketamine, a street drug used to relax muscles, renders the victim defenseless. It's sometimes used by date rapists. She had enough in her to stop her heart, injected at the base of her neck near her descending carotid artery. She suffocated first, then went into cardiac arrest."

Jake nodded. "The overkill by ketamine doesn't make sense, not if this was a hate crime. Ketamine poisoning is a Russian spy trademark."

Ensign Blanco's dark gaze met his partner's, then lasered into Jake's. "Our thinking, exactly, Agent Bernstein. Hate crimes are usually committed with guns, knives, cars, or bludgeoning instruments. They're usually impulsive acts committed with or without direct, personal provocation. A syringe loaded with ketamine takes planning. Perps who act out hate crimes are usually cowards who prefer to act in groups. Whoever attacked her was big and strong. Sam was not a large woman. Her file indicates she was five-six, close to one hundred and thirty pounds—not petite but slim. She had self-defense training, so she was no stranger to close-quarters combat. There was evidence of a hell of a struggle, too. Her back bumper was dented. She must have kicked like crazy to get free." He slowly shook his head.

"Call me Jake," he said. "I'm consulting informally as a favor to Admiral Snider, so please, just Jake."

Ensign Taylor collected herself before continuing her report. "Okay, sir. Sam was a fighter. The lab techs found fabric under her nails where she must've clawed the arms of the attacker. The lab identified it as a synthetic, a mix of polyester and spandex used in workout and running outfits. We think the perp was a very big man in gym clothes who maybe gave the impression he was jogging by and took the alley as a shortcut. In case he was spotted. A killer for hire? Tracking her until he got the opportunity?"

Ensign Blanco jumped back in. "Also, the forensic field techs extracted a single strand of hair. The genetic markers indicated Asian or Asian-Caucasian mixture."

Jake's pulse sped up. That was a real break. "Hmm, Asian or part Asian. Interesting. Not your usual hate-crime perp."

Ensign Blanco nodded. "There's more. Admiral Snider said he'd already told you that the lieutenant's shoes had been taken. They left the jewelry and expensive watch she was wearing. Plus, we found a wrapped box inside her garment bag, a pair of diamond earrings worth close to five thousand dollars recently bought at Worth's Fine Jewelry store at the mall.. According to the salesman who sold them to Sam, they were a gift for her girlfriend. To quote the guy, *She was excited and anxious that her girlfriend would love them.* He had the impression the gift was for a very special occasion, maybe on the level of an engagement or commitment gift. He knew Sam was gay, he said."

Ensign Taylor broke in, "A bigoted killer who takes her Navy-issue shoes but leaves behind all that bling? Even the car? The killer had access to her car keys. He took her purse—a wallet-sized thing, according to the waitress—and her cell phone, too. So why leave the jewelry behind and take her ID, credit cards, and her phone? Doesn't make sense."

Jake nodded, impressed with the two young ensigns. They obviously had some experience with crime investigation and were also critical thinkers. "He probably didn't have the time to do a more thorough search. Maybe he was looking for something. Maybe he takes shoes as trophies of his kills. "Were there shoes on her bod—" He amended his question. "Was she wearing shoes when you found her?"

"Yes. Casual shoes, black flats. She had on blue jeans and a red sweater."

Jake squatted down to examine where the rear of the car would have been. "Put a trace on the lieutenant's cell phone. Let's see her contacts, personal and otherwise. Any blood drops around her car?"

"No, sir," Ensign Blanco said. "Scuff marks on the ground, very faint. No footprints."

Jake stood up. "Okay, I want copies of all your interviews, every single one. Her co-workers, her social friends—here and elsewhere." He looked directly at Ensign Taylor. "A Navy officer with a sterling record killed behind a gay-lesbian hangout. There might be a connection...might not. Might have been a set-up to make it look like there was a connection. If this murder was premeditated, why kill her here? Why not closer to her home? Whoever did this was prepared. Also, I want her service record file. Her work duties. Admiral Snider'll approve it."

"Certainly. We already have copies for you in this folder." Ensign Taylor handed him a thick, navy blue envelope with the US Navy insignia in gold and sealed shut with a large gold star. "Would you like to speak with Lonnie Pezzerella? She's in the café right now. We called her, so she's expecting us."

Jake followed the two young NCIs as they walked down a long, spotless corridor that ran from the rear of the café to the front. Inside, the sales counter, stools, and tables took up most of the public space. The décor depicted comic book superheroes, including framed posters on walls painted primary colors. The place was bustling with customers, male and female. Lunchtime, of course. The staff consisted of two servers—tall women in their thirties or forties. At the back of the café was a hallway with doors leading to supply rooms, a busy kitchen with three female cooks, customer restrooms, a staff break room, and a surprisingly large conference room.

They entered the conference room, where an older woman was waiting. Jake took a seat at the long, wooden table that had chairs for eight. The two ensigns joined him and introduced the woman who sat at the head of the table. Her expression showed a mixture of what Jake interpreted to be sorrow and anger—anger perhaps at the intrusion on such short notice and during a busy time of day for her café. Jake estimated her age to be mid to late fifties.

Lonnie Pezzerella wore her graying brunette hair in a short, mannish hairstyle. At first glance, she appeared at least fifty pounds overweight for her tall height, six-foot-one or two, at least. Her clothes, a baggy cotton top and baggy knit pants covered with a white cook's apron. Her lack of makeup and any pretense for fashion matched the masculine vibe she exuded.

With a quick glimpse around the room, Jake concluded that Pezzerella had found another purpose in life besides serving up soup and sandwiches. Posters of GLBT activists adorned the clean, painted walls. Information from organizations she no doubt supported, lay side-by-side with government outreach flyers offering financial help and legal aid to desperate women. Lonnie Pezzerella was clearly a woman with a mission.

"Thanks for seeing us on such short notice," Ensign Blanco began. "We'll make this as brief as possible. This is FBI Special Agent Jake Bernstein, called in by NCI to assist us in our investigation."

Pezzerella nodded unsmilingly, looking at each of the Navy officers in turn before settling her blue-eyed gaze on Jake. Her mouth creased at the corners into a smile. "I'm a movie buff. Has anyone ever told you that you look like Ben Affleck?" She had a high, soft voice, not what he had expected.

Jake grinned. "All the time." He waited for her to settle down before getting on topic. "Ms. Pezzerella, I would like to know everything you know about

Lieutenant Carlton. Everything, from gossip to any conversations you've had with her. Your impressions..." He trailed off and waited patiently, giving her time to think. Although she'd already been interviewed by local homicide and the NCIs, Jake knew she'd had a few days for the shock to wear off. Something new in her memory bank may have arisen since the initial interviews.

Pezzerella sighed. "Please call me Lonnie. Everyone's informal here. Well, there's not much to tell. Sam—Samantha Carlton—was a regular customer, mostly at the nightclub. We knew she was one of us, of course, because she'd pick up women on Friday and Saturday nights in the club. My business partner, Lisa, can tell you more about her. I don't think you have interviewed her yet. She's been ill with a bad cold this past week, as I told these investigators a few days ago."

This was confirmed by nods from the NCIs. Ensign Taylor informed Jake they'd spoken by phone.

Pezzerella nodded. "Lisa will be up to seeing you tomorrow. I gave her"—she indicated Ensign Taylor—"the address. We own both buildings, but I run the café. Lisa manages the nightclub." She paused to heave another sigh.

"We let Sam park in back after she got her new car," she continued. "A Christmas present from her rich father. He's a big-shot businessman in San Francisco. Harbor Boulevard gets a lot of traffic, not only from tourists but, y'know, troublemakers, bored kids looking for targets. We've had our share of vandalism."

Also confirmed by nods from the NCIs.

"Sam was a good customer, so I didn't mind the favor. It was actually Lisa's doing, and I went along. We've had absolutely no problems back there. None whatsoever. I can't believe this." She sucked in a deep breath. "I think someone was stalking Sam. Lisa thinks so, too."

"Why do you say that, Lonnie?" Jake asked. He glanced over at Ensign Taylor's copious note-taking.

"We've had death threats ever since we opened two years ago." Lonnie swiped her eyes with the back of her knuckles. "That was expected. We don't believe in fairy tales. Lisa and I are pragmatists. We know there's an element of society that still fears and resents gays and lesbians. Some of our patrons are transgender, too. They come to the café or nightclub in the gender they identify with and feel comfortable in."

Lonnie paused. "Anyway, after our first year, the threats stopped. Just out of the blue, they stopped. Lately, though, the past month in fact, those threats started up again."

"Emails?" Jake asked.

"No. We gave the notes to the cops when they first started. Typed notes, threatening all kinds of things, from shooting up the club to poisoning the café food. All kinds of sick stuff."

Jake looked at the NCIs. Their baffled looks confirmed what he suspected. The homicide detectives were withholding. Why, he wasn't sure. "Who did you turn over these notes to, Lonnie?"

She drew a sheaf of papers from a folder on the table. "A Detective Lorenzo. I made copies. There was something about that cop's attitude that I didn't like. Like he didn't take the threats seriously. So as a precaution, I copied every single threatening note. I dated them on top, and as you can see, these started coming in around four weeks ago."

Ensign Taylor took possession of the papers, and Jake noticed more copies inside Lonnie's folder. Backup copies.

"Sam was here in the café that night, obviously waiting for someone." Lonnie frowned. "She looked so disappointed when whoever it was didn't show up. I saw her, myself, but one of my gals, Jerry, served her. She said Sam was on her cell phone a couple of times, I guess calling that person."

Jake's head whipped around. Ensigns Blanco and Taylor were shaking their heads. A reminder that no cell phone was found with the body.

He turned back to Lonnie. "Did you or Jerry notice the kind of purse she had? Did it have a pocket for a cell phone?"

Lonnie glanced over at Ensign Taylor. "Jerry described it to this investigator."

Ensign Taylor shuffled through her notebook pages, then looked up. "Yes, that's right. Jerry—Geraldine McAllen—said that Samantha's wallet-purse had a pocket for her cell phone. She had it out on the table." Her forehead creased as she glanced at her phone. "I requested that trace you wanted on the way in here, and I just got the list of her calls."

Presumably, the lieutenant had the phone with her when she left the restaurant, so the killer must have taken it. Perhaps the phone was a key to the killer's identity. Jake nodded at Ensign Taylor. "Good. We'll go over it later." He looked at Lonnie. "There were no witnesses?"

"Not from the café," she said. "I would've known. Someone would've said something. Maybe someone at the nightclub saw something. We were shut down that night, but an electrical crew was making repairs. Lisa was sick but came in, anyway, to supervise. She said they all left around eight-thirty. Also, she mentioned the bar manager, Jimmy Park, was training a new hire. You'd have to ask Jimmy and the new bartender if they saw anything."

She shot him a look of weary resignation. "I suppose you want to know what I was doing that night, Agent Bernstein. I was in the kitchen until about seven-thirty. Then I welcomed the social worker—a Paula Dell—who'd come to give a talk to battered women who needed help. She spoke to a group of six...no, seven women from eight until ten o'clock in this very room. I stayed here to serve coffee, tea, some snacks, and to offer my support where needed."

Jake nodded, glancing at the posters on the walls again. "I see." He glanced at the two ensigns with a pointed look. Had those seven women and the social worker been interviewed at some point? Perhaps one of them heard or saw something.

Ensign Taylor jumped in with the answer. "I spoke to all seven women and the social worker by phone. One of the women denied being there, said we were mistaken. She sounded frightened that we had tracked her down, probably a victim of abuse whose husband was nearby. Anyway, I didn't pursue it since the rest said they saw nothing out of the ordinary at the café. Although none of them went into the back alley that night or any other night."

A few more routine questions brought Jake up to date on the café. He'd have to return later that night to see for himself how this nightclub was run. He wondered if Meg would mind dropping in after dinner.

He nodded to the Ensign Taylor, thanked Lonnie for her cooperation, and shook the woman's hand. Her grip was strong.

"I hope you catch the bastard who killed Sam," Lonnie said. "We liked her a lot. She not only brought in some of her Navy friends to the café and club, but she was always polite. Just a quiet, unassuming woman looking for love. Like everyone else."

"We'll do our best," Jake promised as he filed out after the two ensigns. Outside in the parking lot, Jake turned to the NCIs. "Okay, the phone trace?"

Ensign Taylor nodded and pulled out a sheaf of computer printouts. "Four numbers stood out as frequent calls. Her father in San Francisco, the NBC"—Naval Base Coronado—"where she was stationed, and a friend and fellow officer. The fourth was the number of a throwaway burner phone. Sam called this number four times that evening. We think this was her girlfriend's number. Haven't identified her yet."

Jake frowned. "A girlfriend who uses a burner. Interesting. Well, set up a meeting with the club manager, this Lisa…"

"Lisa Chance," Ensign Taylor said.

"If electricians were working at the club that night, and she was here overseeing things, one of them might have seen something. In any event, I want to get a feel for this place that played such an important role in the vic's social life. Meet me here at nine tonight. I'll bring my girlfriend."

"The nightclub? Tonight?" Ensign Blanco looked puzzled.

Jake shrugged and repeated, "I want to get a feel for the place. We're going undercover, so both of you dress the part."

The two ensigns exchanged glances, then nodded.

Chapter Four

JAKE HELD THE DOOR open for Meg when they reached the Daoud's Persian Restaurant in east San Diego.

"All right, I did say yes," Meg conceded.

He exaggerated a flinch when Meg pinched his belly as she proceeded him through the door. He'd talked her into postponing her homework and going to The Lido with him. Since they couldn't show up at a Middle Eastern-themed restaurant in swinging-sexy club clothes, they had each brought a change of tops to go with their jeans.

"Besides, you love this. You said you wanted to work for the Special Support Group," he reminded her in a low voice, "so tonight's your chance." He burrowed his hand under her sweater to touch her bare skin, then added a mock challenge. "Don't disappoint me. I expect to see some really sexy vamping out there. And sharp surveillance work."

She smiled and leaned in as she moved past him and whispered, "Yes, but pretending to be gay's not what I had in mind."

He shrugged, pulled out his hand, and playfully ran it down her back. "Hey, you do what the job calls for. You'll see, the job's not all glitz and glamour. The point is to blend in."

They paused inside the restaurant. The lighting was subdued, and the mocha-colored walls were covered with framed posters of Qur'anic verses written in calligraphy. The large main room was spacious and held about fifteen tables.

The hostess, wearing a hijab, led them to a Formica-topped table where the cheap flatware was wrapped, burrito-style, in a paper napkin. The chairs were utilitarian, and the two-sided paper menu left a lot to be desired. As Jake expected, the menu stated that all the food was *halal*, meaning cooked in the traditional Muslim rite of food preparation. There were the usual kabab and shawarma choices with wild rice or orzo, but Jake noted several unusual dishes which probably appealed more to their orthodox Middle Eastern clientele.

"I told Sarah we might come tonight, but I don't see her," Meg said. "Maybe she's helping out in the kitchen. She cooks sometimes when her mother is ill." Her face brightened suddenly. "Oh, there she is. Good, she's our server. Now you'll meet her, Jake. She's a bright girl, just a bit behind in her English class."

A pretty teenage girl with her head covered by a black *hijab* and sporting a loose gray tunic over her blue jeans, appeared at their table. Sarah silently set down two glasses of iced water, then quietly said hello. Meg stood up and hugged her. Sarah shyly hugged her back, then turned to face Jake as Meg introduced them. He held out his hand, but after sneaking a glance at the kitchen door, the girl shook her head.

"Sorry, my father does not allow me to touch men who are not my relatives. He's very old school." She smiled and shrugged.

"Of course, sorry about that."

From Arabic and Middle Eastern culture training at Quantico, Jake knew he'd pushed things a bit by offering to shake the girl's hand. But he wanted to know how conservative the family was. Pleasantries over, he sat back and watched Meg work her charm on the girl.

"I read your essay, Sarah, and it was so good. A big improvement over the last one."

Sarah beamed for a second, then seemed to remember something. Her face darkened, and her smile faded. Meg glanced at Jake but kept her attention on her tutee. Jake suspected something was off about the girl, even as she politely replied to Meg's praise.

"I'm so glad. I worked hard on that essay. *The Great Gatsby* is a strange story. I understood only a little of it."

Meg nodded. "It's a typical American twenties-era rags-to-riches story. And the terrible costs of those ill-gotten riches."

Jake jumped in, the book had been a high school requirement for him and remained vague in his mind. "Sarah, I felt the same way when I read it. The only thing I understood was Jay Gatsby's need to impress the woman he was in love with...what's her name."

"Daisy," Meg said.

"Yeah, Daisy—his need to impress her with his wealth and accomplishments. Even though he'd gotten his money the criminal way, he had to show her what he could do. He had to win her over."

Although the girl nodded and smiled, her gaze kept flitting toward the kitchen door.

Meg smiled and changed the topic. "Is your mother here, Sarah? I'd like to meet her and tell her about your progress at the Tutoring Center."

Sarah's dark eyes snapped wide, and her body stiffened. "Oh, my mother's not here tonight. Well, she *is* here, but she's in the kitchen. Working hard. She can't come out here. Not tonight." She quickly lifter her pad and pen. "If you're ready to order... I really have to get back..."

"I'll take the shawarma dish," Jake said. "And hot sweet tea."

Meg said she'd take the same.

When the girl left, Meg frowned. "I'm going to the bathroom." She hurried after the teenager and caught up to her at the entrance to the kitchen.

The door opened, and Jake spied two *hijab*-clad women beyond Meg and Sarah. They appeared to be working at a large stove while three men bustled around them. A dark-haired, bearded man, large and stocky, came into view and barked something at the women.

When the man moved on, one of the women at the stove looked up from her stirring and stared at Sarah in the doorway. One side of her face bore dark bruises, her right eye was swollen shut, a reddened cut angling upward from the side of her mouth. Her expression appeared afraid or resigned—Jake couldn't tell for sure. He made out only a few Arabic words the man shouted at Sarah, still standing in the open doorway, which didn't sound pleasant. Then the door shut behind Sarah, leaving Meg staring at the floor.

When Meg returned to their table, she slumped to her seat. The crushed look on her face said it all. "Maybe I shouldn't have probed. But Sarah told me once that she and her mother were having a hard time."

"Hard time, how?" Jake asked, even though he already suspected he knew how and why.

"Her mother was born in Egypt. I guess she's a more secular Muslim, but she married a fundamentalist Iranian man. It seems..." She trailed off.

"Is her mother the one that looked like she'd had the shit kicked out of her?"

"You saw that, too?" Meg shook her head and lowered her voice. "I don't feel like staying now, but it would be rude to leave." She followed the direction of his gaze to a poster on the wall. "Can you read that? The Arabic?"

"Yeah. I know that verse. We had to learn to decipher even Arabic calligraphy. That's one of the Qur'anic verses we had to memorize at Quantico when training for that undercover assignment. It's often used by jihadists as proof that Westerners can't be trusted."

Meg looked at the calligraphy. "What does it say?"

"I think it's chapter five, verse fifty-one of the Qur'an. If I'm not mistaken, it reads literally, *O you who believe! Do not take the Jews and the Christians for friends; they are friends of each other; and whoever amongst you takes them for a friend, then surely he is one of them...*"

Meg looked chagrined, her forehead furrowed, her pretty mouth downturned. "Really? That's what it says?"

Jake glanced around the walls. "The owner has chosen some of the most antagonistic Qur'anic verses." He indicated another Qur'anic saying with a toss of his head. "That one says, *Those Muslims who befriend unbelievers will abide in hell.* I'd say the owner was an orthodox Muslim, maybe an Alawite. They're extreme Shia Muslims. If his non-Muslim customers could read Arabic, they'd probably stop coming."

Meg scowled. "Why do you think Sarah's father follows that philosophy?"

Jake shrugged while rubbing the stubble on his cheeks. "Muslim business owners choose the verses from the Qur'an that resonate with their personal viewpoints. Just like Christians choose Bible chapters and verses and Jews pick their Torah excerpts, the ones that resonate with them. Of course, most Americans don't read Arabic. If they did, they'd be shocked. It's clear how Sarah's father feels about Americans. Mr. Daoud is showing his fellow Muslims that he's devout and ultra-conservative. To us, it seems close-minded, even hostile."

Like many Americans, Meg was naïve about Islam and the Muslims who lived among them. They didn't realize that Islam was not only a religion but also a political ideology. Their holy book contained enough hate speech to shock the average American.

"But he came here by choice. He chose to live here."

He quirked up an eyebrow. "True. Clearly, the man has issues. Not only with Americans but with his own family. From what you've said about Sarah, she's caught between two conflicting worlds."

"What can I do?"

One of the traits he liked best about the woman he'd fallen in love with was her abundance of empathy. He took a moment to contemplate an answer to Meg's question. "Nothing."

Sarah approached their table again with their meals. Her father might not like them, but he'd be more than happy to take their money.

Jake added under his breath, "My advice, Meg, don't interfere."

Chapter Five

JAKE REACHED FOR MEG'S hands as she unbuttoned his shirt halfway down his chest, exposing the dark, curly hair on his chest. A chill pierced his skin through the warmth of the polyester fabric. "Wait a minute," he protested.

She slapped his hand away. "Jake, you can't take that buttoned-up look into a gay club. I'm trying to transform you from a straight FBI agent into a swinging gay dude. Work with me here."

They were standing by his rental car on the fourth floor of the parking garage a half-block from the nightclub. After dinner, they'd stopped at a gas station where Meg used the restroom to change from schoolteacher to vamp in about ten minutes. She wore a glittery black top with holes cut out to expose her bare shoulders and her tightest jeans, emphasizing all her curves and setting off her slim ankles and high heels. She'd lavished on the makeup, too, adding dashes of rouge and thick fake eyelashes. Her luscious lips, painted a slick, bright red, pursed into teasing moue. Jake stared at her mouth, then her made-up eyes, followed by her bare shoulders and shapely hips.

He was beginning to dig this undercover operation.

"Okay, that'll do." Meg patted his chest and stepped back. "So we pair up and go in with those Navy investigators? Act the part and keep our eyes peeled for a big Asian guy."

Jake had already talked Meg through the plan to go undercover with Ensigns Blanco and Taylor, who insisted on using first names—Javier and Mary Lou. He also double-checked to see if Meg had brought her smartphone. It would be less noticeable for a woman to flash her camera phone around in a playful manner and take shots, even if their target was somewhere in the background. Also, it made more sense if Meg and Mary Lou asked about Samantha Carlton and her whereabouts. Acting as casual acquaintances, they'd naturally want to know why she wasn't there on a Friday night. After all, the Fleet was in port, and they knew Sam had been a regular at the club.

Jake and Javier planned to casually circle the perimeter, searching for a big Asian man. It was probably a long shot that the perp would frequent the club, but they had to give it a try. Javier had contacted Jake earlier with a rundown on their briefing with the local homicide detectives, who insisted on working off the theory that the attacker was a homicidal homophobe with a shoe fetish.

For Jake, the theory was laughable, but the local detectives were sticking to it based on the hate-filled threats the owners of The Amazon and The Lido had received in the past month or so. Though too simple to believe, in Jake's opinion, the locals were just responding to the hate crimes committed in the greater San Diego area over the past few months.

For the time being, the ensigns hadn't brought the local cops up to speed on the details they'd learned about the attacker. If the PD preferred their own rush to judgment, so be it. If the NCIs did their job, the truth would eventually win out.

The line outside the nightclub trailed halfway down the long block. Same-sex couples slung arms around each other, either chatting and laughing with other couples or texting furiously. Jake noted a few singles in line, eyeing the other singles and several leering at him. The crowd represented an age range of early twenties to forties. The common dress theme...sexy casual.

Jake felt so much older than his thirty-two years.

"See, I told you," Meg said. "You have to strut your stuff. See how many guys are coming on to you."

"You sound like you've done this before. The club scene, I mean."

"C'mon, you talk like you're middle-aged."

Jake pointed to his head and grinned. "In here, I am. Comes with the territory."

He spotted the ensigns toward the end of the line, who waved them over and let them cut in. As they blatantly assessed each other's looks, he introduced the two women.

"Meg. Mary Lou."

Mary Lou wore her hair in a straight pageboy. Her ample curves filled out her snug-fitting gold-sequined tube top and black mini skirt. She had gypsy bangles all up her arms and large sparkly gold hoop earrings dangled low over bare shoulders. She and Meg giggled at each other.

"We are so stereotypical clubbers," Mary Lou cooed with her hint of a drawl. She licked one finger and touched her hip, adding a hissed. "And so hot."

Meg, appearing a trifle embarrassed, dug her elbow into Jake's side. "This could be fun, but boy, do you owe me."

"Remember, this is your tryout for SSG." Jake waggled his eyebrows at Meg as he sidled up to Javier, who wore a snug-fitting mesh shirt paired with tight-fitting jeans. Meg took her place alongside Mary Lou.

"We all know the plan," Jake said. "We leave at twenty-three hundred and meet up to compare notes. You know where."

The crowd inched toward the entrance, where a male bouncer and a tall, husky female stood. The brunette woman, with shoulders like a linebacker, looked to be in her late forties and wore her dark, frizzy hair cut close to her head. More muscular than bulky, she was at least six-three. Jake would have a hard time throwing her to the mat in under ten seconds.

The woman's big, meaty hands held a clipboard that she referred to from time to time. As singles and couples entered, she took their names—or aliases—and stamped the backs of their hands. The colorful stamps bore The Lido's logo. Next to her, the young but powerfully built blond bouncer stood in a military stance, a black T-shirt stretched over his pec-sculpted chest and muscular arms. The man looked everyone over. Occasionally, he'd bend over and speak into the female's ear.

"Is that Lisa Chance?" Jake asked Javier.

"Yep, we're cool. We interviewed her yesterday and her alibi holds up. She left at the same time as the electricians and the two bartenders. The time they left was corroborated by all concerned as eight-thirty. Sam didn't leave the café until nine o'clock. Anyway, Lisa said she'd cooperate any way she could. I told her we were coming, and she said she'd play along."

Just as their turn to enter came up, a black Mercedes sedan pulled up to the curb. The Asian driver, dressed in a black suit, got out and ran over to the curbside rear passenger door. A young, strikingly beautiful Asian woman stepped out. Wearing a red mini dress that hugged her breasts and hips, she swept her dark almond-shaped eyes over the crowd, pausing over Jake, then Meg.

Lisa spoke to her immediately. "Sheila, come in! So great to see you again!"

The Asian babe strolled over to Lisa and shook hands. Her long black hair flowed down her curvaceous back like a sleek waterfall. Average height, slim but curvy in all the right places, she carried herself like a gliding swan.

Sheila spoke quietly to Lisa. Jake heard her lightly accented English as the owner clearly held up the line to give Sheila the VIP treatment. Javier nudged Jake's arm, drawing his attention to the Mercedes.

Sheila wasn't alone. A hulking Asian male emerged and rose to his full height, exiting the rear passenger seat on the street side. Jake estimated the man to be at least six-foot-four. The guy, who appeared to be bulked up on steroids and weightlifting, was obviously her bodyguard. He wore a black t-shirt under a black sports coat and was smooth-shaven. Jake guessed he was in his late twenties or early thirties. His longish hair was glossy black, worn straight back behind his ears in a short ponytail. His left ear held a diamond the size of an *M&M's* candy. His arms were covered and so was his bulldog neck. If he bore scratch marks, the jacket and white scarf he wore around his bulldog neck concealed them.

The bodyguard joined Sheila, placed his hand at her elbow, and escorted her inside after their hands were stamped. After the VIPs disappeared inside, Lisa addressed Jake and Javier.

"So, new Navy guys?"

"Yeah, just transferred in," Javier said. "I'm Jose, and this here's my friend, Johnny."

Lisa jotted down their aliases, stamped their hands in red with The Lido's logo, and ushered them inside. She apparently liked her Navy customers and welcomed them with enthusiasm. Meg and Mary Lou soon followed. The girls paused at the edge of the dance floor. A cocktail waitress dressed like a can-can dancer approached them with a tray of drinks held aloft and pointed to a vacant table with four chairs. Couples and singles obviously shared tables on a busy night.

While the girls and Javier took seats, Jake remained standing and scanned the black walls adorned with colorful nineteenth-century Toulouse-Lautrec posters of the Folies Bergère and the Moulin Rouge. Must be French night, Jake thought. Or Parisian fantasy night. Whatever.

The music was excruciatingly loud. Jake morphed his automatic wince into a wolfish grin. He noticed men around him giving him the once-over. Javier made a snide comment that Jake ignored.

Strobe lights in ever-changing colors flashed and raked the dance floor while an old disco mirror globe glinted overhead. A stage on the café side of the club held a female DJ and her equipment—two human-sized woofers, her table, stereo, and mics. On the other three sides of the square-shaped club, three tiers ran up like stadium seating. Instead of benches, there were tall round bistro tables and chairs. On the uppermost tier, upholstered banquettes, tucked away into shallow alcoves, faced the action below. Drinks littered silver cubes that acted as tables. The overall tones were black and silver.

Already, Sheila and her bodyguard were climbing to the top tier. The hulk flicked their *RESERVED* sign off the cube table onto the wooden floor and settled onto the couch closest to the alcove's entrance.

Dancers were writhing and grinding against each other on the packed dance floor, and the girls joined the fray. Strobe lights, now pink morphing into yellow, streaked across their bodies as Meg bumped hips with Mary Lou and threw her arms up in wild abandon. Or a facsimile thereof. Laughing like a drunk schoolgirl on spring break, Meg held her phone high in the air as if taking photos of the dancers around her.

Yep, she was a natural. Jake caught her gaze shooting up to the top tier. The phone in her hand swiveled upward. That girl didn't miss a thing.

"Ya think that's our guy?" Javier dropped his hand over the wooden railing and discretely hooked his thumb in the direction of the upper tier.

"Yep." Like most law enforcement officers, Jake did not believe in coincidences.

He looked at Javier, wondering if the ensign's thoughts were churning in the same as his. "Okay, let's work the room. Find out who they are."

"Got it. If we get separated, twenty-three hundred."

Chapter Six

JAKE WORKED HIS WAY over to the bar that ran the width of the rear wall. Four bartenders scurried back and forth: two men and two women. One of the men appeared to be part Asian. His black shirt pocket bore the name *Jimmy* on a white badge. As soon as a barstool opened up, Jake took it and waved him over.

"Coors on tap if you have it," he said, throwing the bartender a wise-ass smile. Acting like a flamboyant gay guy was an undercover ploy he'd never used before. He doubted it would come off, so he turned dark, moody, and mysterious instead. More his nature, anyway.

"You got it," Jimmy said, drawing a glass. He had to shout above the pulsating noise. "Never seen you before. You with the Navy?"

Jake nodded. "Yep. Just came back from leave. One of the officers I used to work with told me about this place. Maybe you know her. Sam Carlton. Lieutenant Carlton. She's supposed to be here tonight, but I don't see her."

Jimmy leaned over the bar when he set down the glass. Jake obliged him and leaned in to meet him halfway.

"I'm surprised you haven't heard. It's all over the club. Should be all over the base, too. She was found in the trunk of her car. Right in back. Murdered. We think some asshole's targeting the club to drive away business. It's working, too. This place is usually twice as crowded on a Friday night." He stood back and busied himself filling a bowl of peanuts. "I'm Jimmy Park. And you're…"

Korean-American, Jake surmised. They'd discovered a hair on the lieutenant's body—an Asian hair. Wouldn't hurt to check out this Jimmy Park.

Various aliases churned through his mind while he examined Jimmy's exposed skin. No marks on his face or neck, but his arms were covered by his long-sleeved shirt.

"John. John Bianchini." They shook hands while Jake assumed a look of dismay and shock. "Shit, no one told me. I've been on leave, visiting family up in NorCal. Just got back today, so no...I didn't hear. Damn."

"Yeah, no shit. We're all on alert. That's why Lisa's out front tonight, checking people out. You saw the two plainclothes cops? They're roaming around. Packing, too, just in case. We think someone or some group's targeting the club and the people who come here."

"Hmm, sorry to hear that. Thanks for the tip. I'll watch my back."

Jimmy glanced around the bustling bar. "Gotta go. If you're around at closing time, let me know. Maybe we can...y'know..." He shot Jake a knowing smile, wriggled his black eyebrows, then moved down the bar.

Jake sipped his beer and gazed absently around the bar. Although a little muscular, at approximately five-ten and one-hundred-fifty max, Jimmy was probably too thin to overcome a medium-sized, frantic woman fighting for her life. Still, a strong headlock and powerful sedative would counteract Sam's defensive force. However, according to Lonnie and Lisa, Jimmy Park had been working Tuesday night, training the new bartender, and the NCIs had already interviewed him. He'd left with everyone else at eight-thirty and hadn't heard a thing either.

Also, what would have been his motive? Certainly not robbery. Jealousy? Revenge? Why would a gay guy kill a gay woman, especially one of his patrons? Did he have an accomplice with a motive?

He glanced at the other three tending bar and presumed the anemic blond male must be the new bartender. Of the two female bartenders, one was of average height and a size six, the other was more Amazonian size, like Lisa and Lonnie. Belatedly, he recognized her as Jerry, one of the café servers, apparently doing double duty behind the bar. He'd noticed her earlier that day in the café, waiting on customers. She shared a brief stare of recognition with him, and he wondered if she would expose his true identity to Jimmy. Nothing he could do about it at that moment. He turned his attention to the other patrons in the bar area.

When Jake caught the attention of several men on the prowl, one of whom approached him and boldly touched his thigh, he left the bar. Time to circulate. Beer in hand, Jake went over to the far end of the railing that overlooked the dance floor. Meg was still dancing with Mary Lou. He caught Meg's attention, and she immediately scowled and turned her back. Her swaying rump transfixed him for a full minute.

He leaned against the railing and casually glance up toward the highest tier, scanning slowly from left to right, aimlessly. The hulk still guarded his gorgeous ward, who was now standing next to him, her hand on his massive shoulder, speaking at his enormous, bent head. And staring down directly at Jake.

Had they made him? Self-consciously, he shot her a lazy grin before turning to watch the writhing bodies on the dance floor. At that moment, Javier slid up to him and slung an arm around his waist. Possessively. Like a male-male lovefest.

This was not Jake's scene. He had three more weeks of medical leave, and what he really wanted was to be with Meg on Santa Catalina Island, soaking up the sun on some charter fishing boat. Not chasing the killer of a Navy officer. Let the NCIs and local cops do their job. However, he'd promised Admiral Snider. And Snider was Meg's substitute father.

Jake let out a soft groan. Damn. It was going to be a long night.

MEG THRUST OUT HER hip, first to her right, then her left. The blaring music and thumping beats were giving her a headache. Her heart pounded in rhythm, although the rest of her cried, *Get me outta here!* She would be twenty-seven on Sunday, but her mind and body already rejected the club scene. Her life plan, like an internal compass, had a needle pointing in a far different direction. Marriage, kids, career, a life with a loving family...if she was lucky.

Meg turned to Mary Lou. "I'm going to the bathroom. Just saw you-know-who head in that direction. I'm going to see if I can strike up a conversation."

"Be careful. Want me to come along?"

Meg shook her head and exited the dance floor. By the time she wended her way through the first layer of dance-floor spectators, she glanced over her shoulder to see Mary Lou already had a new partner. Meg waited in a short line, then entered a stall. Taking her time, she sat there until she heard a female exclamation.

"Sheila! I'm surprised to see you here tonight. Did you hear about Sam?" A moment of silence, followed by another exclamation. "*Omigod*, you didn't know? I thought you two were close. Well, anyway, they found her body in the trunk of her car Wednesday morning. She was murdered!"

The next thing Meg heard was a stall door latching shut and then a woman retching in the stall next to hers. She looked under the wall of her stall. Red satin stilettos faced the toilet, then did an about-face.

"Are you okay, Sheila?"

A soft, strangled voice replied, "Yes. Something I ate for dinner. I'm fine now."

"If you need help, let me know. Okay?"

"Yes, leave me, please."

The woman must have left the bathroom, for nothing more was said between them. There was no more retching. In fact, it sounded like the Asian woman was using her phone. Meg took her cell phone out of her purse and turned on the microphone app. She held her phone in the direction of the next stall.

Meg heard Sheila's low voice, speaking Mandarin or Cantonese, apparently talking into her cell phone. Her rapid-fire speech showed no undue emotion, just a breathy urgency in a language Meg couldn't understand, followed by a low, strangled sound, which could've been a sob or a chuckle. Then she stopped speaking.

Meg put away her cell phone, stood up quickly, flushed, and went to wash her hands over the granite basin. A half-minute later, Sheila emerged from her stall. Her lipstick was gone, and her dark almond-shaped eyes were clouded over.

She stood next to Meg and glanced over. "You're new here. Are you Navy?" The woman's tone was matter-of-fact and bore traces of upper-class British English.

A heartbeat later, Meg found her voice. "Yes, I'm Lieutenant, uh, Meg Snider. I was just transferred to North Island." The location of the Navy base on Coronado.

Sheila smiled as though she hadn't a care in the world. As though a good friend of hers hadn't just been murdered. She reapplied her lipstick and added a coral smudge to both cheekbones. "I'm Sheila Lee. I'm a graduate student at San Diego State University."

"Glad to meet you." Meg smiled back. More than a little curious, Meg was about to ask Sheila to join her for a drink or dance when the bathroom lights suddenly blinked off.

Shrieks from a few of the other women in the bathroom made Meg jump. She found herself in the utter dark with a strange woman who apparently knew the murder victim very well and had a predatory air about her. A thought struck her, so she retrieved her cell phone from her little purse. The flashlight feature gave them a cone of light that enabled them to make their way to the door. Several others followed them.

A milling crowd and total darkness, except for little floating islands of light from other cell phones, greeted them outside the women's bathroom. Sheila's bodyguard blocked their path, presenting a black obstruction in the narrow corridor. He spoke to Sheila in rushed tones, again in one of the Chinese dialects.

Sheila's strong hand grabbed Meg's arm. "The whole club lost power somehow. I have to leave. Meg, will you be here tomorrow night?"

"No, I'm on duty."

"You're not attached?" The woman's meaning was obvious.

Meg's cheeks heated involuntarily. "No."

Sheila swept Meg along the corridor with her, her bodyguard serving as a linebacker to the crowd in their way. "I'd like to get to know you. Can I call you?"

"O-okay," Meg replied, distracted by the crowd blocking their way.

"We must get together. Give me your cell number," Sheila said before turning away. They reached the edge of the bar area and ran into a wall of people waiting for the lights to come back on.

"Okay." Without thinking of the possible consequences, Meg verbally gave her real cell phone number.

Strangely enough, the hulking bodyguard whipped out a notebook and wrote the number down. Sheila nodded to the man before grasping Meg's hand in a kind of farewell gesture. Then she and her bodyguard disappeared into the darkness.

Someone screamed. Others joined in. An acrid smell reached Meg's nostrils. Smoke. An elbow smacked her in the head. Someone shoved her hard against the wall. Shouts to remain calm morphed into frantic screams. People pressed into her, pushing her in their relentless human current toward the rear of the bar. An exit sign flashed with the aid, no doubt, of an emergency generator.

When the jostling grew uncontrollable, Meg threw her purse strap over her head and tucked her phone back in. She wasn't going to lose her cell phone, not when she'd captured Sheila's unguarded words. Someone in full panic mode shoved her roughly against the wooden railing overlooking the dance floor. One quick glance at the disc jockey's stage platform chilled her. The curtain behind the woman's table curled into jagged ribbons of orange flame. The wooden stage burst open, swallowing the woman into an inferno. The dance floor had already emptied.

Jake. Mary Lou. Javier.

Swimming against the human current was impossible, so Meg scurried along, doing her best to remain standing. A small woman beside her tripped over someone and began to fall. Meg clamped a hand on the woman's waist and boosted her up, walking her fast in the direction of the rear exit door. The club's temperature rose as the flames spread. Meg heard shouts of desperation.

Finally, the sprinklers turned on. Water drenched them but fed the spread of smoke, which thickened in the hot air. People, including Meg, coughed. Her eyes burned, and she squeezed her lids shut. There was nothing she could do but allow herself to be blindly swept along, all the while groping with one hand and holding onto the woman beside her with the other. She stumbled and felt her shoulder strap fall loose. With a yank, she righted it and kept her arm around the woman.

Keep moving. Don't get trampled. Jake! Jake! Where are you?

Cool air slapped her face as the exit door opened wide, and she glimpsed a patch of black sky. Another wave of panic ensued. People scrambled to escape the club's now out-of-control fire, the ceiling sprinklers inexplicably drying up. The pushing and shoving increased, along with the screams. For the first time, genuine fear raged within Meg. Her adrenalin spiked, and her pulse ran rampant. The noise was unbearable. She wanted to clamp her hands over her ears. Her head swam and her knees buckled.

Someone's forward momentum jerked her away from the woman beside her. Meg fell against a hard male body, then collapsed against the side of the bar. Her head hit the wood, and she saw stars. Air left her chest. In fear, she curled up into a ball next to a bar stool.

Heavy shoes stomped on her leg, and she cried out in pain. Meg wrapped her arms over her head, tucking her legs under her. Ten feet away, shoes trampled on the same small woman Meg had tried to help. Then a man lifted the woman into his arms—

Jake.

Meg screamed his name.

He rushed to her side and tried to help her up. "Meg."

"No, Jake, help that woman first."

"You sure? For God's sake, stay there. Under the bar. I'll come back for you."

Jake and the small woman vanished amid the crush of bodies moving like a tsunami of flesh and bone. Smoke clogged the air, making it impossible to breathe. Meg buried her nose into the space between her knees and shut her mouth. A feeble thought intruded her waning conscious mind. She wondered what would come first. Would she suffocate to death or burn alive?

Jake.

Chapter Seven

JAKE EMERGED INTO THE night air. People scattered past the flashing lights of two massive fire trucks, which took up most of the back alley. He set the small woman down on the asphalt. She wept and coughed as he called an EMT.

The first responder arrived with an oxygen tank, gave Jake a couple of whiffs, and then asked, "You okay, bud?"

"Yeah, take care of her." Jake indicated to the woman on the ground. "I'm going back in."

Jake waved off the man's objections. A thought made him pause. He whipped off his polyester shirt, tore one of the sleeves off, and soaked the whole mess in a water-filled bucket one of the firemen had placed on the ground. Slinging the drenched shirt over his shoulder, he wrapped the sleeve over the lower half of his face and tied it in back.

As he approached the door, the exodus of people had trickled down to a few late stragglers, and Jimmy came into view.

"Hey, man, don't go back in—"

Jake inhaled deeply, then plunged in, narrowing his eyes to slits as the roiling smoke hit him. He crouched down on all fours and crawled quickly to the end of the hall and veering to the left toward the bar. He paused briefly to pull the mini-Maglite from his pocket and clenched it between his teeth. The smoke screen was thinner closer to the floor, and the small circle of light bobbed around as he searched for Meg. Then he saw her. His eyes and nose burned with unshed tears, and his throat clogged with smoke despite the damp cloth wrapped around his face.

Suddenly, a piece of ceiling, licked with flames, came crashing down on top of the bar. He ducked his head and flattened out to avoid the flying sparks.

A moment of racing heartbeats later, he reached Meg and wrapped his arms around her bowed back. She turned over in his arms, half consciously gazing at him. He took the Maglite out of his mouth and pocketed it, then ripped off his wet shirt and swathed her head and face in it. With a groan, he lurched to his knees, holding her limp body and wondering about the thirty feet or so to the exit. He wasn't sure he could make it. He felt exhausted, dizzy, and weak from smoke inhalation.

The sound of heavy boots pounded on the floor, and Jake squinted to see two firemen coming his way. One of the men lifted Meg, and the other helped him.

"She–" He couldn't finish. His nose and mouth filled with acrid smoke and his chest heaved in a desperate attempt to breathe. He clamped his mouth shut and held his breath. Those thirty feet seemed like a hundred.

At last, he inhaled cool air and tore off the wet sleeve. He sank down to the hard ground as someone pressed an oxygen mask onto his face. His fear for Meg's safety resurfaced. Once his eyes cleared, he realized that she was no longer there. His legs trembled as he stood and scanned the chaotic scene.

He saw Meg on a gurney, an oxygen mask strapped to her head, and an EMT taking her pulse. When raised to her elbows and scanned the area, Jake let the tears flow. By the time he reached her, his tear-streaked face matched hers. The fierce embrace he gave her swept her up and off the gurney. She ripped off the oxygen mask and gulped in the cool air. A spate of coughing racked her before she settled down. With a smile, she let the medic know she was fine. The EMT moved the gurney and oxygen on to the next survivor.

"You sure, Meg?"

She nodded wearily, then dissolved into his embrace again, leaning her whole body against him.

He kissed the top of her head, filled with relief. "Okay, let's get outta here. Find the others."

Meg took another deep breath, coughed again, and then stared down at her feet. "I lost my shoes. Damn. But my purse—" She touched the strap on her shoulder and grinned. "I've got it. I didn't lose it. Good, good..."

Jake and Meg made their way to the parking garage, where they linked up with the two NCIs. The four started talking at once before Jake made a cautionary gesture. Club patrons filed past them, either shaken and subdued or talking excitedly. Javier waved down a group of six young men, who stared at Jake's bare chest for a moment before turning back to Javier.

"Did everyone get out?" Javier asked.

"Yeah, they think so," one guy replied. "We heard Lisa say that everyone got out. The club's a friggin' mess, but the fire's nearly out. They don't know why the sprinklers froze up. It was just fixed Tuesday night. Lisa thinks it's arson. Those same damn homophobes who've been threatening them for months. Probably the assholes who killed that Navy officer." The group moved on, pairing off as they continued down the street.

Jake, Meg, and the two NCIs kept their counsel as they climbed to another level and reached Jake's rented Explorer, leaning wearily against it.

"Okay, recap," Jake began. "We don't know much about the fire right now. You two contact the SDFD tomorrow and find out what you can. It may be a coincidence, maybe not. Coming on the heels of that murder, this is strange timing. What do you remember up to the fire breaking out?"

Javier spoke first. "I was chatting up some guys sitting inside one of the upper alcoves. Asking about the Asian Iron Man. He's supposedly a hired bodyguard for a rich woman from Hong Kong. I'll check them both out tomorrow. I was finishing my first beer when the curtain on the stage behind the DJ caught fire, and we got the hell out of there. The bodyguard and Sheila were already gone by then. They weren't near the stage."

Next, Mary Lou offered her viewpoint. "I was on the dance floor but kept watching for any movement on the upper level. I was scanning the crowd around the dance floor when Meg decided to follow Shelia to the restrooms. Another girl started dancing with me, when all of a sudden, I heard some pops, a whoosh of air, and all hell broke loose. Lisa yelled for everyone to leave and had the front doors wide open. She was pretty quick about it, I have to say. Very proactive. I was one of the first ones to leave. The fire trucks showed up within minutes, five at the most."

Jake looked over at Meg, who leaned against the left-front fender and stared grimly at her phone.

He put his hand on her shoulder. "Did you learn anything, Meg?"

"Probably nothing, but in the bathroom, I was in a stall and heard some woman telling Sheila that Lieutenant Carlton had been killed. Sheila entered the stall next to mine and made vomiting noises, so maybe she was sick or drank too much. Then I heard her making a call and speaking to someone in Chinese—have no idea whether it's Mandarin, Cantonese, or some other dialect."

She held up her phone and played back the slightly muffled recording. They all shook their heads.

"Nice work, Meg. Send that to me, and I'll get it translated tomorrow," Jake said. "What else?"

"She was very friendly with me. Asked me if I was Navy and wanted my name. I gave a fake name and rank, Lieutenant Meg Snider, and told her I just transferred to the Navy base. I hope that didn't sound suspicious. Anyway, she wants to see me again."

Jake noted Meg's smirk. "So she flirted with you?"

"Yep. I was even flattered. Rather, Navy Lieutenant Meg Snider was very flattered. She asked for my cell number, and I gave it to her." Her hand flew to her mouth. "I didn't think. I gave her my real number."

Jake frowned but said nothing.

Meg shrugged. "She wants to see me again. Looks like the club'll be out of commission for a while, so we can't hook up there."

He snorted. "You're not hooking up with anybody who's got a gorilla for a bodyguard. If she calls, put her off. Your involvement in this case ends here and now."

"I'd classify her interest in me as mild, so let's see. Who knows? I might be able to learn something that'd help the case." She broke off and surrendered to another coughing jag.

Jake whipped a bottle of water out of his Explorer and urged her to sip. He held her around the shoulders while her panting subsided, and she began to breathe normally again. If the coughing continued, he'd take her to the ER. Maybe she got off the oxygen too soon.

Meg splashed some water into her hands and scrubbed her face. It was then that Jake noticed the ends of her long blonde ponytail were singed black. He said nothing. When she saw it later, he'd deal with it. He blamed himself for her participation in this ad hoc investigation.

Though she'd wanted to help, he should have refused her.

Yeah, good luck with that.

So far, he hadn't refused her anything.

"I spoke to the bar manager, Jimmy Park." He held up a hand to halt Javier's comment. "I know you already interviewed him, but I had the opportunity and took it. Likely of Korean descent, he also fits the Asian profile of the hair found in Samantha's trunk. Got a fingerprint off the glass he gave me. I always carry these on me." He showed them several plastic strips coated on one side with special adhesive. He had one of the strips flattened against a dark, plastic seal. "We'll run it through the national criminal database and see what pops up. He was one of the last guys out the back door tonight. What was he doing? Helping people? Or helping himself to the till?"

Jake felt a chill as the adrenalin coursing through his body banked off. Meg had already grabbed the shirt he'd worn to the restaurant earlier and handed it to him. He gave her a wink, letting her know he appreciated the gesture, before shrugging on the button-down shirt.

"I was by the railing on the far side of the bar when the fire broke out. Jimmy Park wasn't behind the bar, not that I can recall. Maybe on a break." He shrugged. "After that, I got busy trying to locate Meg and helping a woman that Meg was half carrying. Quite a night."

"Amen to that," Mary Lou said. "We'll check in tomorrow after we finish reviewing Samantha's cell phone records and run the background on Sheila Lee and her bodyguard. The forensic lab should also be finished with Samantha's personal laptop."

Jake and Meg said goodnight and climbed into the Explorer. Before turning on the ignition, he slipped an arm around her. He kissed her cheek, her neck. Finally, her mouth. Long and hard.

She smiled and kissed him back until another bout of coughing quashed the kiss. She turned away in her seat, her face buried in her hands.

"So, Meg, you still want to work for the FBI?"

She nodded between coughs. "Sure do." Her ponytail had settled over one shoulder. With a sudden start, she seized her hair. "Shit, shit, shit!"

"You sure? Burnt hair isn't the worst that can happen, you know."

She shot him a mock scowl. "This was the most exciting night I've had in a long time."

"Hey."

"Present company excluded." She grinned.

He rolled his eyes and fired up the car.

Chapter Eight

SATURDAY MORNING was the first thought that entered Jake's mind as he awoke. Free time, leisurely sex, coffee, golf... Sunday was Meg's birthday. He had to buy her a special gift, but what? He'd be leaving in three weeks, maybe without her. What was he going to do about that?

Then all that happened the night before rushed back. The nightclub sounds, whirling mirror ball, the gyrating couples on the dance floor, and the beautiful Asian woman and her massive bodyguard. A plausible suspect? In terms of size alone, twenty percent of the clubbers would be plausible suspects. Motive? Means? Opportunity? Then thoughts of the fire swamped his mind—the crackling flames, the dense smoke, the pandemonium...

Meg...overcome by smoke.

Meg. He rolled to his side and opened his eyes, facing the back of her head, nestled in her pillow like a child's resting form. Her hair still smelled of smoke even though they'd both taken showers before going to bed. She'd toweled her hair dry before laying her head on a towel covering her pillow. Sometime in the night, during one of her coughing spells, she'd removed the towel.

She lay still, quiet now, her breathing sounding normal. God, what would he have done if he'd lost her? He scooted closer and spooned her warm body in a rush of emotions, relaxing as he wrapped one arm around her and pressed his belly against her backside. What if he'd found her body cold? What if she'd died during the night from smoke inhalation? He shook off such morbid thoughts, but a resolve burrowed deep inside him. Meg had no business joining any field office's SSG. She was a civilian and should stay a civilian.

He had to keep her safe and as far removed from his line of work as possible. Hadn't he learned—hadn't she learned as well—that getting involved in bureau investigations was dangerous? Why hadn't her fake drowning, back in early

November, cured them both of that foolishly romantic notion? He was to blame for involving her at the club the previous night. His work at the FBI was not going to be her fate. She was destined to be a teacher of languages. Maybe his wife. The mother of his children. But he would keep her removed from the danger he faced in his line of work.

He stilled.

Where did that line of thinking come from? Wife? Mother?

Though it seemed natural in light of his concern for her. His love for her. Was she destined to be his wife, the mother of his children? He couldn't answer that right now. He could make it happen, though, as long as he could keep her safe. But did he want to take them both that far? Did Meg want to take their relationship that far? He'd never asked her.

With his thoughts churning unproductively in a circle with no answers, Jake kissed her bare shoulder before silently getting up, careful not to disturb her sleep. If she continued coughing, he'd take her to the ER and—

His cell phone buzzed. Slipping on a clean pair of khakis over his black briefs, he punched a button. "Jake Bernstein."

"Can you talk?" Javier asked. "Got lots to share. Can you meet us somewhere?"

"Give it to me on the phone."

"Well, I need you to meet someone, hear from him in person, and assess whether he's credible."

Jake sighed and glanced over at the bed. "Yeah, sure."

Javier named the place to meet them, then rang off. After leaving Meg a note on the kitchen table, Jake threw on a clean polo shirt, socks, and loafers, leaving his smoky, soot-stained clothes on the floor in the bedroom. He'd help her do laundry when he returned. He put that in his note, too.

Would he be so considerate if they were married? He wondered about that. Marriage tended to make people complacent. He had been as guilty of that as the next man.

He frowned at the thought while he drove down the hill and south along the 405. How would things be different if they were married? He knew things changed after marriage—hell, he'd been married before, and look how that turned out. Still, his first wife was career Navy and more ambitious than any male officer he'd ever known. Meg was different. She'd put her husband and family before a career...wouldn't she?

Jake was still frowning as he pulled into the parking lot of a strip mall a mile north of downtown San Diego. Starbucks held court on the corner, where most of the cars had converged. Inside, he found Javier and Mary Lou. A large coffee drink awaited him on their table. Both officers looked exhausted.

"Didn't know what you liked, so I got you a venti vanilla latte." Mary Lou smiled.

"It'll do, thanks. How long have you guys been up?"

Javier huffed. "Actually, we never went home. Went to our office on base and dug in all night. Our boss, Lieutenant Commander Wickham, wants to meet you on base at oh-nine-hundred Monday morning. Admiral Snider will also be present. They want to know what we've been up to, so Mary Lou and I thought we should bring you up to speed. Hope you don't mind."

"My involvement in this investigation is not official. I can only give advice, and that's because I cleared it with my supervisor and..." He was about to say *Uncle John*, which was how Meg always referred to the admiral. "...and because Admiral Snider specifically requested my help."

"Yes, we know, Agent Bernstein."

Jake waved a hand. "Jake."

"Jake. This is our first big homicide case. We lost the other two NCIs to Seattle, so we're it until we get replacements for the two petty officers that left. We need your help. Our boss agrees and so does Admiral Snider."

Mary Lou nodded emphatically. "Yes. We absolutely need your help."

"Okay, what do you have? What've you spent all night learning?" Jake sipped from his drink, which was too sweet, but the caffeine would help focus his brain.

Javier scanned his notebook, took a deep breath, and dove in. "Sheila Lee has an H1-B temporary foreign student visa, the daughter of a bigwig from the People's Republic of China. Her real name is Xing Lee Peong, but she goes by Sheila Lee here in San Diego. Her father's the Minister of Culture in the PRC politburo. Her bodyguard, Xu-wen Ton, is a Chinese bodybuilding champ and works in security for the PRC consulate in Los Angeles." He shrugged. "A little over two hundred thousand students from the PRC come to the US every year. They attend colleges and universities all over the country and the percentage goes up yearly." He snorted. "Did you know that? I had no idea so many... Anyway, the cops have no local sheets on either of them. Clean as my mother's kitchen."

Mary Lou elbowed him. "The translation."

"Oh, yeah. We had Meg's phone recording of Sheila Lee translated. It's a little strange. It translated as, *Checking in. Rather dull tonight except for news of the navy officer's murder.* Then a break in her speech as she probably listens. We couldn't pick up the other end, so we don't know who she's speaking to. She continues with, *I should be in the cinema. Tell them I expect a movie contract.* Then she breaks off abruptly, no goodbye or anything." Javier raised his eyebrows. "So, Jake, what d'ya think?"

Taken out of context, Sheila could've been referring to anything or anyone. "Okay, what else?"

"Jimmy Park has a sheet. Petty theft, misdemeanor assault, small stuff mostly, during his juvie period. He was arrested two months ago for a DUI and possession of controlled substances but under the dealing limit. He got off with a fine and a six-month probation." Javier flipped over a page of his notebook and continued. "The San Diego Fire Department is still investigating the cause of the fire and is clamming up. But my one contact let it slip that they found a melted plastic liquor bottle—the liter size used by bartenders—with traces of kerosene. The accelerant. And the remnants of a couple of flares. The igniters. Hardware store supplies. It would've been worse if the stage curtains had been more flammable. The owners replaced them a few months ago after a club fire on the other side of town. The Lido's curtains were made from fire-retardant synthetic materials. The investigators are still checking out the ceiling sprinklers. They should've come on immediately."

Jake gulped half his drink and considered the information. The evidence suggested an inside job. But the motive? To ruin the business? Scare off the gays in town? Promote the theory of a hate crime?

Mary Lou jumped in. "All of Lieutenant Carlton's phone contacts were accounted for. Her father, Navy friends, co-workers, a couple to Lisa, and that burner phone number we can't trace. That same number was called multiple times during the months of November, December, and up to the evening of her death."

Jake frowned. "Someone close to her used a prepaid disposable. We'll never know who, most likely. My question is, why?"

"Could've been a friend from abroad," Mary Lou suggested. "He or she would probably buy a disposable phone. Sam traveled a lot with the fleet. Her last deployment was in the Arabian Sea. She might've met someone from one of her tours of duty who came to town. Most of those calls originated from disposables bought in California. We tracked the manufacturer's production numbers. Disposables bought here."

Javier cast her a skeptical glance. "Possibly, but calling Lieutenant Carlton two or three times a day? I don't call my girlfriend that much."

"Twice a day for a month and several times on the evening of her death, yeah, that's more than a casual friend." Mary Lou yawned loudly and excused herself.

Jake shifted impatiently. "This is all speculation. Interesting, though, that someone in frequent touch with our murder victim didn't want to be identified or merely found it expedient to use a burner. Sounds like Samantha was emotionally connected to that person. A friend or lover?" He blew air out of his cheeks. "Dig deeper into her personal life. Friends, family, co-workers, fellow seamen, and officers on her ship..."

"The USS Dixie. Triple A-class, two-year-old guided missile cruiser," Javier said.

"...the USS Dixie. Set up an interview with the medic on board. The ship's doctor usually knows all the personal dirt on the crew." Jake smiled. "That was the case when I was Navy. The doc was always the first to hear any gossip. Also, talk to her father. Maybe he found something in her condo that will shed some light."

Mary Lou nodded as she rejoined them. "Her father's still in town."

Jake nodded solemnly. "What else?"

Javier twisted in his seat and gestured to one of the two baristas behind the espresso machines. "I was talking to this guy in the club last night. Had to finally ID myself to get him to open up. He's the reason we're meeting here."

A tall, stick-thin young man sauntered over, his straight shoulder-length hair was as black as a crow. Reddish pimples dotted his face, but despite his unfortunate looks, he had an engaging smile and straight, white teeth. On cue from Javier, the young man approached their table.

"You must be the FBI guy." He thrust out his long arm. He spoke perfect, heavily accented English. Jake shook the fellow's slender hand and invited him to sit down. "I'm Domenico Fabrizio. Call me Dommy."

Javier introduced Jake as Special Agent Bernstein, then added, "Dommy and I were talking in The Lido last night about Sheila Lee. He has another connection with her—sorta roundabout, but interesting. Go ahead, tell him."

Dommy, clearly excited to speak to a real, bona fide FBI agent, directed his remarks to Jake. "Ensign Blanco asked me about Sheila last night before the fire happened. I moonlight as a server there on the weekends when they need me or when one of their regular servers is sick. My roommate—we're both students at San Diego State University—my roommate's dating a sailor who used to go out with Sheila. Angie says Sheila had this guy over at her place several times before he shipped out. They were hooked up—you know what I mean? Hooked up?"

Jake nodded, suddenly feeling more patient with the kid. "This sailor, what's his name? His rank?"

Dommy paused uncertainly. "I don't want him to get in trouble. Angie would be angry."

"No trouble," Jake assured him. "We'd just want to talk to him, confirm what you're telling us. Your roommate, too." He shot a pointed look over at the two NCIs. They both went to work in their notebooks.

"His name is Mack—Mike Mulvihill, but everyone calls him Mack. He's an engineer on an aircraft carrier. He and Angie email back and forth while he's deployed."

"Where is he now?"

"Somewhere in the Pacific. He can't tell Angie exactly where. Some top-secret mission." Dommy smiled at the three investigators. "I'm an engineering student, too. Mechanical engineering, mostly cars, not like Mack. He studied aeronautical engineering."

Javier exchanged looks with Jake, their tacit observations obviously followed the same inductive reasoning channels.

"So he's an officer or seaman tech?" Jake asked.

"I don't know. I only met him once, but I think he said he was an ensign. Ensign First Class. He told me he does something with missiles. Calibrating and testing the guidance systems. You have to ask Angie. Or Mack."

"How long did Mack date Sheila?" Javier asked.

"Mack told Angie he dated Sheila about three months before he shipped out last year. Before he met Angie."

"When did Mack ship out?"

"September—no, mid-October. He hooked up with Angie in August. They fell hard and fast. You know what I mean?"

"They had a sexual relationship? Mack and Sheila?" Jake needed to make it clear for the record.

Mary Lou furiously jotted notes in her notebook. Javier took a break from writing but listened intently.

Dommy grinned. "Oh, yeah. Mack told me that Sheila was hotter than anything he'd ever had before. Smoking hot. She would do anything." He punctuated the word *anything* by waving two hands in a circle gesture, and Jake got the point. "Now Sheila goes to a gay club and hooks up with women. That's not right."

Mary Lou stepped in rather curtly. "Maybe she's bisexual. Swings both ways."

Dommy shrugged dramatically. "That's possible, but I don't trust people like that."

Jake kept the young man on track. "So after a hot and heavy sexual relationship between Mack and Sheila Lee, they break up? Is that right, Dommy? Then Mack meets and falls in love with your roommate, Angie? You get to know him, then he ships out on his aircraft carrier?"

Mary Lou's pen froze in mid-air as she waited for Dommy's reply.

"That is right, all you said. What Mack told Angie," Dommy said, intertwining his long fingers, "was that he broke up with Sheila. He would not tell Angie why. Why would Mack get tired of all that hot sex? Something happened, I think, that turned him off. I don't know what. He didn't tell me, but he looked angry and embarrassed about it."

Jake sat back in his chair and glanced over at the two NCIs. They needed to speak to Angie and Mike Mulvihill next. If Mulvihill was temporarily incommunicado, they would have to go through Sec Nav—the Secretary of the Navy—and set up a satellite uplink transmission with the carrier. If everything Dommy said was true, Mack might be an important lead.

So who was this Sheila Lee really? An oversexed bisexual student from the People's Republic of China who just happened to have a thing for Navy personnel? Was she just another example of a girl gone wild while far from home?

Jake's experience in counterintelligence and counterterrorism told him differently.

Dommy abruptly frowned, tapping his long fingers on the table and attracting their full attention again. "After I learned this about Sheila, her relationship with Mack, and all of that, I began to look for her at the club. You know, thinking I could hook up with her. Maybe she would like *me*, have hot sex with *me*." He grinned in a self-deprecating way. "So the nights I worked there, I flirted, you know, brought her free drinks, said nice things to her. But, no, I was invisible to her. She, how do you say, only had eyes for the Navy men and women at the club. The officers, mostly. One, especially."

Jake sat up straight. So did Javier and Mary Lou. The tension grew so thick you could almost cut it with a knife. He sensed what was coming and cocked his head, riveting his gaze on Dommy. "Which Navy officer?"

"The one who was murdered. Samantha. Lieutenant Carlton. Everyone called her Sam. She was a little old for The Lido, but hey—"

Jake interrupted, "You're sure that Sheila was having an affair with Lieutenant Carlton?"

Dommy bent over and bowed his head, his embarrassment acute in the slump of his entire body. "Yes. I liked Samantha. She always gave me good tips. Smiled and was friendly. So when I saw her spending a lot of time sitting and drinking with Sheila, I wondered if they were together. I followed them one night, over the bridge to Coronado Island, to Samantha's place." He quickly added, "I wasn't stalking them. I just followed them once. No, twice."

Silence followed as the two NCIs stared at Dommy. Jake's pulse began to race—a familiar reaction he always had to a solid lead in any investigation. The unexpected turn in Dommy's testimony, however, was just speculation. They would need proof that Sheila and Sam had carried on a secret liaison together. And maybe something more.

"They could've been just friends," Mary Lou said.

"No." Dommy shook his head. "Not possible. They were kissing as they went up the steps to Samantha's place. From that night on, I watched them at the club. They always sat together in a group of women who go there. I could see that Samantha was—what's the word?—moonstruck. Sheila, not so much,

I think. Sheila and her bodyguard would follow Samantha in a separate car. I followed them one more time, you know, to satisfy my curiosity. Maybe to convince myself that Sheila did not reject me, the man, that she really preferred women. Ask Lisa. She knew what was going on."

Javier darted a glance at Jake. Javier's mouth twitched in anger, and Jake knew the reason. Why hadn't Lisa said anything about Samantha's relationship with Sheila when the NCIs interviewed her on the phone the morning Samantha's body was found?

Surely, Navy personnel were warned against fraternizing with citizens of a country notorious for stealing national secrets. The Chinese didn't just pirate DVDs and Prada handbags. For years, a majority of the FBI's known cyber terrorists were private citizens and government workers of the PRC. Their government gave tacit approval to all forms of theft.

Why would Samantha take the risk and get involved with a citizen of the PRC, especially a young woman with such political connections? As a Navy officer, Samantha should've known better. She should have been less trusting.

Jake questioned it but didn't say anything. Had Samantha betrayed her country? Was Sheila a spy? Was she also a killer? But if she'd turned a Navy officer, then why kill her?

Jake recalled a passage from an FBI report he'd read as an analyst a couple of years before.

American universities are an ideal place for foreign intelligence services to find recruits, propose and nurture ideas, learn and even steal research data or place trainees for the purpose of spying on that nation.

More than any other country, the PRC sent their graduate students to the US to *learn* what they could. All the FBI could do was damage control when students turned out to be spies.

He felt the weight of Javier and May Lou's stares.

Apparently, Javier had another line of thought, which he was quick to express. "So, Dommy, why should we believe you? You're the rejected wannabe lover of this beautiful Chinese woman. This could all be sour grapes. Retaliation for Sheila giving you the brush off."

The young man's black eyebrows rose in surprise, and his mouth fell open. "Do you think I am lying to the police? Lying to the FBI? Just for revenge against that woman? No!" His flat palm slapped the tabletop. "No! I am not that stupid. There are laws about lying to the police. Why would I risk losing my visa for that? I want to stay in this country. I'm trying to help. Nothing more."

His complexion colored to match the dark pimples. Javier stared him down and said nothing. Bad cop.

Mary Lou intervened and reassured Dommy they would investigate further, that they tended to believe what he had said, and that he was in no danger of losing his student visa. They appreciated his honesty and courage in coming forward. Good cop.

A moment later, Dommy was no longer apoplectic and had calmed down enough to sputter, "I must get back to work." With a tired sigh, he gave the two NCIs contact information for Angie, details about Lieutenant Mike Mulvihill, and his own personal details and student visa status.

Minutes later, Jake stood by his rental car and reviewed Dommy's testimony with the NCIs.

"Do you believe him?" Javier asked.

Resting his arms on the hood of his car, Jake gazed across the lot at the Queen palms lining the perimeter of the strip mall. The graceful, feathery fronds rustled in the balmy breezes coming off the ocean. The day was lovely, cool, sunny, and the sky a vivid blue. He longed for a stroll on the Torrey Pines fairways. A chance to walk and think. Alone.

Meg would be busy with her tutees most of the day and then hosting a meeting of the German Club later. Jake intended to stay away until the German Club met at four. Then he'd make an appearance and convince Herr Shit-Face that Meg was spoken for. He'd make his message clear. *Bug off, bro.*

He faced the two Navy investigators. To them, the world was still fresh and somewhat innocent. Despite their training, they probably wanted to believe the best about people. At least, that was Jake about fifteen years ago. Not anymore. For him, the world was a dangerous, deceitful place, even in beautiful, sunny San Diego.

"Yeah, I believe him. So follow that connection but verify everything he said. Set up a SATCOM link if you have to with Mulvihill's ship and talk to this guy. Something spooked him off hot, free sex. Maybe it wasn't so free."

Jake took his key fob out of his pants pocket and unlocked the car doors. Nevertheless, he remained standing. *Be thorough. Leave no stone unturned.* "Also, verify with Angie everything Mulvihill told her. It's all second-hand information but something new might shake out. And let's meet early Monday morning at Samantha's condo before the oh-nine-hundred briefing. I want to see her place. Arrange for Samantha's father to meet us there. We need to interview him before he leaves with Samantha's body. Find out what you can about her, her background, values, personality, and habits. How much does any father know about his adult daughter? It might turn up something useful."

Mary Lou had given up her notebook and used her smartphone to record Jake's instructions. He reminded himself to choose his words carefully.

"Have either of you been approached by the media about this case?"

Mary Lou and Javier looked a little surprised, glanced at each other, then shook their heads. Just as Jake surmised. The local reporters were following the local PD's rush to judgment. Well, good. It'll make the real killer complacent and maybe let his guard down.

"Even if you're approached, *no comment* is the official reply. Okay, well, let's follow this lead to its logical conclusion," Jake said. "It might peter out to nothing or open up an international can of worms."

The two NCIs stared at him with eyes wide and mouths open.

Jake smiled grimly and climbed in his Explorer. His golf clubs were in the back, waiting.

Time to walk and think.

Chapter Nine

LOUD VOICES ASSAILED Jake as he ascended the outside staircase to Meg's corner apartment. He stopped on the landing to gaze at the winter's pale sun, sinking behind the row of palm trees to the west of her apartment complex. Instead of an intimate dinner along the wharf, Jake was about to face a roomful of German language students led by the man he referred to as *Herr Scheisse-Gesicht*—aka Herr Shit-face. Jake shook off his murderous thoughts and pasted on a phony smile as he opened the door.

He immediately headed to Meg, sitting on a stool by the kitchen counter. She greeted him with a hug, and he returned the embrace tightly, then kissed her thoroughly. Whatever discussion in German going on temporarily halted, then slowly resumed following a tittering of chuckles and comments.

He eased back and smiled at her. Her long blonde hair hung over her shoulder, not pulled back in her usual ponytail. Her ears were adorned with the large gold hoop earrings she often wore when they went out at night. She wore a light brown knitted tunic over black leggings and black ankle boots. Around her neck hung the gold chain and amber pendant he'd given her in Germany six months before, after the conclusion of his investigation into her grandmother.

Bernstein, he'd told her, pronouncing the word in the German way. *That's my name and the German word for amber. To remember me by.* He had thought he'd never see her again. Meg had been so upset at him over her grandmother's suicide.

Meg released him but held on to his arm. "So glad you made it back in time. I want you to meet my German Club. But first, there's beer in that cooler over there. And bratwurst, *krautsalat, und kartoffelsalat* on the table. Paper plates and forks there, too."

He helped himself to the food while Meg introduced him to the group of nine students and one professor. While receiving greetings in German, Jake nodded and held up his beer bottle in a kind of toast to acknowledge them. Instead of speaking, he dug into the plump, savory bratwurst and German-style potato salad—*kartoffelsalat*. The salad was heavy in mustard, just the way he liked it, and the wurst dripped with juices. The sweetened coleslaw—*krautsalat*—wasn't bad, either. Meg locked gazes with him, a question implicit in her expression.

He simply smiled and concentrated on his food, realizing he hadn't eaten all day. Five young men sat on the carpet, swigging their beer, and four young women were on the couch and one chair. Professor Heinz sat in the second chair, clearly moderating the discussion spoken in German. Half listening, Jake picked up the gist of it. They were debating over one of two articles they'd all read in the weekly German newspaper, *Die Zeitung*. The students had chosen sides, the socialist democrats versus the more conservative party of Chancellor Angela Merkel.

Heinz interjected, "I'd ask Jake to chime in, but he can't speak German, obviously, and seems more inclined to stuff his face." He glanced at Meg, probably to gauge the effect of his snide remark.

When a few students half chuckled, Meg looked at Jake and seemed about to object. Jake gave her a silent signal to let it go. She responded with an ironic smile and raised eyebrows. Jake nonchalantly pretended to ignore the snide remark and swallowed the last bite of his bratwurst before taking a long draw from his beer bottle.

Rather than drop his lame attempt at ridicule, Heinz continued his foot-in-mouth routine, this time in German. "Fraulein Larsen's friend is firmly glued to that table, I believe. She should make him the centerpiece. Like a hog with an apple in his mouth."

Some students looked at Jake, others looked away. It was clear to Jake that they'd already picked up on the professor's attraction to Meg and thus the implied rivalry in the man's gibe.

One young woman attempted a mild admonishment with, "Herr professor..."

Jake sighed. Time to step in. He walked to the outer fringe of the circle in Meg's small living room. He wasn't about to take a patch of floor, so he leaned against the wall behind one of the young men.

How long had it been since he'd spoken German? He'd translated a briefing report from the *Nachrichtendienst*, the German Intelligence Service about four months ago. Two months before that, he was in Hannover, Germany, saving Meg and her grandmother from the ringleaders of a neo-Nazi organization.

His knowledge of the German language went back at least twenty-five years, as long as he could remember. He'd originally learned the language from his German-born grandfather, Nathan Bernstein, who'd immigrated to the US in the early nineteen-thirties to escape the Nazi pogroms. High school and college German classes followed, put to useful work in Navy intelligence, FBI reports, and various undercover assignments in which his fluent German became necessary. Evidently, Meg had neglected to inform the group of this. Which was okay with him. It made the moment all the more satisfying.

"*Entschuldigung bitte.*," he began, speaking flawless Berliner-accented German, "On behalf of Herr Heinz, I wish to apologize. Müncheners, like the professor, are usually not so impolite to the friends of their hostess, in this case, Fraulein Larsen. But we all must make allowances for petty brinkmanship."

Heinz's chin jutted upwards, and his eyes flashed a mix of humiliation and fury. His pale skin, from the neck up, flushed a nauseating shade of mottled pink. Dead silence ensued as the students comprehended what Jake had said and snuck furtive glances at Heinz. Meg's expression defused the situation. She even apologized to the professor for not warning him that Jake spoke fluent German.

A floodgate of questions from the students followed. How long had Jake studied German? How long did it take to become fluent? When they learned he was an FBI agent, they wanted to know if he ever used German at work. What was the career path like for Americans who spoke German? On and on, the barrage of interest directed Jake's way did not let up for thirty minutes. Jake answered all their questions, deflecting some about the FBI that were too sensitive, but answered a few. All in German.

The newspaper articles in *Die Zeitung* were forgotten until Heinz finally stood up to take his leave. "We'll discuss these political articles in class on Tuesday."

Everyone filed out after the professor, shaking Jake's hand and thanking Meg for her hospitality as they went.

When they were finally alone, Meg wrapped her arms around his waist. "Jakey boy, you were very naughty."

He gave her a lopsided grin and a one-shoulder shrug. "He had it coming. *Schadenfreude* works for me. And you're just as guilty, foxy lady. You could've told him beforehand I spoke German. What was that all about?"

"Yes, well," she quipped, her tone a bit flinty, "I was trying to tell him to back off. He's an arrogant know-it-all. Thinks he's God's gift to women. He chased me all last semester, wouldn't take any of my hints. Finally, I had to threaten to report him. I had to invite him today. He's head of the German Club."

Jake felt a release of anxiety deep within him. Meg had never told him, but he'd sensed something between her and the professor. He half-turned away and expelled the tension through a sigh, which he quickly covered up.

"Good. So you gave him rope and let him hang himself, so to speak?"

She nodded. "I think he got the message. So, want to help me clean up here?"

He surveyed the damage that nearly a dozen college students could do to an apartment the size of his condo's walk-in closet and decided the German Club bunch was fairly well-behaved.

"Wanting to is a stretch, but yeah, sure. By the way, great bratwurst."

"I know you like German food. We're having barbecued wurst at Uncle John's tomorrow."

"Wurst, I like." He gathered all the empty beer bottles and tossed them into her kitchen trash can. Helped her put the meager leftovers in the fridge.

Then he remembered her birthday was the next day and he'd gotten so caught up in the Lieutenant Carlton case, he'd forgotten about shopping for a gift. *Scheisse!* Maybe he could run and pick up something. "What's going on the rest of tonight?"

"Whatever you like," Meg said, bending over to tie the ends of the trash bag. She turned her head back to him and waggled her behind.

That made him smile. And reach for her.

And forget again about her birthday gift.

Much, much later, Jake sat up in bed and cradled Meg's head against his chest. They spoke in hushed, relaxed tones, still basking in the afterglow of sexual release. A time to build intimacy and trust, yet he picked up a different vibe from Meg, a kind of melancholy.

"One of my students didn't show up for my tutoring class today," Meg whispered, referring to her helping the students at the local high school. "The girl from the restaurant Friday night. Sarah Daoud. Her friend, Marsha, was there and told me Sarah's mother was in the hospital."

"What happened?" Jake asked.

"Marsha said Sarah's mother was beaten up just outside their restaurant Friday night. She was closing up, and some men attacked her."

"Where was her husband? Don't they close the restaurant together?"

Meg raised her head and looked at him. "That's exactly what I asked. Marsha didn't know the details other than Sarah's mother told police her attackers were strangers. And while they were beating her, they were yelling threats against Muslims and Middle Eastern immigrants."

Jake continued to stroke her bare shoulder.

"I called Sarah's cell phone, but it went to voice mail. Marsha said Sarah's father took away her phone."

"Don't get involved, Meg. I know you're concerned, but don't get involved. You don't know the details or what's going on in that family. Escondido has one of the nation's largest Muslim communities, you know. They help each other, and they don't rat on each other to the cops."

"What're you saying?"

Jake kissed the top of her head. "I saw Sarah's mother in the kitchen the other night. She had a black eye and a bruised face. The way your student behaved...all the signs are there. Sarah's mother is a battered wife. We don't know what else is going on."

A deep sigh escaped Meg. "I wonder if there's anything I can do to help Sarah."

"Probably not. Just be her friend. Listen if she wants to talk."

She stiffened in his arms. "I also got a call from you-know-who."

He didn't make the connection. "Who?"

"Sheila."

Jake sat up slowly. "No shit?" He raised a knee, rested an elbow on it, and rubbed the whiskers on his face.

"What shall I do? She wants to meet for drinks. I put her off, but I could always change my mind."

"Don't call her back, Meg. She's a person of interest in the Carlton case. It's is too dangerous."

"That's all the more reason why I should call her. I can help the investigation. When she found out I was a Navy officer, she showed a lot of interest. Maybe I could wear a wire and draw her out."

"That's too dangerous. I'm not going to use you as bait. No way."

"Are you sure? I could find out what she knows about Samantha Carlton."

He lay back down and wrapped an arm around her. "No way, no how," he repeated. "Let's go to sleep."

"I'm too keyed up."

He grinned, flipped back the covers, and eased her down on the soft mattress, then rolled on top of her. "I've got just the thing to help you relax."

Chapter Ten

THOUGHTS OF SARAH DAOUD and her mother wouldn't leave Meg's mind. The following day, as she and Jake prepared to head to her Uncle John's house on Coronado Island, she insisted they take a quick detour for a brief visit to take Mrs. Daoud some flowers. After plying Jake with her charms, he finally gave in and drove her there.

About thirty miles northeast of and inland from San Diego, Escondido remained a working class, mostly suburban town. Near the center of the downtown area, Sarah Daoud's mother lay in a ward at the local hospital. Meg stopped and bought a vase of flowers at the hospital gift shop on their way to the ward.

After Meg explained to the nurse at the check-in station that she was one of Sarah's teachers and wanted to bring flowers for the girl's mother, the woman gave her the room number. They stopped and bought a vase of flowers at the hospital gift shop on their way to the ward.

Two men stood in the hallway outside of Mrs. Daoud's room, sizing up Meg and Jake as they approached. Both men were in their mid to late forties, with dark hair and heavy beards. Although they were dressed in casual Western attire—from their jeans to their button-down shirts—they still appeared Middle Eastern. Aware their visit might not be welcomed by Sarah's father, Meg approached with her chin raised defiantly. It was within her right to see her student and her student's mother. The nurse had said it was okay for her to visit, and Meg was determined to do so.

Meg turned to Jake. "I'll just be a moment. You should wait here, okay?"

"I'll be over there." Jake pointed to a small alcove a couple of feet away with a small cube-shaped table and two uncomfortable-looking molded plastic chairs. Clearly, visitors weren't encouraged to stay long.

Grateful for the absence of his I-told-you-so smugness, Meg nodded to him while she grazed his hand in thanks.

Quietly, she eased open the door and passed a sleeping woman on her way to Mrs. Daoud's half of the room. Behind the drawn curtain, Sarah hovered over her mother, weeping softly. The girl looked up suddenly, gasping in surprise as Meg appeared with a vase of roses in hand. Meg suppressed her own gasp as her gaze settled on Sarah's mother.

The condition of Mrs. Daoud's face shocked her. The woman's features were so obscured by the purplish, swollen skin and eyes they were nearly unrecognizable. Meg assumed the woman was either unconscious or sleeping. Probably sedated. Mrs. Daoud's chest barely moved, her breathing shallow and labored. One arm was in a cast, and two IV lines snaked from the other bruised arm. Swaths of bandages covered her upper torso. One of Mrs. Daoud's legs stuck out from under the blanket, also casted from thigh to ankle and supported by a sling suspended from the ceiling. One side of her body had clearly taken the brunt of the beating.

Recovering her composure, Meg placed the vase on the tray table near the foot of the bed, rolled the tray out of the way, and sidled up next to Sarah. She fought back tears and slipped a hand on the girl's shoulder. A heartbreaking moment later, Sarah clung to Meg, letting go and sobbing.

"It's going to be okay," Meg murmured against the scarf that covered Sarah's dark hair.

During the tutoring sessions at school, Sarah never wore the *hajib* that most religious Muslim girls and women wore. Yet now, in the presence of her mother and the other men, she covered her head and wore no makeup. The poor girl was jockeyed between two worlds, trying to fit into one while simultaneously attempting to appease the other. When Sarah's sobbing subsided to occasional shudders and sniffs, Meg led her to two nearby chairs.

"What happened, Sarah?" Meg took a seat.

The girl gazed down at the linoleum floor and wiped her nose and eyes with a tissue. Meg waited.

Sarah shook her head slowly. "Some men, bad men, attacked her. They beat her with their fists and kicked her. One used a...a bat."

"Is this what you told the police?"

Sarah nodded. "I found Mama on the ground. Father was still in the restaurant's kitchen and said he didn't hear or see anything. I came back to the restaurant because...because I was worried for her. I rode my bike. The restaurant is just half a mile from our house."

"You saw the men who attacked your mother?"

Sarah hesitated, then nodded.

"Was your mother able to give a description to the police? Was she able to describe her attackers?"

Sarah looked toward the half-open doorway and lowered her voice to a whisper. "Not really. They were strangers, big white men. Americans. Father told the police this was another hate crime by Americans against Muslims. He said there have been many hate crimes lately in the San Diego area. Father said he's going to sue someone. Maybe the government. Maybe the police for not protecting Muslims. My father's very upset."

Sarah's voice cracked and quivered so much that Meg wondered if her student was in shock.

Meg patted the girl's back. Her sympathy notwithstanding, she felt something was off. Maybe she was imagining things, but Sarah's explanation sounded rehearsed, memorized.

"They took out my mother's spleen. The doctor said it was ruptured, but she can live without a spleen. Is this true, Miss Larsen?"

Meg wasn't sure, but if the doctor said so, who was she to say otherwise. "Yes, if the doctor says so, it's true. Your mother will take a long time to recover, though. Does she have family in the area? Besides your father? Someone who can help her and you? Parents, sisters, brothers?"

Sarah wilted. "My mother was born and raised in Egypt, but her family came here when she was young. Her marriage was arranged by her and Father's parents. Except for my brother Jafar and me, she has no one else nearby. Her whole family lives in Detroit." A tear escaped the girl's sad, dark eyes. "So you see, here we have only Father. What he says, we have to do." Her quivering voice dropped to a whisper. "What he says, we have to say."

Meg could only nod in sympathy and understanding. She felt the girl's choice of words and confidential manner of speaking were telegraphing another message. Everything about the girl registered fear.

"Is your father one of the men in the hall?" Meg asked.

The girl glanced at the door and shook her head. "He's at the restaurant. Sunday's always a big day. He told me I could come and stay with Mother."

"Who are those two men, Sarah?"

"Friends of my father's." A moment passed before she stood and took her spot by her mother's bedside. "Thank you for coming, Miss Larsen, but you should go now."

Meg hesitated and was about to advise Sarah to always tell the police the truth, when her attention diverted to a commotion in the hallway. Raised male voices drew her glance toward the doorway. Not that Jake couldn't hold his own with such men. Months ago, he'd gone undercover to become one of them. Had joined a violent, extremist Islamic group in Silicon Valley to uncover a plot to blow up Candlestick Park at game time. He even spoke Arabic and probably knew more about Islamic history, religion, and the various Islamic sects and cultures than many Muslims. There were still many details about that operation that she would never know. Jake said much of it was classified.

Meg could only wonder why the two men in the hallway spoke so heatedly. Were they outraged at what had happened to Mrs. Daoud? Angry over what Sarah presented as a crime of hatred against a religious minority?

She patted Sarah's arm. "If I can do anything for you and your family, just let me know. If you need extra tutoring help, let Marsha know. I can send home some assignments."

Sarah nodded, on the verge of tears again. "Thank you."

JAKE CONTINUED TO PERUSE the magazine, turning the pages every thirty seconds or so, pretending to browse the articles. Occasionally, he handled his cell phone atop the magazine and pretended to text with both thumbs when he wasn't reading. In truth, he was listening to the two men's angry voices, not more than a dozen feet away. Apparently confident an American male wouldn't comprehend their language, they spoke freely with each other in Arabic at a low volume acceptable enough for a hospital setting but loud enough for Jake to hear snatches of their conversation.

What he heard shocked even him. Although not familiar with their particular dialect, enough formal Arabic was used to understand the topic of their discussion.

Honor killings. Which were not that common in the Muslim American communities, but they did occur. Of course, there was nothing honorable about them, but Muslim men justified such violence as necessary to maintain the honor of a family. Most Americans would be deeply disturbed if they knew the extent of these *honor killings*, but the media under-reported such crimes. After all, such reporting wasn't considered politically correct these days.

Jake knew the FBI in every city where Muslim populations were increasing hosted seminars for the local law enforcement agencies on this topic. The usual male-on-female violence, usually perpetrated by a male close to the female victim, often ended with the girl or woman refusing to identify the assailants. The cops would spin their wheels for a few days or weeks, hunting down phantom attackers, only to give up the chase when their supposed leads proved false, or the trail went cold.

The most frequent reason for these so-called *honor killings*? Nothing more than the girl or woman was becoming too Westernized. Rebellion against the authority of the Muslim male in her family was tantamount to the girl or woman committing treason against her country. In some Islamic sects, punishable by death.

So much for cultural assimilation into American values and traditions, Jake groused to himself. Other ethnic immigrant groups had difficulty assimilating, but none were so violently opposed to Western values as conservative Muslims, in his experience, anyway. He'd never hear this conclusion from the official FBI media releases, however, nor from the current Attorney General. Even the FBI manuals had been changed. The word *Muslim* or *Islamic* had been stricken before any reference to terrorism.

So much bullshit.

Admittedly, Jake could only hear half of what these men said, their heads turned away from him most of the time, and their voices lowered as they paced in the hallway. Still, he thought he'd gotten the gist. And his smartphone's digital recorder captured the bulk of it. With volume enhancement and the miracles FBI techs could perform, nearly every word should be accessible. His Arabic might be a little rusty and leaned more toward the formal language taught to school children, not their idiomatic dialect, but he understood enough.

Jake gathered from the men's conversation that Sarah's mother's beating was an honor killing gone wrong. The two men spent most of the time in the hallway, trying to understand what had gone wrong. Their plan should've worked but failed. There was something else about the attack. Something about Sarah coming along too soon and screaming.

The rest, Jake couldn't hear or comprehend. Still, the men circled on and on, gnawing at their failure to achieve the honorable killing of Fatimah Daoud. What Jake couldn't catch from their heated discussion was the reason for it.

The deep voices of the two men resonated with dishonor and shame. And warning. Now that the police were involved, what could they do? They had to be cautious. There was something about Sarah telling the police. She said two American men did this. The police would blame bigots, militant Jews and Christians, the enemies of Islam, whoever...

More was conveyed in their tone of voice. The rest, Jake cobbled together from separate words that he could understand. They would wait and bide their time.

Jake pocketed his cell phone, threw down the magazine, and stood up. He'd heard enough to want to toss their sorry asses in prison for years, but a lot of good it would do.

Without the testimony of Mrs. Daoud and her daughter, who'd evidently witnessed the tail-end of the attack, the cops wouldn't arrest, and the DA wouldn't prosecute. The two men's discussion—basically an admission of their complicity in this crime—was inadmissible in a court of law, ill-gotten without a warrant. No judge, jury, or courtroom audience would ever hear it.

Just then, Meg exited the room, clearly dazed with sorrow. She seized his hand, and they left the ward silently. When she asked him how the visit had gone for him, he avoided her eyes and deflected her question with a shrug.

"That bad, huh? I was worried the men might bother you. They sounded a little angry."

"Those cowards? They're only tough with women and children. How was your visit with Sarah and her mother?"

If he told Meg what he'd heard, she would want to immediately run to the cops. By interfering, she'd only accomplish making herself a target and putting Sarah in even greater danger than she already was.

Meg hung her head. "It's a miracle Mrs. Daoud didn't die. I hope they find the bastards who did this to her. Poor Sarah. She said she saw the two big white men. Americans. They ran off when she got there and started screaming."

He heard the catch in her voice, and her deep blue eyes filled with disbelief and pain. They exited the hospital and paused in the afternoon sunlight. Outside, the world was sunny, hopeful, even normal. Not perfect but...well, normal. The shit he'd heard inside seemed to evaporate a little when he gazed up at the blue, cloudless sky.

"Yeah, I'd like to see those cowards rot in jail. Or worse."

He took his cell phone out of his jeans pocket. He was going against what he thought wise, but the look on Meg's face, a shocked, naïve civilian, made him change his mind.

"Remember what you did Friday night? How you taped that Chinese woman in the bathroom with the digital recorder on your cell phone?"

Meg nodded, her eyes growing wide as her mouth opened slightly. "You taped those two men? Without their knowing?"

"Yep, without a warrant."

Meg looked puzzled, so he went on.

"I pretended to be texting someone. The local cops might want to hear this and get it amplified and translated. Or maybe not. What they do with it, it's their call. But keep this in mind, Sarah's life might be in danger if I play this for the police. They'll pressure her to turn state's evidence against her father. Others could get to her before she testifies. I'm telling you, Meg, I've heard of this happening before. Michigan, Missouri, New Jersey, Florida... More times than you can imagine. Even here in sunny California."

Meg's jaw dropped, and her hand flew up to cover her mouth. Her vacant stare told him she was processing the horrible truth and having difficulty with it. "I don't understand. What're you saying?"

"I'm saying, I think it was an attempted honor killing. Follow the narrow Islamic path. Or else."

She bit her bottom lip. "You're sure?"

He zigzagged his hand. "I'm not familiar with the dialect they were speaking, but I think I understood enough."

Meg remained silent until they reached his SUV, and the dam finally burst. She climbed in and doubled over, covering her face and weeping like a child.

He pulled her against his shoulder, laid his cheek against her hair, inhaled her distinct scent of lavender and citrus, and waited. "Maybe I shouldn't have told you."

Civilians were always shocked at the evil among them. When it surfaced, that is. He was officially on leave, but still a federal law enforcement officer. Did he want to involve the San Diego field office based on his overhearing a conversation in a language he wasn't fluent in? And based on an inadmissible tape recording?

Hell, yes.

"Sarah, poor Sarah..." Meg's keening cries, broken by soft sobs, dwindled to panting sniffles. "Her mother, Jake, you should've seen what they did to her..."

"Meg, you can talk to Sarah, but don't expect her to implicate her father or her father's friends. Sarah knows what's truly at stake."

"Wh-what do you mean?"

Meg wasn't thinking logically about the situation, too caught up in the horror of what she'd seen and what he'd just told her. She hadn't even begun to see the complexity of the situation, much less seeking justice.

"Sarah's life is at stake," he said gently. "Put yourself in Sarah's shoes. All the way, Meg. Then take a good, deep look. If I take this to the cops or the bureau, her very life might be threatened."

Although they were no longer in the mood for a lighthearted family barbecue, they continued in tense silence toward Meg's uncle's house. Just as Jake exited Interstate Eight onto the Mission Valley Freeway, he noticed the tail. He'd been too distracted to spot it before.

Had they been followed all the way from the hospital?

Chapter Eleven

JAKE RE-CHECKED HIS rearview mirror. That late-model red Honda had dogged their tail for miles, and he now recalled seeing a similar car in the hospital parking lot. A lone male driver kept moving his mouth as if speaking on a Blue Tooth device.

So Daoud was a little more than curious about his wife's visitors. He'd sent one of his pals to conduct surveillance, though it was sloppy and amateurish.

Jake immediately formed a plan and laid it out for Meg as calmly as he could. In response, she snapped out of her mental fog and straightened in her seat. Their latest jog around the UC campus had presented some possibilities for them to shake this tail.

He mentally took inventory of what he had on hand. In the back seat on the floor, hidden under an old sweatshirt, was a backpack that held some of his work gear, as he called it—his locked and loaded .40 caliber Glock pistol and two full magazines and his old Navy combat knife with knuckle guard and two parallel blood grooves to keep it from getting slippery in his hand. He recalled vividly—how could he forget?—the last time he'd used both. His last black op with SEAL Team Three.

"Meg, take out your cell phone. I've got an idea."

She'd done as he asked just as they pulled into the parking lot behind the basketball gym on the north side of the university's campus. Jake grabbed the backpack and swung it over one shoulder, locking the SUV with his key fob as they headed for the gym at a slow trot.

Meg stayed on full alert and kept pace with him as she held her phone in camera mode. They entered the gym, which had been converted into a grid of eight volleyball courts. Women teams engaged in a tournament, and their raucous shouting fans had turned the gym into a cacophony of reverberating noise. They walked around the edges of the bleachers and exited the gym on the south side. Running at a medium jog, they traversed the campus and arrived at the south-side parking lot. Two blocks later, they found Meg's Dodge Durango in her apartment building's carport.

"Stay here, Meg. You'll be safe in this crowd, but let me take your car." He bent over to catch his breath, realizing he wasn't physically up to par yet. His ankle and shoulder both throbbed. He looked over at Meg, who was faring better than he was. She'd barely broken a sweat.

She shook her head. "No way. I'm going with you."

In mild exasperation, he sighed audibly. "Okay, but do as I say. No heroics. We're there to surveil, not engage."

When they arrived back at the north-side parking lot outside the gym, Jake pulled Meg's Durango to the curb. He spied the red Honda parked at the curb, facing them about thirty yards away. The driver was staring at the gymnasium building, his mouth still moving, obviously communicating with someone.

Jake pulled a navy blue baseball cap from his backpack, tamped it down over his head, and gently pushed Meg down in her seat. His backpack sat at her feet, but her cell phone nestled in her lap.

"Take photos when I start moving, but don't get out. Don't know what this guy has on him." Jake grabbed his cell phone from his pocket, opened the car door, and eased out of the driver's seat onto the roadway. He knelt beside the cement curb, clicked a series of digital photos of the red Honda's license plate, and then waited. He thought of something and reached back to grab the sweatshirt he'd left on his car seat.

As Jake expected, the driver of the red Honda emerged from his seat with something in his hands. A few clicks of the camera and a closer look through the viewfinder revealed a dark-haired bearded man in his twenties. He wore Western-style clothes—jeans and a button-down shirt with the tails hanging out. It was the younger guy from the hospital, and he carried a baseball bat.

Jake swore as he watched the man approach his parked Explorer, knowing what the asshole was about to do. A simple vandalism charge would get the guy a slap-down and he'd be out on bail in two hours. Valuable potential intel would be lost.

Meg leaned over in the driver's seat and whispered softly through the open car door. "Jake, Sarah said one of her mother's attackers used a baseball bat. Do you think—"

He reminded her to stay down and eased the door shut. He'd learned with his bureau training and experience with the SEALs Team Three that intel was everything. Having already made up his mind, Jake shrugged on the sweatshirt, snagged his lethal combat knife and held it in his left hand. On second thought, he flicked the safety off his Glock and eased it into his back waistband. Then he pocketed the phone, rose from his haunches, and rounded the front left bumper. A big sycamore tree concealed his position, but he was prepared to confront the asshole. And if the guy was packing, Jake intended to be ready.

The guy rapidly scanned the parking lot before he strode up to Jake's black Explorer. He could've been a ballplayer, the way he held the bat back and then switched balance from his right leg to his left. The bat swung in an arc and crashed into the Explorer's left taillight. The sound of the impact could be heard as far as Jake's cover. The car alarm shrieked as the guy batted away. Meanwhile, Jake noted Meg was catching all the action on her camera.

Next, the Explorer's rear bumper took a beating, then the cargo hold's hatchback door, shattering glass over the parking lot.

Fuck it, the asshole was strong and wielded the bat like a pro. He was also a coward of the first order, most likely having used it on a poor, defenseless woman during his last time at bat. Jake wanted nothing more than to teach the schmuck a lesson he'd never forget.

Finally, Jake pulled the sweatshirt hood over the baseball cap and the back hem over his pistol. With most of his face concealed by the hood, the cap, and dark aviator shades, his cover as a university student was now complete. He emerged from behind the tree and strolled across the street.

"Hey! What the hell you doing?" Jake shouted loud enough from his position at the edge of the parking lot to be heard over the car alarm's continued two-beat wail.

Jake's sudden appearance clearly surprised the vandal, and the bat froze mid-swing. The guy's eyes flickered over Jake's tall height and sturdy build before settling on his fists. Caught off-guard, the man appeared to weigh his options. Then panic—or prudence—set in, and the guy dropped the bat and took off, rounding a row of cars on the far side of the parking lot.

"Hey!" Jake shouted again, standing still instead of pursuing the man. *Let him get away... Right now, grab the bat. We'll get him later.*

The evidence was more important than tackling the guy, subduing him, and holding him until the cops arrived. They'd want to know who Jake was... Too soon to let that happen.

Seconds later, the asshole was leaving rubber along the street as he peeled out, took the nearest side street, and disappeared. Jake hollered over to Meg to bring her phone over and take some pictures. In short order, having kept her emotions in check, she'd snapped photos of his vandalized car, the glass shards on the ground, and the bat lying near the rear tire. A moment later, Jake bent down and picked up the bat, using his sweatshirt hem as a glove. He examined it closely. It was a wooden bat, thank God. The FBI forensic lab would probably find blood and tissue traces in the tiny grooves.

Carefully, he brought the bat to the Durango and had Meg snap another photo before wrapping it in a paper bag she had in the trunk. After shedding his sweatshirt, he realized he was covered with perspiration.

Meg studied him, her dark blue eyes widening with sudden knowledge. "I wondered why you didn't go after him... Now I know." She stared at the bat, resting in its paper bag on the back seat. "You sacrificed your car for...that."

"Rental car. Besides, it's evidence. Should get the asshole fifteen years instead of"—he hooked his thumb in the direction of his wrecked SUV—"fifteen minutes. With bail and some cocked-up story, he'd bargain down to community service, if that. Like you said, we've gotta get the bastards who tried to kill Sarah's mother."

Meg's anxious expression dissolved into a tentative smile. "I see your point."

"Well, there might be more fish to fry than we think. So tomorrow, I'll take a trip to the bureau's San Diego field office. See what kinds of vermin they can scare out of the dark."

The men's paranoia and hostility were so extreme that even somewhat naïve Meg caught the connection between Mrs. Daoud's attack and this vandalism. Something else was going on, and Jake was determined to find out exactly what it was.

He took out his cell phone and called the rental car company. He sure wasn't going to end up on their favorite customer list.

"Got another Explorer on hand?" he asked the rental car clerk.

Chapter Twelve

MEG INHALED THE MUSK from Jake's warm, naked body lying next to her, his head turned away on the pillow. She gently played her hand over his smooth, firm rump, stopping to squeeze a cheek, then dancing her fingertips up his spine until they came to rest on his left shoulder. Moving on, she traced his upper trapezius muscle to the nape of his neck and threaded her fingers through his dark hair, now longish after nearly two months of growth.

Vacation suited Jake. The crow's feet around his eyes had smoothed out along with other facial wrinkles. His FBI work taxed him, she had no doubt about that. Especially that last undercover assignment in Silicon Valley as a Muslim scientist with an ax to grind. He got shot and nearly blown up. Was that always part of the job? She hoped not.

If he ever asked her to marry him, would she want to? She wanted him, no question about that. But could she be the tolerant, understanding wife an undercover specialist on an FBI's counter-terrorism team would need? Did she have the strength and nerve to be that kind of supportive spouse?

Dead to the world, Jake continued sleeping, his breathing steady if a bit shallow. His mouth opened and his breathing morphed into soft snores. She had to act quickly before he awoke fully. Meg slipped out of bed and into her terrycloth bathrobe. An idea had occurred to her as she awoke.

She found both their cell phones in the bedroom before heading to the kitchen. Jake's secure FBI phone was always kept in his locked, aluminum case, which now resided under her bed. His regular phone—his private line—rode with him at all times, a way to keep in touch with his family and friends. Civilians, Jake called them. She knew that reference included her. She was a civilian in his world of intrigue and violence.

While reflecting on the differences in their chosen careers, she made coffee, poured herself a cup of black hazelnut-flavored brew, sat at the kitchen table, and copied the digital recording from Jake's phone onto her phone using the mic mode. With the volume down low, she replayed her copy to make sure the recording transmitted clearly. The two men were speaking a language she could not understand. What Jake had told her about the men's conversation continued to trouble her profoundly.

At her uncle's barbecue yesterday, no mention was made of the Navy lieutenant's murder nor of Mrs. Daoud's near-fatal beating. Instead, she and Jake had buried their concerns for the length of their three-hour visit and had, she thought, put both cases out of their minds. They'd shared Long Island iced teas with Uncle John and his wife, Pat, and had played flag football before jumping into the family's pool with Uncle John and Aunt Pat's two teenage sons.

Then they had celebrated Meg's birthday with ice cream cake, replete with a forest of lit candles. Her cousins had bought her two charms for her bracelet. Uncle John and Aunt Pat had given her a light blue cashmere sweater for those cool winter nights in San Diego, and Jake, in typical form, presented her with a Nordstrom gift card. He apologetically explained that he'd kept it generic since he didn't know what to get her. She hid her disappointment with him and thanked everyone with hugs and kisses.

Still, for three lovely, carefree hours, she'd pushed everything out of her mind, and Jake appeared to have done the same.

Now, staring at the microphone icon on her phone and hearing the Arabic-speaking men, her worries flooded back. Maybe Jake had misunderstood, she reasoned. After all, he said he did recognize the dialect the men were speaking. She knew how difficult understanding different dialects could be. Her Parisian French had been little help to her in Quebec during one visit with a former colleague.

Maybe the men were talking about the beating but not with the sub-text that Jake had thought. And maybe because of his recent case with Islamic terrorists from overseas, he was seeing Islamic extremists everywhere. His ability to be objective might be impaired. After all, those particular Islamic thugs had kidnapped, brutalized, and shot him. She'd be jaded, too.

She sighed, feeling better already. They'd uncover the truth, no matter what. She had faith in Jake, but it wouldn't hurt to help him out, too.

Convinced that what she planned to do was reasonable and justified, Meg took her coffee and the two cell phones back to the bedroom. She tucked Jake's phone back into his jeans pocket and hers back into her satchel-style purse. Then set the coffee on the nightstand, shed the bathrobe, and crawled back into bed.

Jake turned over, drowsily opening one eye and reaching for her. "Hmm, nothing beats a morning like this."

She snuggled into the curve of his arms. "What do you mean?" Bless his heart, but she wanted to hear him say it.

"The smell of you, the smell of coffee. Perfection, bliss, nirvana. Paradise on Earth. I'm one lucky guy, Meg, to have you in my life. A damned lucky guy. And I promise to make up for that lame birthday gift. Just gotta get my head cleared. Get this case out of the way."

"But you're always on a case. Even now, on medical leave."

For a long moment, he said nothing as his hand played up and down her upper arm and finally rested on her shoulder. "But I couldn't turn down your uncle's appeal for help. He's your family."

"I know. Uncle John appreciates what you're doing. But Sarah Daoud's not your family. You told me not to get involved. Why are *you* getting involved?"

This time, he didn't miss a beat.

"Because, Meg, those bastards are practicing Sharia Law in our country. *Our* country. Westerners always assume that all religions encourage respect for individual dignity. Sharia, or Islamic Law, teaches that non-Muslims should be subjugated or killed. It teaches two systems of ethics, one for Muslims and another for non-Muslims. Islamic Law builds on the tribal practices of the seventh-century Middle East. It promotes the subjugation of others who do not follow Islam, and it's especially brutal against Muslim women who don't toe the line. I'm sure Mr. Daoud and his pals feel justified in attacking that woman so viciously. It's a miracle she didn't die. But that's what happens—these so-called honor killings happen—when a woman rebels against their law. Sharia Law goes against everything we stand for, everything generations of Americans have died for. Don't you understand this?"

His harsh, raspy delivery softened as he went on. "I know the press hasn't covered this very much—more's the pity. Unfortunately, a lot of Muslims in this country want to see Sharia Law accepted, like the Sharia Law courts that now exist in France. France won't fight for their rights, but damn it, we Americans had better."

Although Meg knew little about Sharia Law, just the bits and pieces she'd cobbled together from random TV news reports, what he said made sense. She'd have to do more research on her computer and try to catch up to what Jake already knew. Keeping up with the big, bad world would be one of the challenges of being an FBI wife.

If he ever proposed marriage.

He bent over and kissed her shoulder. "Okay, I'm getting off my soapbox. Rant officially over."

For now, such expressions of love would have to do. Meg smiled and raised her head to kiss him.

Chapter Thirteen

AN HOUR LATER, JAKE had showered and was dressed for his meetings with Samantha's father and the NCIs, then later with Admiral Snider and the base's NCI commander. Five days had passed since Lieutenant Samantha Carlton's murder, and though there had been developments in the case and persons of interest had been identified, no physical evidence pointed conclusively one way or another. There were still more questions than answers.

Jake had a few theories floating through his mind, but nothing concrete yet. Since the local cops would probably be handing off the Daoud *hate crime* case to the FBI San Diego field office, he'd identify himself, drop off the bat, give them a copy of the recording, and explain the circumstances. It'd be up to them to determine whether a warrant to search and seize was justifiable or whether establishing physical and electronic surveillance was needed first. Most likely, both would happen, but it wasn't his case. He'd merely stumbled onto something that required investigating.

He never wanted to be involved in the first place. Still didn't.

He had three more weeks of medical leave before the CTC in DC wanted him. He longed to squeeze in a fishing trip off Catalina before he left California this time. He wanted to visit his parents and brothers, too. Not to mention just three more weeks to persuade Meg to join him in DC when she finished her winter and spring quarters at UCSD.

Crossing over the two-hundred-foot-high Coronado Bridge onto Coronado Island took him back in time. Ten years before, he'd crossed this very span with a Navy recruiter, toured the North Island Naval Aviation base, and decided that becoming a Navy pilot was not his thing. The guy had taken him back over the bridge south to the Navy Amphibious Center, where the SEAL teams trained. The idea of joining the SEAL—Sea, Air, Land—special forces had grabbed him immediately. The rigorous physical and mental training had challenged him like nothing ever before in his life. But he toughed it out, passed every test they threw at him, and served his country proudly as a member of SEAL Team Three. He'd been based in San Diego and loved it. That was followed by four years of in-country black ops, assigned to various Special Forces groups.

Over time, the senseless waste of men and material got to him. To the politicians in DC, the teams were just grunts, no matter how sophisticated their training and toys were. They'd become puppets of the pols and their lackeys in the Pentagon. Intel suffered. Black ops forces were often sent in to clean up a foreign policy mess. From one administration to another, American loyalties to various foreign regimes in the Middle East changed like a damned weathervane in the wind.

He'd lived by the SEAL motto—*The only easy day was yesterday*—and loved their spirit. He'd loved his SEAL team buddies but had grown to hate how the pols abused their power and misused the skills and dedication of the SEAL teams.

The only thing that made sense to Jake was justice. Gathering intelligence kept him in control of the outcome. He liked it that way.

At heart, he was an analyst who had to gather intel in the field. Maybe Meg was right. Maybe being a SAC in a field office somewhere in California wouldn't be so bad. Not as exciting as an undercover field assignment, *maybe*, but he could help strategize intel collection and analysis. He could make a difference and God knew, the devil was always in the details. If certain information had been studied and followed through on, maybe the Boston Marathon bombing wouldn't have happened.

His mind snapped back to the present as he meandered the south island neighborhoods. He drove down Second Street, where he'd shared a cottage with his first wife. They'd married in his second year with the SEALs. He was twenty-four at the time and knew jack shit about women. His ex-wife Kay was a blonde like Meg but more curvaceous. They'd had one year of blind passion and bliss followed by two years of hell. She turned out to be different from the woman he thought he'd married. After a disastrous exfil op in Lebanon, he decided to quit the SEALs, and she decided the Navy was more important to her than Jake.

Or maybe she'd always felt that way.

Maybe they'd both changed or were so deaf, dumb, and blind in love that they'd married delusional, fantasy versions of each other at the start. Who knew? He probably still knew jack shit about women.

Jake pulled up to the curb in front of the familiar bungalow. The front yard of their old Craftsman was still as tidy as when they'd lived there. Houses and yards stayed, marriages ended, and sometimes careers, too.

Life went on.

Did he feel any residual affection for Kay now? He stared at the tidy walkway bordered by orange and white flowers and tried to picture his ex-wife fiddling in the garden. She'd once planted something along that walkway, then abruptly declared gardening was a drag and never picked up a trowel or hose again. What a pistol she was. She never had any hobbies, no, she was all Navy.

He couldn't help but smile. That's it. He had been drawn to the pretty, blonde pistol.

Had he always fallen for strong, sassy, independent women who fell in and out of love with him? And why, he wondered. Would Meg do the same—become disillusioned, turned off, disgusted, and that would be that? He'd certainly struck out with that gift card.

He switched off that depressing line of thinking and concentrated on his destination. He turned off the main boulevard onto Orange Avenue, which held another tidy row of small bungalows. Javier and Mary Lou waited outside a white house with green window trim. Samantha's house. The Naval Air Station was a mile to the north of this residential neighborhood, convenient for a female Navy officer living alone and whose job, according to the NCIs, entailed being on call at all times. She'd been assigned to Captain Snider's guided missile cruiser, the USS Dixie. Samantha had been one of the engineers engaged in advanced weapons operations.

Jake and the NCIs had no sooner entered the little house when a sixtyish-year-old man of medium height, husky build, and thinning gray hair met them in the living room. He was casually dressed, but his clothes spoke of wealth and privilege. Obviously, he was expecting them.

"I'm Sam's father. George Carlton."

The two NCIs and Jake shook his hand in turn, somberly expressing their condolences for his loss. Jake always took special notice of the eyes of the victim's families. He could tell the extent of their grief by how steady and purposeful their gazes were. A truly grieving family member wanted answers, wanted the truth, wanted justice for their loved one. Their eyes burned with those desires; they weren't shifty, evasive, or embarrassed. Mr. Carlton's eyes burned.

"We've already looked around, sir," Javier said. "However, Special Agent Bernstein wanted to do his own search."

Mr. Carlton nodded at Jake. "I'm packing some of her things. Her younger sister would've come, but she just gave birth to my third grandchild. The two girls, Samantha and Catherine, were all we had. After their mother died two years ago, I was glad they both stayed on the West Coast. Cathy's near Seattle. I live in San Francisco, but you probably know that." His rambling made his discomfort apparent.

Here they were, except for Mary Lou, who had known the lieutenant, strangers for all intents and purposes.

"Mind if I look around?" Jake asked.

Given permission from Sam's grieving father, Jake surveyed the living room after tugging on the white latex gloves Javier handed him. Bookcases lined one wall, a large LCD TV screen along another, and a sitting area against the third. The room was neat and clean and decorated with muted colors. He moved to the adjacent kitchen and small dining nook while listening to Javier speaking in hushed, respectful tones with Mr. Carlton.

"Sir," Javier said, "we couldn't find Samantha's laptop. It wasn't in her car, either. Several co-workers who'd visited her at home informed us that she had one, a newer model MacBook. It was her personal computer. Would you know anything about that?"

"No. I found it strange, too. She used it to video chat with her sister and me. She also kept in touch with university friends, travel companions, as well as some good friends she used to play softball with on a women's league."

The kitchen appeared to have been arranged by a compulsive neat-freak—the dish towels were hung just so on the oven handle, and all the canisters were turned with their labels facing outward. The tiled countertop was hygienically clean, with nothing out of place. There was no clutter, no dirty dishes or cups in the sink, or drying on a rack. The small, round, reddish-oak dining table displayed no crumbs or glass rings; there were no napkins skewed in their brass-colored napkin holder. With Samantha's military training, Jake expected a certain amount of order, but what he saw went beyond anything he'd ever seen before.

"Any pets?" Jake asked Mary Lou, who'd followed him around. She shook her head, and he lowered his voice, "Any evidence of another woman sharing the place?"

If what Dommy, the barista, had said was true, Samantha may have gotten hot-and-heavy with Sheila Lee. Wouldn't there be some residual evidence at Sam's place?

Mary Lou shook her head again. "We went over everything with forensic techs. They left everything the way they found it. No fingerprints except Sam's. Strange, isn't it? Especially if she was seeing...someone. Samantha wouldn't broadcast any special relationship even if she had one, but you'd think we'd find something. Another woman's toiletries, at the very least?"

Jake nodded. "That's what I'm thinking."

In the living room, Javier asked, "What about her shoes? Her work boots? The ankle boots her co-workers said she always wore on the ship? Have you found a pair?"

Samantha's father said nothing.

Javier continued, "The reason I ask is that her work boots weren't on her when she was found. She'd worn them that day on the ship, according to her co-workers. The waitress at the café said she was wearing them while she had coffee that night. Later, er, when she was found, she wasn't wearing them. They were nowhere in her car, either. We found that odd."

Mr. Carlton and Javier had entered the kitchen as Mary Lou showed Jake into the lieutenant's bedroom. The bed was made with the bedspread folded over the pillows and tucked in. The bed reminded Jake of Meg, who liked to do the same with her covers. There was a hint of neat freak in Meg, too. He wondered about that. She'd grown up in a military family, also. Her grandfather was an Air Force career officer.

His peripheral vision brought his attention to the framed photos of Samantha's family and friends on the nightstand, the double dresser, and a shelf above an upholstered chaise lounge. However, he saw no pictures of the beautiful Chinese girl, Sheila, with whom Samantha allegedly had an affair.

He mentally took note while looking into the lieutenant's pristine walk-in closet. Except for a row of Navy uniforms—from camouflage fatigues to summer whites to dress blues—it looked like racks of an upscale women's boutique. He pulled aside the jacket of her dress blues. The gold bars and two medals proudly stood above her left pocket. Jake recalled his own bar and medal. If he'd stayed in, he'd have a chest full by now.

He pawed through the tailored cotton tops, wool jackets with matching trousers. Sam apparently preferred pantsuits like a lot of career-minded women. Not Meg, whose taste in clothes ran from jeans and colorful, trendy tops to leggings and tunics to sexy sundresses. Sam clearly spent a lot of money on tailored clothes. Nice civies. Even nicer shoes below on their tiered stands. But the whole place was as sterile as a lonely, single woman on the cusp of middle age.

Jake checked a few random items for stray fingerprints but found none. The house was super neat and clean, with nothing out of place like no one lived there.

According to the NCI reports, Sam's last day on earth followed her usual routine. Her neighbor on the left saw her jogging at six in the morning. She'd logged into her assigned station on the cruiser at seven and logged out at four. She had come home, made some phone calls—mostly to that untraceable cell phone—and spoken with her father once. She'd then joined a fellow Navy officer for cocktails and dinner at Peohe's on the east side of the island. The officer reported that San had mentioned she had a meeting with her girlfriend. Sam wouldn't divulge the girlfriend's name, saying their relationship was secret. The woman's family wouldn't approve, so they'd kept it hush-hush. At eight, Sam left for that meeting. An hour later, she was last seen alive at The Amazons, having coffee and waiting for someone—the girlfriend?

She had been a busy woman with a busy life. And yet her place showed none of this.

Something felt off. The place was either staged, or Samantha Carlton was an OCD-certified neat freak. Had someone gone to great lengths to wipe out any trace of Sam's lover? Why?

Jake whipped around as Samantha's father and Javier entered the bedroom. He was about to ask the father about his daughter's habits when the man went straight to a large box in one corner of the closet, brought it out with Javier's help, and set it on the bed.

Mr. Carlton silently rummaged through the box's contents and finally held up a pair of worn ankle boots. "Are these what you mean, Ensign Blanco?"

"Yes. Where did you find them? We looked all over."

Mary Lou shook her head. "These weren't the boots she was wearing that night—" she began, then clamped her mouth shut.

Mr. Carlton sighed. "It's all right. I've come to terms with Sam's death. Not her murder, but when you have a kid in the military, you know in your heart that anything can happen. Her overseas deployments gave me many sleepless nights. I just never dreamed it...this would happen when she was in home port." He took a deep breath before continuing. "I flew down right after the Navy called me. When I got here on Wednesday, there was a postcard from a San Diego shoe repair shop saying her boots were done. It said the outer sole had been restitched. Sam took those shoes in the week before she... Anyway, I picked these up that same day, thinking...well, I don't know what I was thinking. Maybe hoping for answers, I don't know."

He held up the left boot. The upper was made of black leather, and the sole was regular wood and leather composition with the heel about an inch thicker than the rest of the sole. He twisted it out to reveal a secret inner compartment. The compartment was empty.

Mr. Carlton smiled to himself. "I started having all her shoes specially adjusted when she was a teenager. Samantha had a bad habit of forgetting her house key. No matter where she went or what she was doing, she'd forget or lose her house key. I know an old Italian guy who makes my customized loafers. He did the same with Sam's work boots, made the heel with the secret compartment." He swung the heel shut, and a tiny click sounded as it snapped into place.

"What if she twisted her foot while walking in those shoes? Would that heel come open?" Javier asked.

"No." Mr. Carlton shook his head. "That's the beauty of this type of heel. It takes a certain twist and downward pressure on the outward, curved part of the heel before the spring inside works. There was no danger of it popping open accidentally." He passed the boot to the NCIs, who examined the mechanism.

Jake was familiar with the old-school spycraft trick since the Russians used something like it during the Cold War. However, this particular shoe device went back to Napoleon's time when spies from various European countries were trying to figure out when and where the Corsican Butcher and his armies were going to invade next.

"Anyway, it became kind of a joke with us," Mr. Carlton continued. "She'd put her house key in her heel and always knew she could get in. She'd sometimes wad up a bill, a twenty or fifty, in case she forgot to put cab fare in her purse. I always thought Sam was so forgetful because her mind was up in the clouds. Like any brilliant person, always thinking on a higher level. Know what I mean?"

Jake and the two NCIs nodded sympathetically before Javier's eyebrows shot up as he looked questioningly at Mary Lou. Had Sam's female friends known about Sam's secret heel? Mary Lou shook her head, looking as surprised as Javier. But would Sam share this secret heel with an intimate friend, a lover? Not fellow Navy officers? Did she fear her secret heel would be reported and the wrong conclusions drawn?

"Her local shoe repairman didn't work on the heel," Mr. Carlton said. "He just had to stitch the upper sole along the side. He did discover the heel's cavity—that's what he called it. He was naturally curious, but he did nothing to it."

The NCIs nodded gravely but said nothing.

Jake decided to pursue the issue of Sam's habits. "Did Lieutenant Carlton continue to be forgetful about important matters? Even as an adult? I mean, from what I've seen here, she's super neat and organized. Why wouldn't this...compulsion apply to carrying a house key or spare money?"

Mr. Carlton began to smile as if shrugging off his daughter's idiosyncrasies, then mid-smile, he frowned and glared at Jake. "What are you implying, Special Agent Bernstein?"

Jake held up his hands, palms outward. "Nothing, sir. Just trying to understand your daughter, her living habits and lifestyle."

Mr. Carlton appeared troubled as he glanced around, his mouth twisting to the side. "I don't recall her being this...well, domestic. She was never very organized or methodical in how she kept her house. Ensign Blanco said they found her house exactly the way it is now. But she may've had a cleaning service come in that day, I don't know. She said nothing about it when I spoke to her on Tuesday afternoon. She said she was calling from home after a long day on the job."

Javier jumped in. "What was the gist of that conversation, sir?"

The older man frowned, appearing to search his memory. "She asked about her trust account. If she had enough money in it to buy a house. I handled her bank accounts and investments. I told her she did. Even as expensive as San Diego real estate is, Samantha could easily afford to buy her own home. It sounded like she wanted to put down roots." His voice caught as he clearly struggled to compose himself.

Jake probed further despite the man's obvious pain. "We understand she had romantic relationships. Did she ever tell you about her latest...relationship? Whether it had become a serious?"

Mr. Carlton's color rose to bright pink, and his eyes bugged out, appearing as though he might keel over from a heart attack. "If you're suggesting that her relationships with women had something to do with her murder..." He sputtered, pausing to take a breath, which sounded like a gasp. "Yes, I know she's a lesbian. I've known for a long time. When she was younger, I sent her to therapy, thinking it was all a phase she was going through. God help me. Poor girl, what I put her through, trying to change her and make her act like Cathy. She suffered...her mother and I suffered...so needlessly. Sam was different, no doubt about it. She had problems with people, getting along, and fitting in. But she never talked to me about her private life. Her love life. I think she respected us enough to keep it to herself. We were uncomfortable hearing about her girlfriends, especially her mother. But Samantha was a good person."

His voice cracked, and he pulled out a handkerchief to wipe his eyes and nose. "As I said, she had brains and was a loyal, dedicated officer of the United States Navy. And anybody who tries to make her into... I don't know, but anyone who tries to malign her, I will sue that person for slander. Do you hear me?" He grabbed the boots, dropped them into the box, and stormed out of the bedroom.

Jake and the two NCIs stared at each other and said nothing. Javier pulled out the pair of boots with latex-gloved hands, gingerly as though they were a blood-soaked garment, and placed them into a large evidence bag.

He then turned to Mary Lou and Jake And whispered, "Maybe the lab can find out what else she might've hidden in that heel. The boots she wore the night she was killed—they're still missing. This explains why her shoes were taken. The killer must have known about the heel, and taking one shoe would've looked strange, so he took them both. He didn't know about this second pair of boots, however."

"Or he knew," Jake interjected, "but couldn't find them when he searched the place."

Javier nodded. "The killer went to a shitload of trouble here if he tossed the place, then straightened it all up. According to her neighbors and friends, Samantha had no cleaning lady. And the friend she had dinner with that evening, Lieutenant Deborah Michaels, she said she'd been over several times to play poker with Sam and a couple of friends. Said her place was always a little messy."

Jake rubbed his chin. "But no fingerprints? That's a pretty thorough murderer. A pro?"

"Yeah. I'm guessing the killer searched, then wiped clean and staged the place. We were here the next day, so it happened the same night she was killed. He wanted to make sure all trace evidence vanished. One cold dude, and yeah, a pro."

Mary Lou stared at the floor while Jake clapped Javier on his shoulder. Javier nodded grimly, obviously on the same mental wavelength. But Jake's thoughts were already leaping ahead to another possible thread. The heel's somewhat square dimensions were approximately three inches across. Plenty of room for a thumb drive filled with top-secret data on the Navy's latest weaponry. Even two thumb drives would fit.

The numbers were adding up. Put a lonely, love-starved Navy weapons engineer and a gorgeous foreign babe together, plus a way to smuggle out classified data that the babe will do anything to get, and they might have a military officer turned traitor.

For Sam's father's sake, God, for everyone's sake, Jake hoped to hell he was wrong.

Chapter Fourteen

DEEP IN THOUGHT, MEG walked the four short blocks from her apartment to the UC San Diego campus. Her German classes were in the six-story concrete and glass Foreign Language building. Her nine o'clock German language class would begin in fifteen minutes, and she'd then be occupied the entire day with a book report in German due Monday. She hadn't even started to read the novel, and her anxiety level was rising as each day passed. She was accustomed to deadlines and having lesson plans to prepare for each week, but living with Jake and forays out and about in San Diego with him were taking time away from her studies.

But in less than three weeks, he'd be gone. Then what? She'd be moping about and missing him. Their time together was important to her, but so were her studies and achieving a teaching minor in German. Still, she'd decided that if he did not propose marriage or at least a long engagement by the end of January, she would let him go. Instead, she'd look for a teaching job in San Diego and make this city her new home. She'd sell her grandmother's big home in Dallas and buy a small house somewhere near Uncle John and his family. Gran was gone. Gramps was gone. Her mother would stay gone with her current husband.

Meg longed for a family, pure and simple.

She had an errand and just enough time to get it done. On the third floor, she came to the office of Dr. Ibrahim Basheera, her European history professor. Although Syrian-born, he'd spent most of his life in Turkey and Germany before immigrating to the States just five years ago. He was a kind, gentle man in his fifties with a dry sense of humor. He was fair in grading his student's essays, which had to be written in German, and he made allowances for the language mistakes of his less-than-fluent students. She liked him and found him easy to speak to.

Although not his formal office hours, the light behind his glass door indicated he was in. Meg knocked and entered when he called out.

Professor Basheera sat behind an enormous desk with wire-rimmed spectacles halfway down his long nose. A large book was propped on top of student papers, which she interrupted as his preparation for a lecture. His brown eyes studied her calmly as she approached his desk.

Dressed in his usual tweed jacket, button-down shirt, and tie, he stroked his short, trim brown beard, which she suspected was dyed to conform to his dark brown hair. However, his facial wrinkles and deep lines betrayed his true age, no matter how youthful he tried to appear. His face and neck were fleshy, his body corpulent. His huge belly strained against the edge of the desk as he attempted to rise to his feet.

Meg waved him down when he invited her to sit on one of the two chairs facing his desk. She declined and apologized for the interruption. "I can't stay, Dr. Basheera. My German class is in a few minutes." She hesitated, having second thoughts, but it was too late now since she'd already committed herself. She took a notebook, pen, and cell phone out of her large purse. "I was hoping you'd have some time to help me. Not with German or German history but something else. You see, my...I made a recording of two men speaking Arabic. They're related to one of my...to someone I know whose mother was attacked and almost killed a few days ago. I was hoping you could translate this for me."

His bushy, black-dyed eyebrows jolted up, but he was clearly intrigued. "My first unusual request of the day. Well, why not? Let's hear this recording."

Meg opened the app, turned the volume up, and played the recording. There were places where the voices faded to almost whispers and other moments when the male voices rose clear and distinct.

She watched Professor Basheera's expression while he listened. A muscle twitched near his left eye, and he looked down at his book while running a hand over his beard. Whatever he was hearing had grabbed his full attention. He grew tense, then visibly stiffened. When the recording ended, he asked that she replay it, this time holding her phone close to his ear. The professor's expression morphed from curiosity to anger to genuine fear, then back to anger. His countenance hardened, and a mask seemed to fall in place.

Meg realized she'd made a grave mistake.

"I'll need time to listen to it and make notes. These two men are speaking in an Iraqi dialect that I'm not very familiar with. If you want a precise translation, you'll have to give me some time."

"No, that's okay," she said, apprehension making her skull shiver. She put away her notebook and cell phone.

He stared at her for a long moment. "The content is dreadful. They're discussing the man's wife and her beating. They're upset, of course. Where did you hear this, Miss Larsen?"

Again, Meg wavered, but only for a few seconds. She had trusted the wrong person. "I'm not at liberty to say, Professor."

Professor Basheera's gaze bore into her. "These are strangers to you. Why would you violate their privacy in this way? To help the police?"

"No, no. It just seemed like a good idea at the time." Meg recalled Jake's words. *Sarah's life could be at stake.* "I mean..." She clamped her mouth shut. This was a bad idea. Too late. Now a bald-faced lie, however lame, was necessary. "Professor, I have no intention of going to the police. This is not my business, and I'm sorry to have...violated their privacy. You see, any time I hear a foreign language spoken, I want to know what it is, where it comes from, the dialect. I'm a foreign-language teacher and naturally curious about Arabic."

"How did you know they were speaking Arabic?" Basheera asked pointedly. He steepled his hands and rested them against his bearded chin. His voice was kind again, but his dark eyes blazed with suspicion.

She lied again. "I've been to Arabic-speaking countries. I've just never studied the language. I know a few words like a tourist learns. *Shokran, salaam aleikum*, things like that." These were Arabic words that Jake had taught her because they were close to the Hebrew equivalent.

"Did these men know you were recording them?"

She paused before muttering, "I don't know."

A ripple of fear ran through her. She should never have come to Dr. Basheera. Hadn't Jake warned her? Look what had happened to Jake's car after visiting Sarah and her mother in the hospital. That man might have attacked them with his bat if they'd been in that rental car. If he could do such a thing after just a friendly hospital visit, what else would he do? These were not people who would dismiss her meddling into their private affairs.

"I suppose you're not going to reveal their names," Basheera said.

"No," she admitted, "I don't know their names. I just wanted a translation. Look, Professor, I made a mistake. I didn't mean to offend you. Or them."

He blinked, glanced down at his book for a second, and then smiled. "Of course, Miss Larsen."

Meg looked at the professor one last time before moving to the door. There must be tens of thousands of Arabic speakers in California, certainly many thousands in Escondido. According to Jake, Escondido had the highest population of Muslim immigrants in southern California. Most likely, the professor wouldn't know the Daouds.

"Thanks," she said and hurriedly slipped out of his office.

BASHEERA SPENT THE next fifteen minutes on the phone. But not his office phone. He used his personal mobile phone and called the first two men listed in his directory of contacts. These were men who attended his mosque in Escondido and had befriended him. He trusted them with his life, just as they trusted him. He made an emergency appointment for that very evening. After receiving instructions from one of the men, he called the university's Office of the Registrar on his office phone.

"Yes, I'm looking for the address of one of my students. She happened to leave a bracelet that looks rather valuable in my classroom last Friday. An heirloom, perhaps. I thought I could drop it off at her place on my way home today."

The student clerk firmly stated the student privacy policy, accompanied by profuse apologies.

Professor Basheera glibly dismissed the young man's concerns. "No problem. I'll just hold it for her until the next class meeting."

He hung up and pondered. Professor Heinz was the advisor for the German Club on campus. Didn't the club have a social get-together recently at Meg Larsen's apartment? Basheera had declined the invitation because alcohol would be served, and he was a strict Muslim. All those years in secular Turkey and decadent Germany could not crush his devotion to Islamic ways. The German professor, Rudolf Heinz, would know where Meg lived. Approaching him and requesting such information would require stealth, however. He'd have to think about this carefully and make a plan.

Foolish *fakir*. Western women were out of control. They behaved and even thought like their emasculated men. They didn't know their place in Islam's great global scheme. They behaved and dressed like whores and their unclean habits polluted the minds of their children. Someday, when Islam took over the world and Sharia Law was the law of the land in this country of heretics, they would all learn and pay the price.

Allahu akbar!

And still, he taught them and treated them with courtesy and respect. Such was his burden to bear and his own price to pay.

For his own small role in this holy war, he would make the sacrifice.

Chapter Fifteen

JAKE DROVE HIS NEWLY rented ruby red Ford Explorer, following the NCIs as they stopped at the so-called Stockdale Gate, named after Vice Admiral James B. Stockdale. NAB, the birthplace of Naval aviation, was the Naval Air Base on North Island, Coronado. The entrance sported a white-stucco, red-tile roofed, Spanish-style gatehouse with heavy black iron gates. Jake waited while the NCIs showed their IDs.

The base housed every class of Navy ship the Pentagon and its congressional committees could appropriate and approve. It was home to one of two Pacific fleets, which served as the country's only protection against sea attacks. Seattle and San Diego remained the two points along the west coast that maintained a substantial Navy presence after the San Francisco and Alameda bases were closed.

Since 9-11, admittance to all military bases was tightly restricted to authorized personnel only. NASNI, Naval Air Station North Island, was only accessible to staff bearing hologram IDs, and Jake knew his former SEAL status wouldn't be enough to gain admittance. The NCIs signaled to Jake, who showed his FBI badge and ID to the guard on watch. Even so, his visit and access had to be approved. One phone call later, Jake was waved through.

The quaint exterior of the gatehouse gave way to utilitarian buildings, old Quonset huts from the 1930s, rows of huge hangars for various Navy aircraft, huge white fuel storage tanks, a control tower, and two long runways that took up half of the base's vast acreage. Despite it all, palm and jacaranda trees waved in the ocean breezes and ships of all sizes, classes, and categories clogged the docks along the bay front.

Jake paused a moment to watch an NH-60 Rescue helo hover near one of the helicopter hangars. A row of Sikorsky Navy Sea Hawks rested like giant birds, letting the cool winds from the ocean dry out their wings. A gigantic C-17 cargo and troop transport plane was waiting for takeoff facing north, just as an F-18 Hornet jet landed on the west runway.

There were six other Naval stations around the bay—Undersea Rescue Command, the Naval Amphibious Base, the Submarine Base, the NASSCO shipbuilding facility, the Sea Lions and Dolphin Training Center, and more—but NASNI was the busiest. South of the Coronado Bridge were numerous dry and wet docks and at least fifty ships of all classes and categories.

They parked alongside Rear Admiral Snider's USS Dixie, a one-hundred-thirty-foot Ticonderoga class guided missile cruiser painted gunmetal gray. They showed their IDs to the duty guard and climbed the gangway. The NCIs saluted the officer on watch and requested permission to come aboard. Again, Jake showed his badge and ID, saluted for the hell of it, and looked up to see the colors flying. For a couple of seconds, he felt a stirring in his chest. A sense of pride enveloped him. It was hard to let go...

Memories shattered as Javier called out to him. He snapped to and reminded himself for the tenth time that day not to stroll down memory lane.

That life's over and done with. You've begun a new chapter, Bernstein. Get on with it.

AS JAKE FOLLOWED THE NCIs across the ship's sleek deck, he estimated about half of the one-hundred-odd crew and officers appeared to be on duty topside at this hour of the day. Below deck, more men and women in working camo fatigues were bustling about purposefully. The NCIs led him to the officers' mess on the second deck, where they met Rear Admiral Snider and the base's NCI commanding officer, Lieutenant Commander Wayne Wickham. Both men wore camos and high-top boots, appearing serious over their cups of coffee and sitting at a table clearly reserved for their meeting. The large, windowless mess was vacant of all other personnel.

The NCIs saluted sharply and stood at attention while Jake shook hands with Lieutenant Commander Wickham. He nodded and smiled at Rear Admiral Snider, then shook hands with Meg's uncle for formality's sake. The sandy-haired fifty-five-year-old had just served him ribs at his barbecue the day before, regressing with Jake into boyhood and doing cannonballs into the swimming pool. For this meeting, however, a certain distance and officiousness were expected.

"Take a seat, Special Agent Bernstein. Ensigns Blanco and Taylor. We're ready for your briefing on the case of Lieutenant Samantha Carlton." Lieutenant Commander Wickham sat with a notebook and pulled out a pen while the two younger NCIs consulted their electronic tablets.

Javier, after his partner's nod, launched into a detailed account of the investigation.

Lieutenant Commander Wickham interrupted only once. "What about that fire at The Lido nightclub? Any connection to the murder?"

Mary Lou spoke up. "The San Diego FD declared it arson sparked by a flare and fueled with kerosene. Their chief suspect all along was one of the bartenders, Jimmy Park. Motive: using the distraction to steal money from the two cash registers and an office safe. During his confession four days ago, Park claimed he expected the sprinklers to work immediately and did not intend to put lives at risk. The sprinklers' emergency turn-on sensor malfunctioned, but that was due to an electrician's screw-up on Tuesday."

"The same day Lieutenant Carlton was killed?"

"Yes, sir. The Fire Marshal believes there's no connection between the murder and the fire."

"Did you pursue this line?"

Javier broke in. "Yes, sir, we did but there doesn't seem to be anything there. The electrician was a new apprentice working under a journeyman. He thinks he didn't double-check the sensor's battery, which had corroded. Therefore, causing the sprinkler system failure."

Javier continued, having satisfied the NCI commander with their conclusion regarding the fire. He next summarized the testimony of Domenico Fabrizio, the coffee shop's barista, who'd hinted at Sheila's, or Xing Lee Pong's, relationship with Lieutenant Carlton and included Sheila's propensity to develop sexual relationships with Navy personnel, male or female, whom she'd met at The Lido. Her bodyguard, Xu Wen Ton, was attached to the security detail of the Los Angeles People's Republic of China Consulate and both frequented The Lido nightclub, always together. "If the woman's a PRC spy, she might've been trolling for targets," Javier concluded.

"You need to establish this Chinese national's credentials," Lieutenant Commander Wickman said. "If she's done nothing wrong, then we need to tread lightly. If she has a bodyguard, she most likely has government connections. Let's not blow this out of proportion. You also need to confirm whether Lieutenant Carlton had an intimate relationship with this Chinese national or not. We've warned our officers not to fraternize with Chinese nationals."

Javier nodded and said, "Yes, sir. I have already confirmed the relationship."

Javier glanced in his direction, and Jake wondered when the ensign had confirmed the relationship. He hadn't had time to speak to the Master Chief Petty Officer since they boarded the ship. Jake's latest phone call to the NCI indicated the MCPO was next on his list to question. The MCPO served as the ship's counselor, counseled the crew and officers, and assessed the morale on board and on shore—kind of a big brother to lean on and confide in.

"I spoke to MCPO Hunter last night," Javier said. "He said Lieutenant Carlton had come to him one day the week before she was killed. She was struggling with an emotional dilemma, saying she was torn between a person she loved and her career and had some decisions to make about her future in the Navy." He paused, glancing between the commander and admiral. "She told Master Chief Hunter she was in love with a Chinese national named Sheila, a beautiful woman younger than herself who apparently returned her love. Lieutenant Carlton mentioned wanting to marry this woman, and if that was impossible, then at least set up house with her, and have a family. Y'know, the whole enchilada. She was considering leaving the Navy if and when this woman, Sheila, agreed to move in with her to avoid her next deployment. She felt a six-month overseas deployment would probably destroy their romance. She also mentioned wanting to sponsor the young woman's immigration and permanent residency status in this country."

The shocked expressions on Wickham's and Snider's faces did not surprise Jake. If Dommy was correct, this young Chinese woman was most likely the same beautiful Sheila from The Lido. If someone fell hard for that babe, he could understand it. But a Chinese national and possible spy? What was Lieutenant Carlton thinking?

But how could they prove the possible spy aspect beyond a shadow of a doubt?

A stunned Snider muttered, "I had no idea."

Javier relayed what they'd learned earlier about Samantha's personal habits, the likelihood that her rented house had been searched, her laptop stolen, and the place staged in the aftermath. Lastly, he included finding out about the woman's work boots and their secret heel-hole. At that point, the commander exchanged an alarmed look with the admiral. Snider nearly dropped the coffee mug he held, splattering a little coffee on the table. He swore under his breath.

If what they apparently feared had actually happened—that Samantha had given military secrets to a PRC spy—the careers of both these men had just crashed and burned.

Jake jumped in during the tense silence that followed. "Exactly what was Lieutenant Carlton's expertise?" He noticed that Snider's face had turned ashen and that one hand shook slightly.

Before replying, the rear admiral picked up a napkin and wiped the coffee off the table, an obvious cover for regaining his composure.

"Lieutenant Carlton had mastered the Aegis Weapons System, which controls our guided missile system. Her background was in advanced, classified military computer language, logarithms and coordinates, and all the protocols associated with this weapons system. Her workstation was inside the locked weapons room. Our missile electronics are so precisely calibrated that they can travel thousands of miles and land on a dime."

"Can I see her workstation?" Jake asked.

Snider shot him a weak smile and shook his head. "Sorry, Jake, off limits. You'd need top military clearance from the Pentagon."

"What about her work computer? I assume that couldn't leave the ship?"

"Affirmative."

Even Wickham looked stunned and grim.

Snider stared at his mug of coffee, looking as if a black-hooded executioner had just stepped into the room.

"Carlton was being trained on the new Predator drone guidance system. The one that delivers Tomahawk missiles."

The two NCIs stared at Jake. He hated to ask the question, but the investigation's direction demanded it.

"What about the use of a thumb drive? Would Carlton have been able to make copies, let's say, of coordinates or the logarithms involved in either of those two systems? Anything about the Aegis system's inner workings?"

Snider grew still. The integrity of his ship's operation was being called into question, and everything in his countenance and posture showed he didn't like it. Not one damn bit.

"Not without the system noting and recording such an action. Her teammate's computer is an identical copy, a security clone. The twin system would notify her teammate of such a violation of protocol. The failsafe buddy is built into the system. Red flags, alarms, and goddamn bells and whistles would go off all over the ship. I'd know about it within seconds."

Jake nodded, softening his tone. "Good to hear. Sorry, but I had to ask. A PRC spy might not know that detail. What about the Aegis Weapons System training manual? I assume Lieutenant Carlton and the other systems engineers had to get special training."

Snider's gaze met Jake unflinchingly. "Yes. They were trained at the Pentagon. Each trainee was cleared to store a manual and its CDs. on their home ship. Those manuals and CDs do not leave the ship. They're locked up and have to be logged in and out."

"Would she or any of the other engineers be able to make copies of those CDs?" Jake asked.

Snider's face colored a bright pink underneath his tan. Jake inwardly winced, wondering if he'd done irreparable damage to his friendship with Meg's uncle. But how could he not ask these questions?

"The same failsafe security system would apply, but I'll check into it."

Jake nodded solemnly. "For now we have to assume that Lieutenant Carlton was probably approached to make a copy. The Chinese are good at reverse engineering. If they got their hands on a flash drive copy of the manuals, they could duplicate the engineering." He turned to Javier and Mary Lou. "We can also assume that Lieutenant Carlton refused and possibly threatened to expose them, so they eliminated the threat. That's my current theory. All we have to do now is prove it. So far, we only have hearsay evidence linking Xing Lee Pong, or Sheila Lee, romantically to Lieutenant Carlton. No admissions from the person of interest. No hard evidence."

Mary Lou cleared her throat and bent over to retrieve something from her briefcase. She pulled out a small, black velvet box inside a transparent evidence bag, looking a little guilty. "We haven't shared this evidence with Special Agent Bernstein yet."

"That's right," Javier said. "We were waiting for this meeting." He shot Jake an apologetic look.

"We discovered this inside a garment bag," Mary Lou continued, "which we found in the trunk of her car under her body. The killer obviously overlooked this. The first time we went through her belongings, we overlooked it, too. It sat at the bottom of the nylon garment bag that held Lieutenant Carlton's uniform. Only her fingerprints were found on the paper wrapping and the velvet box inside, sir." She slid the box over to the NCI commander.

Wickham pried open the lid of the black velvet box. On a silky white bed lay a pair of diamond earrings, brilliant cut, and at least five carats apiece. A tightly folded note popped out and unfurled under the man's long fingers.

Wickham read the note, which was brief and simple as a child's Valentine. "*To my love, Sheila. Let's make a life together, Sam.*"

"There may be another Sheila," Taylor said, "but I don't think so, sir. Not after learning that Xing Lee Pong was also known to her friends at The Lido nightclub as Sheila Lee. Several witnesses claimed to have seen Sheila Lea and Lieutenant Carlton sitting together at the club many times during the last three months."

Jake nodded to himself but remained silent. The evidence, while circumstantial, was piling up.

"There's another wrinkle in this case." Mary Lou paused to take a deep breath. "Xing Lee Peong is the daughter of a PRC minister and has diplomatic immunity. The Cultural Minister of the People's Republic of China is her father, and she has official status as the cultural attaché with the PRC consulate in San Francisco. We just found out about her status this morning."

Wickham's expression turned livid. "Great. What the hell is she doing here in San Diego?"

"She's enrolled as a student at San Diego State U." Mary Lou threw a pleading look at Javier and Jake.

"It took us a while to track it down," Javier explained. "She has classes only on Fridays and spends almost every weekend in town. She goes by several aliases and is listed as a cultural attaché assistant, one of several at the PRC consulate. In China's diplomatic web of spies, that could mean anything. Like a roving spy or spy at large."

Snider swore aloud and swiped a shaky hand over his face. "Any ideas for proving this Chinese national's engaged in espionage and murder? Without causing an international incident? She may have diplomatic immunity, but the State Department could expel her for reason."

The two NCIs glanced at Jake as if expecting their FBI consultant to show his creative problem-solving brilliance.

Jake took a swallow of his now tepid coffee. "We could set up a honey trap. A sting operation. Use another weapons officer as bait. This Chinese national appears to have a precise type of target but isn't particular about the gender, male or female." Another memory struck, and Jake was surprised Javier had neglected to bring it up. "The only physical evidence of the perp found at the crime scene was a single strand of straight black hair, which DNA tests revealed as Asian or Asian-Caucasian. If we could get a sample from Sheila's bodyguard and lucky enough to find a match, we'd have cause for a warrant."

Even with diplomatic immunity, such a diplomatic privilege would be waived in the case of a homicide investigation.

Jake remembered Meg saying that Sheila had pursued her phone number, thinking she was a Navy officer who'd just been assigned to Snider's guided missile cruiser. A shred of an idea formed, which he hastily discarded.

No way. He wouldn't put Meg at risk.

Snider frowned and shook his head. "I can't authorize this. Can't and won't expose my weapons officers to such danger."

"We'd control and monitor every step of the trap," Wickham offered, cautiously looking toward Jake. "Would the San Diego FBI field office lend some manpower and tech support?"

"You'd have to ask, sir," Jake said, "but they've helped me before. My last undercover case wouldn't have succeeded without their assistance. Call their Special Agent in Charge. His name's Tom Alabastro."

Wickham and the two ensigns looked to Snider for final approval. A long moment later, the ship's commander raised a now-steady hand, and rubbed his clean-shaven chin. His dark blue gaze, reminding Jake of Meg's, pierced each one in turn, first Jake, then the two ensigns, and finally resting on Wickham.

"Only with my officers' permission," Snider said. "They didn't sign up to be spy catchers or homicide investigators. They're engineers, for God's sake. Most of them are married and have families."

"Even to catch the murderer of a fellow Navy officer?" Wickham asked.

"Even that," Snider rasped.

Despite the rear admiral's reluctance, Jake had to admire the man's priority. His officers and their work came first, and solving this crime was above and beyond the call of duty.

Snider stood and everyone stood with him. "Stay and have lunch," he muttered, then turned to Wickham. "When you have a plan for this operation, run it by me. I'll assess it before I approach my officers."

His cobalt gaze settled on Jake for just a moment before he withdrew.

He asked for my help. Now he apparently resents my interference.

Without hesitation, Wickham said, "All right, Ensign Blanco, Ensign Taylor, Agent Bernstein. Let's see your plan by tomorrow morning." He pounded the metal table with both fists, not once but twice for emphasis. "It damn well better be foolproof." Then he stood and walked out.

The two young ensigns looked scared to death as if facing a firing squad. If they fucked up this *honey trap*, they'd torpedo their Navy careers.

Jake scrubbed his face wearily. What had he gotten himself into? He was supposed to be on medical leave, recuperating from his injuries. Instead, he found himself in the thick of a Navy criminal investigation, holding the hands of two rookies.

Smart rookies, but rookies nonetheless.

Chapter Sixteen

NINE DAYS AFTER LIEUTENANT Carlton's murder and five days after Fatimah Daoud's attempted murder, Jake drove north on Highway One-sixty-three. In the hills above the morning fog, Jake veered into the parking lot for the Federal Building on Aero Drive. Having made an appointment with Tom Alabastro, the San Diego field office's Special Agent in Charge, Jake was ready to offer his assistance and in return ask for it. The NCIs had already called and spoken to Alabastro about the Samantha Carlton murder case, but Alabastro wanted to hear the investigation's update from their ad hoc FBI consultant.

Jake was no stranger to the field office. He'd met the SAC right after Christmas when he'd moved in with Meg. As a professional courtesy, he'd debriefed the man and his small counterterrorism team on the outcome of the undercover operation in Silicon Valley.

It was late morning, but the fog still clung to the valley. On the ocean side of the coastal hills, the high sixties temperature was cool but not chilling. Comfortable and pleasant, as everything seemed to be in San Diego. Another day in paradise. On the surface, anyway.

Jake, wearing a lightweight leather jacket over his golf shirt, showed his badge and ID to the guards in the lobby, then again to the guard in the vestibule on the FBI's floor. All Federal offices had tightened their security protocols since 9-11, and Jake faced firewalls in front of firewalls wherever he went. The nature of the beast in today's post 9-11 world. The fact that Jake carried a bat wrapped in a paper bag, enclosed within a nylon sports bag, hadn't greased the skids any. The guards scrutinized the bag's contents and waited until Jake explained.

"Evidence in a criminal case," was all he had to say.

Alabastro greeted him just inside the bullpen after Jake had passed through the vestibule and the electronically locked door. The man looked younger than his late fifties. He had a thick shock of salt-and-pepper hair and hooded dark eyes. Of medium height and slim stature, Alabastro had a ready smile and an almost happy-go-lucky personality. Jake could tell the man's field office liked their boss, for everyone in the bullpen behind him had raised their heads and greeted their visitor with good-natured bonhomie. His visit was pre-announced, evidently.

Jake recognized the agent standing next to Alabastro. He'd played an instrumental role in Meg's fake murder. Jake recalled his name was Chuck. Meg had praised the man's strength during the fake drowning setup when he'd pulled her through relentless underwater currents to the safety of the boat. From her emotional narration of that terrifying event, she owed the agent her life. Jake hadn't met him at the December meeting, so facing this big, strapping young man in person presented the opportunity to thank the guy.

"I owe you two big time," Jake said, amiably shaking their hands.

"Wanted to meet you in person," Chuck said, grinning. "You're the guy who stopped the attack on the Forty-Niners' stadium. From a dyed-in-the-wool Niners fan, my hearty thanks right back at ya. And congratulations on exposing that sleeper terrorist cell. Good work."

"You helped make it possible," Jake said.

Wearing out their mutual blandishments, the trio dissolved as Alabastro led Jake to his private office. Along the way, they stopped at the coffee bar. After the SAC refilled his mug, he brewed a strong black cup for Jake, who added a dollop of hazelnut creamer. Not having had time for breakfast, his stomach growled in protest when he spotted a basket of Italian biscotti and fresh bakery muffins on the side of the counter next to another large bowl of fresh fruit. Alabastro chuckled and nodded, so Jake helped himself, grabbing a plastic plate and stainless steel fork sticking up from another container. Not exactly Martha Stewart, but better than the coffee machine and dirty kitchen on his floor at FBI Headquarters in DC. Impressed with the office's amenities, Jake considered what Meg had said about the SAC possibly transferring or retiring. *Wouldn't it be great if I could transfer here?*

Ditch DC and live and work in Paradise? Settle down with his *shiksa* goddess? What's not to like? Except it would mean giving up an important assignment with the National Counter Terrorism Center.

Jake followed Alabastro into his office, where they sat in club chairs along one wall decorated with commendations and military photos alongside four FBI directors and two attorney generals. Alabastro unbuttoned his suit jacket and crossed his leg over one knee. He nodded at the sports bag Jake had placed on the silver-painted cubist-styled coffee table.

As a prologue, Jake gave a summary of his knowledge of the Daoud family in Escondido. A background check on his secure laptop had revealed all he needed to know about Khaled Daoud—his immigration status, and that of his wife, Fatimah, their American-born children, Sarah, aged fifteen, and Jafar, aged twelve, the mosque in Escondido where they all attended, their restaurant in a little strip mall. He'd also uncovered information Daoud's compatriots and their frequent online use of the Al-Qaeda web site, Shumukh al-Islam, as well as other online contacts with radical Islamic clerics in Yemen, Syria, and Iran. Daoud appeared clean, but his pals were dirty. Jake suspected they created their own little makeshift jihadist cell?

Then Jake played the recording he'd made in the hospital and handed Alabastro a printout of DC's translation. The verbatim translation supported Jake's original interpretation of the two men's indiscreet conversation in the hospital corridor.

Alabastro shook his head. "Un-fucking believable. They had no idea you were FBI, knew some Arabic..."

"Yep, their unlucky day. But something made me even more suspicious that this attack wasn't just an immigrant hate crime. One of their cohorts followed us and used this bat on my rental car. Trying to scare us to stay away." Jake pulled a manila envelope of eight-by-ten photographs from the nylon sports bag.

Alabastro sorted through the dozen photographs. He glanced at the wooden bat Jake retrieved from his bag, the shaft fully covered by the brown paper bag.

"Don't tell me..." The SAC's dark eyes bulged in surprise.

"No, I'm not certain if this is the weapon used against Mrs. Daoud. I'd like your lab to analyze it, though, for traces of blood, epithelial cells, and hair."

"Sure thing. And those bastards have fooled the local cops into chasing after known bigots in the area. An arrest was made. Two members of a white supremacist bike gang. They were seen passing through Escondido on the day of the attack. The cops are convinced they've got the perps. I spoke with the sergeant in charge of the case after I heard from the Navy investigators about the Carlton case. Looks like two parallel investigations but two different directions, two different conclusions. The press, of course, is following the PD's version since the NCIs aren't sharing any info with the meda."

Jake nodded. Alabastro scanned the bat, then looked over at Jake. "What would you like me to do with this evidence? And your testimony?"

Jake shrugged. "Whatever you can to find the truth. It's your jurisdiction. I'm officially on medical leave from HQ and the CTC. Just keep me informed, okay?"

"I'll request a FISA warrant. Might get it by Monday."

The FISA court was a specially federally designated court that catered to NSA and FBI requests. The federal judges on the court were practically on standby in cases of homeland security. By mentioning FISA, Alabastro made it clear to Jake that he was taking these allegations seriously.

"Jake, would you like a protection detail for you and Miss Larsen? Just in case?"

Jake thought a moment. "Not necessary. So far, Daoud and his thugs don't know how to find Meg or me, and we'll keep it that way."

Alabastro nodded and said nothing. He glanced at his watch, a cue that it was time to move on to the primary reason for their meeting.

"As you know, there's the Carlton case," Jake said. "The NCIs from Navy Base Coronado are trying to put together a sting operation to find the killer of that Navy officer. We need your help—manpower, some tech toys, and surveillance. Lab work, too, if we can get a hair sample."

The man's generous mouth tugged up on one side. "For a man on medical leave, you've been a busy guy."

Jake hmphed. "Tell me about it." Then he launched into his plan.

UNDERCOVER IN SAN DIEGO

BY THE TIME JAKE FINISHED eighteen holes of golf at Torrey Pines, Meg's phone message had come through. She wanted to take a break from her insufferable Goethe novel and meet him downtown in the Gaslamp Quarter for dinner. Her treat. Sevilla's on Fifth Street...the main drag. The restaurants in the touristy neighborhood were plentiful and excellent. They'd sampled Donovan's seafood, Greystone's steaks, the brew at The Lucky Bastard's, and the martinis at The Tipsy Crow. Tonight would be tapas.

Late nineteenth-century styled street lamps dotted every block and emitted sodium-yellow light as Jake limped up Fifth Street from the underground parking garage near the Convention Center. He'd twisted his sore ankle on a divot hole on the fifteenth fairway and now could barely walk on it. What he needed was an ice pack and a painkiller. On second thought, JD on the rocks or a couple of shots of El Patron would do the trick.

Sevilla's was dark, and from what he could discern in the gloom, had a Picasso modernistic look. Mixed between the abstract wall fixtures were huge, colorful posters of bullfighters. Jake found Meg perched on a high-backed stool at a bistro table under an image that exalted the courage of El Cordobés. He limped over and gave her an embrace and kiss. Her return kiss was warm, but he sensed, distracted. Dressed in her usual jeans and knitted tunic, she was a sight for sore eyes. She wore her long, wavy blond hair down about her shoulders like cascading gold.

Today, her ubiquitous hoop earrings were silver with little diamonds hanging from the bottom of the hoops. On her left hand's second finger gleamed the ring her beloved grandmother had given her for her sixteenth birthday. The garnet stone, as large as an almond, was ringed by a bezel of gold and diamonds. Her birthstone.

Now twenty-eight, Meg was counting the years until marriage and motherhood. Jake knew the race was on, and her biological clock was ticking away. How did he know this? At her birthday party hosted by her Uncle John and Aunt Pat, she'd told everyone there—just dropped the bomb without notice—that by the time she turned thirty, she wanted to be married and possibly expecting a child. After which, her uncle, aunt, and cousins had looked pointedly at him. Without missing a beat, Meg had gone on to explain how family was important to her. She'd already lost her parents—her mother was

MIA—and grandparents. She was searching for another replacement family. With her background, he just couldn't blame her.

Meg seemed to be full of bundled nerves. One high heel kept flopping back and forth off one foot as she swung a crossed leg like a frenetic drummer's stick. She slugged the last of a large Margarita as he gave his order—two shots of Patrón tequila and another Margarita for her.

He made the mistake of groaning while rolling his right shoulder and rubbing his left ankle.

Meg frowned. "Jake, I told you not to play eighteen holes. Your ankle can't take it yet."

He shrugged and grumbled like a chastised little boy.

She went on as if she expected such a nonverbal response. "I can't tell you how bored, how screaming bored I was. Just had to get out. I was overwhelmed with what Goethe calls *weltschmerz*. Do you know that word, Jake?"

He threw her a lopsided smile. "Oh, yeah, world-weariness. I get it all the time, especially during a case." He placed his hand over her nervously twitching fingers. "So you're weary, Meg. You're bored out of your skull. You're already sick of German?" He asked the last question in flawless German.

She took a long swallow. "I guess. I don't know, *mein liebling*. Just the whole thing. You're leaving soon makes me sad."

He downed a swig of his Patrón. What could he do except launch into his usual sales pitch?

"You know I want you to come with me. I've got a two-bedroom, two-bath condo with plenty of room. You can take German at Georgetown, Virginia State, or Berlitz and be ready for next year's classes. There are lots of high schools in DC, public and private. We'd make it work, Meg. Until I can get a SAC position in California. I saw Alabastro today at the San Diego field office. The man sure doesn't look ready to retire any time soon."

Her thoughtful gaze shut off suddenly as she tipped her giant glass again. They'd spiraled the same topic up and down and around and around all month, to no resolution.

They studied the menu in silence, and when the waitress arrived, Jake let Meg order for them in perfectly accented Spanish. He had no idea what she'd ordered but when it finally came—all eight dishes—the various aromas and choices satisfied him. Mini *empanadas* filled with, he hoped, chicken. *Brochetas de moro*—skewers of grilled lamb, peppers, mushroom, and tomato. A small pan of *paella del mar* packed with seafood. *Calamares en su tinta*—great, although he had to drink and swish the liquid around to wash the black squid ink off his teeth. And a charcuterie with Manchego cheese, chorizo, and other meats.

Jake gulped it all down with relish. The food and tequila helped wash away the day's work clutter. His ankle pain had diminished to a dull throb. He glanced at Meg, wondering if she felt restored as well. She was no longer frowning but watching him as though trying to detect his mood.

She sighed heavily. The look in her dark blue eyes told him something was up. A guilty look as blatant as her burnt-orange sweater canvassed her face. He waited, his full stomach feeling strangely like a hole had opened up inside. Was she breaking up with him?

"I did something stupid," she said.

He waited and downed the last of his tequila shot. His third. Time to switch to his water glass. "Yeah?"

She told him how she'd copied his recording from the hospital and played it for her European history professor, Ibrahim Basheera, and how she'd sensed something was amiss by the look on his face. He'd clearly understood what the men had said yet did not act in outrage at the woman's attack. On the contrary, he sounded defensive, as though he was trying to protect the two men or justify their private actions and words.

Two hours before, her German professor, Herr Heinz, had texted her and revealed Basheera's request for her address. After the fact, Herr Heinz started having misgivings about giving it to Basheera without thinking since he hadn't checked with her first.

Or maybe it was his payback, Jake thought, for that German Club meeting.

"Then today, when I met with the students from the high school, the ones I tutor twice a week, Sarah wasn't there again. But her friend Marsha came up to me after the class. We discussed the meaning of a short story they were having trouble understanding, and she handed me a note from Sarah. It said that her father had taken away her cell phone and was restricting her to school and work at the restaurant. She mentioned overhearing her father speaking furiously on the phone and saying something about her teacher and the hospital. She knew he was referring to the day we visited her mother in the hospital." Meg stared at him, her eyes big with worry. "Don't you see? She wanted to warn me. Her father somehow found out, maybe from Professor Basheera, that we had recorded the men's conversation. And now Mr. Daoud knows where I live."

Jake recalled Alabastro's offer of a protection detail. "Meg, why did you take that recording to your professor? Didn't you trust me?"

"I know, I know. It was a stupid thing to do. I thought you weren't being objective. That you were influenced by that undercover job. I'm so sorry."

"Does Basheera know I'm FBI?"

"No, I don't think so. I've never mentioned it. Ever since you went undercover last year you told me not to tell anyone, remember? But Herr Heinz knows."

"Oh, yeah, Herr Heinz," he growled the man's name, "and the whole German Club."

"I've never told Professor Basheera. I'm so sorry."

His simmering anger at her betrayal sat like a fist in his gut. She'd made a copy of that recording behind his back. And then shared it with a stranger? How could she've done that?

Meg opened her big satchel hanging over the back of her pub chair. She urged him to peek inside, where her snub-nosed, .38 caliber Lady Smith and Wesson revolver rested, no doubt locked and loaded, ready for action.

"Oh, Meg."

"I'm so sorry, Jake. This is just in case, y'know."

He couldn't shake the feeling of betrayal. "Why did you go behind my back?"

She stared at her half-eaten plate and let out another heavy sigh. "I thought you might be wrong. I thought you might be seeing bogeymen behind every bush. I thought your judgment might be faulty because of what those terrorists did to you. Y'know what they call Americans who distrust Muslims? Islamophobes. I was afraid you'd become an Islamophobe."

He snorted derisively. "You know who made up that word? The Muslim Brotherhood, that's who. That bunch of thugs who'd fooled their own Egyptian brothers into believing they'd changed. Then, when they got into power, their true colors emerged, and they tried to force Sharia Law into Egyptian society. Let's get out of here."

"Jake, I'm sorry."

"No, don't say it. The damage is done. But you know what this means. While I'm back in DC, you're here alone, and that Escondido bunch of radicals knows where you live. Think about that, Meg."

She silently paid the bill while he slid off his stool and stalked over to the front door. They walked down the sidewalk, Jake limping in front of her, trying to get his temper under control. He'd never raised his voice to her before. His fists kept clenching involuntarily.

She'd parked in the same underground garage, so they headed in that direction. Closer to the harbor, the cool air turned cold and breezy. Jake caught a scent of brine off the bay as he slowed down so she could catch up to him. He fought to clear his mind as he felt her grab his arm and hook one of hers through his.

While his anger had banked a bit, he was still fuming. "Y'know, Meg, you've put yourself in danger. All so fucking unnecessarily." He glanced at her bag. "And if you're caught with that gun and no license to carry a concealed weapon, you could lose your teacher's credential. Then what'll you do?"

She staggered a little on her high heels, and he had to prop her up on the side of his bad ankle. He gritted his teeth against the pain.

She leaned in close enough to whisper against his shoulder. "I'm sorry. The drinks I had were stronger than I needed. I feel a little woozy. Jake, are you packing your gun?"

He glanced down at her. "Yeah, always. Why?"

"I think someone followed us out of Sevilla's."

Jake sighed audibly.

Chapter Seventeen

JAKE LOOKED DOWN INTO Meg's eyes, glittering in the lamplight like cut sapphires, but focused now on the street scene around them. He fought through the blood still pulsing in his ears.

"Did you say someone followed us from the restaurant?"

Her nod was nearly imperceptible. "I think someone followed me here.." Her words slurred. "In that car over there, the small black one. And I think the man in that car was in the restaurant."

On the other side of Fifth Street, along a row of cars parked at the curb, two dark-haired men sat in a small black sedan. The driver's face reflected in the side mirror, but Jake couldn't see any details. A moment later, the car's engine fired up, and it sped down the street. Cars cruised up and down this popular nightspot street and by now the sidewalks and outdoor cafés were packed with people. The empty spot was soon filled by another car.

"*Now* you're telling me?" He took a deep breath and bit his lip. Meg clearly had too much to drink and barely managed to hang onto his arm. The pain in his ankle had worsened, and so did his limp, but he kept them both upright with sheer willpower. "Did they see you park?"

She nodded curtly, her face registering the import of the situation, the cold air appearing to sober her up a little.

"They were probably our bat-wielding friends, you realize," he grumbled. "Word got back to Daoud and his pals."

They continued shakily down the street another block. Across the street, Jake spied two more Middle Eastern-looking guys emerge from a restaurant's doorway, where the bustling outdoor café had effectively concealed them. They were staring Meg's way, and one of them spoke urgently into his cell phone.

Four of them. These guys were serious this time. They had stepped up from one bat-swinging vandal to an attack team. Jake could kick himself for declining Alabastro's offer for protection. Even if he called now, the SAC wouldn't be able to gather a team in time. For now, he and Meg were on their own. Hobbling the five blocks to the garage made them slow-moving ducks in a shooting gallery.

On their left, Jake spotted a small crowd elbowing their way into the entrance of the seafood restaurant, where he recalled having dinner with Meg a couple of weeks ago. They'd exited on Sixth Street through the steakhouse side of the building. He figured these pricks wouldn't know about the walk-through in the kitchen and restroom hallway that connected the two restaurants. He steered Meg toward the crowd.

Jake marched Meg through the kitchen, amid the staff's protests, and kept going past the restrooms and out into the lavish dining room of the steakhouse. Holding onto Meg, he breezed past the line of waiting diners and out onto Sixth Street. Luckily, a yellow taxi had just dropped off a couple. Jake immediately flagged him down.

He helped pour Meg into the back seat, told her to lie down, and then quickly slid into the front passenger seat and told the driver where to go.

"The Convention Center garage? Sure 'nough." The young Hispanic hooked a thumb at the backseat. "Too much partying, yes?"

"You could say that," Jake said. His loaded Glock was in the glove compartment of his rented Explorer. Was Meg sober enough to use her Smith and Wesson? He looked back at her, lying on her side, her right hand already inside her big bag. He frowned at her. "Only if you can see straight," he told her cryptically.

Another problem arose. "Meg, what floor is your car on?" He couldn't recall seeing it, but in his haste, he'd taken the elevator down to the street entrance.

"Third."

In minutes, the taxi pulled into the garage, pausing while the driver swiped his pass. When they reached the third floor, Jake's heart began to hammer. The small black sedan had parked two spaces over from Meg's Dodge Durango. The two men brazenly stood watch next to their car. Jake sank further into his seat and pulled the collar of his bomber jacket up over his ears.

"Stay down, Meg. We're going up to my car."

The driver looked alarmed. "Want me to call the cops?"

"Not yet. Take us to the fifth floor. My car's there. Drop us off, then call. Stay up there until you see the cops or another car come down. There's probably safety in numbers but I don't want you caught in the middle of something."

"I got lots of cousins," the driver muttered, grinning. "We kick ass."

Jake smiled and slipped one of his FBI cards to the driver. They reached the fifth floor, and Jake pointed out his ruby-red Explorer. He pressed a fifty-dollar bill into the man's hand. "You've earned it."

He hustled Meg out of the taxi and into the back seat of the Explorer, his new replacement car.

"Meg, for God's sake, stay down and keep your weapon at the ready. If anyone opens either of these doors, shoot him. Remember what they did to Mrs. Daoud! Don't give them a chance to do the same to you. Understand?"

He revved up the Ford and placed his Glock on the passenger seat. "Here goes."

Gliding down two ramps, he lightly pumped the brake, letting gravity do the rest. The assholes had blocked part of the ramp with the back end of their car. They must've recognized him in the taxi. One of the two guys had a bat that he slapped against his side, the other—Khaled Daoud—pointed the barrel of a pistol directly at him.

He had no choice. "Meg! Stay down and hold on to something."

FBI field training included evasive driving techniques. While he'd forgotten half of his own training, a simple ram and run was something he'd never forget. He fastened his seatbelt, then eased off the brake and gradually accelerated. The eyes of Daoud and his buddy bugged as they realized what he was about to do. He barreled down on them and aimed for the right rear fender of their small sedan. His training overrode his instincts to brake hard at the last moment before impact.

The subsequent crash jolted him. He was lifted off his seat, hit his lower chest against the steering wheel, and bounced back as the airbag exploded into his face. Meg cried out in back. Metal ground on metal and glass shattered. If he'd damaged the SUV's engine, they'd never get out of there alive.

He pumped the gas pedal, and the Explorer bucked and wheezed before it lurched to life again. The airbag collapsed, and he could finally see through the windshield. His heavier SUV had pushed the lighter sedan sideways into the rear of another car, the sedan's trunk and rear bumper now a mangled mess of metal and fiberglass. A small explosive sound grabbed his attention as a bullet thudded against the passenger seatback. Meg screamed.

"Stay down!" Jake brought his weapon up and pointed at his passenger window, but the attackers were behind him now, and it was all he could do to swerve around their smashed sedan. He would've liked to have popped off a round or two, but he couldn't risk stopping and getting out before aiming. The other two guys, the ones who'd tailed them on foot, were now running up the ramp, huffing and puffing in the middle of the roadway.

They scattered to the side as Jake's SUV zoomed their way. He pointed his pistol out of the driver's window to make sure the two men didn't pursue. Another bullet pierced the rear passenger's window as his SUV spiraled down the ramp. He kept going down the three floors of the parking garage and gritted his teeth as he crashed through the barrier's wooden arm. His Explorer bounced off the curb near the exit as he veered violently to the right.

He doubted the rental agency would rent him another car, but that was the least of his problems. If he'd disabled their only vehicle, he'd get away. But he wasn't sure. The other two guys might have another car.

From the backseat, Meg reassured him that she was okay. Being half-plastered had probably kept her loose enough, like a drunk's limp-doll reaction, which often saved them from broken bones during a crash.

"Stay on the floor," he yelled, "it's safer."

Jake's relief went deep as he panted and slowed down a little to regain control. He couldn't afford a DUI but nevertheless sped up L Street, then turned left onto Eleventh Avenue. A mile or two later, he merged onto Highway Five and headed north to UCSD.

"Meg, baby, are you okay?"

"Yes."

"Okay, sit up, but buckle yourself in."

He checked to see if she'd been hit by one of the bullets or any broken glass. Except for a bruise on her left cheek, she looked fine. And was damned lucky. That one bullet must have missed her head by inches.

Another problem struck him as he glanced into his rearview mirror for the tenth time in as many minutes. Daoud knew where Meg lived. Until he could get Alabastro to assign a protection detail, they had to stay away.

Fuck.

A half mile from the turnoff to Meg's neighborhood, he veered into the parking lot of a Best Western motel. The parking lot was hidden behind the main building and bordering high hedges. He stopped and registered them as Mr. and Mrs. Schoenberg and used one of his undercover aliases' credit cards. He helped Meg out and didn't even look closely at the front of his rented Explorer. His adrenalin rush had eased, and leaden exhaustion weighed him down mentally and physically. Each painful step was an effort, and each strained muscle in his arms, shoulders, torso, and legs screamed out in pain. Meg looked visibly sick with a mixture of tequila and shock. As soon as they entered their room, she made a beeline for the bathroom, knelt over the toilet, and vomited. He deadbolted the front door and made no attempt to console her.

He set his Glock on the nightstand on his side of the king-sized bed. Heavy-lidded, he peeled down to his black cotton briefs and climbed into bed. Later, when Meg turned off the lights and slid into bed beside him, he silently rolled over and turned his back to her. She said nothing.

Jake couldn't stop his troubling thoughts as he slipped into a weary, uneasy sleep. *Trust is everything. She can't love me if she doesn't trust me.*

Chapter Eighteen

"I'M LEAVING NOW." JAKE averted his eyes down to his sports bag. He zipped it up and turned to go.

"Are you coming back?" Meg's voice hitched a little as she fought back welling tears. This was a side of Jake she'd seen before—a kind of relentless stubbornness, a steely pride, and cold deliberation. She'd seen his character emerge in Ireland, and it was one of the reasons she'd fallen in love with him, but she'd never seen this wall of pain and anger directed against her.

He stopped and stared back at her. His big dark eyes, now hooded and full of suspicion, enveloped her.

Dear God, is he going to walk out of my life and never come back?

It was early Friday evening, dinnertime. Meg had spent the entire day, Thursday, with Jake at the San Diego FBI's field office, meeting with SAC Tom Alabastro and SDPD Major Crimes detectives, having to explain what had happened the night before in downtown San Diego, including why there were two damaged cars in the parking garage, why the others—the alleged perpetrators—had fled the scene before the local police had arrived, why a taxi driver was left to excitedly relate his portion of the story. On and on the questions went until the report in the lead detective's notebook ran to ten pages or more.

Alabastro filled in another ten pages or so with his decision to conduct a parallel investigation without the PD's consent. Meg told her involvement in this case of an alleged "honor killing" attempt and her connection to the Daouds. Evidently, the SDPD detective had already reached his own conclusion. In his view, two bikers were involved in what was still considered a hate crime.

While the FBI pursued their line of investigation and a search warrant based on trace blood evidence found on the legally obtained bat and based on the illegally obtained recording, the San Diego PD believed they'd already found their perps—two bikers with a history of white supremacy affiliations and a sheet of assault and battery. The bikers just happened to have eaten at the Daoud restaurant the same evening as the attack and had complained about the food and, although they'd paid for their meals, hadn't left a tip. Sarah Daoud, a witness to her mother's attack, had picked the two bikers out of a lineup the next day.

After the detectives left his office on Thursday, Alabastro wasted no time in setting up a protection detail for both Meg and Jake, contracting out to a private security firm. Friday morning a wireless transmitter was installed in Meg's apartment and two men in plainclothes, wearing earbuds, were now stationed in two separate vehicles at the curb outside. One of them would accompany her to classes while the other maintained watch at her apartment.

Meg slumped down on the kitchen chair. *I brought this all on myself-no, on us.*

Jake's silence was worse than an all-out screaming match. His angry, hurt silence—how could she combat that? She had no weapons in her arsenal for cold silence.

His gaze dropped again as he slung the sports bag over his shoulder.

"Just going up to L.A. to see my folks. Do some deep sea fishing with Dad and Gabe." Before he left, he lobbed back, "Stay safe, Meg. Stay here at the motel or with your aunt and uncle in Coronado. Don't, whatever you do, go back to your apartment unless the FBI security team is with you. Those Escondido thugs could be watching. Just be extra cautious for a few days. If you don't trust me, trust the local field office. They know what they're doing."

His reference to trust stung her but she deserved it, she felt. She should have trusted him—should not have trusted Professor Basheer. Then and there, she decided this was not a good time to let him know that Sheila had been calling her once a day all week wanting to set up a rendezvous at The Lido nightclub that very weekend. She hadn't called the woman back. She'd wait until Jake returned on Sunday night. He looked like he wasn't in the mood to deal with anything else at the moment.

Meg could redeem herself in Jake's eyes by helping with Jake's Navy case. The honey trap plan had reached a dead end. Jake had told her that all of Uncle John's weapons officers on board the guided missile cruiser had declined to offer themselves as bait in the NCIs' sting operation. But she could offer herself. Sheila already believed Meg's lie from that night at the club, just before the fire started. Why not go along and see what she could find out?

Jake glanced at her before he shut the front door behind him. Acutely aware the bug was picking up everything they said, she was reluctant to say anything more than a feeble, "Have a good time, Jake. Tell your family hi for me."

He nodded and was gone.

He hadn't kissed or hugged her. They desperately needed to talk, but this evidently was not the time for Jake.

BY NOON SATURDAY, MEG had returned to her apartment with one of the local FBI security teams in place outside. She'd just finished her Goethe's book report, and her eyes were beginning to cross. She closed her laptop, stood up, and stretched her back by bending over and touching her toes twenty times. Lord, what she wouldn't give for a run around campus. Jogging had always been her therapy, her meditation time, a time to sort out her emotions. Instead, she felt under house arrest—her fault, she knew.

What about Jake? He'd had to drop off the badly damaged Ford Explorer and pay the difference between what the rental agency's insurance would cover and the actual cost for realignment and body work. But that wasn't the half of it. She had damaged, perhaps beyond repair, their relationship, all in the name of finding the truth. In her view, anyway. Of course, he saw it differently. She'd distrusted his judgment and foolishly went to a professor, a stranger, who apparently had his own hidden agenda.

Restless, she went into the bedroom and looked over his half of the double chest of drawers. He'd laid his notebook, digital camera, a pair of cufflinks, his SEAL knife, and other paraphernalia on top of a couple of recently cleaned t-shirts and briefs. She resisted the urge to look through his notebook, knowing it contained information about the Carlton case. She'd heard enough about it at the FBI field office on Thursday and had been briefed a little before their excursion to The Lido. Two business cards were attached to the front of the notebook, denoting the names and telephone numbers of the two NCIs he'd been consulting with. Meg recalled what Jake had said about both NCIs. *Smart but inexperienced. They don't need much direction, just a nudge here or there.*

Impulsively, she picked up one of the cards and punched in the number of Ensign Blanco's cell phone. When he picked up immediately, she was taken aback.

"Hi, this is Meg Larsen. Y'know, Special Agent Bernstein's...friend." What am I really to him, she wondered suddenly. Screw-up friend with benefits? Ex-girlfriend? Her eyes filled with tears, and she had to sniff them back and remind herself to buck up.

"Oh, yeah? Jake called us from L.A. Just to let us know he was out of town this weekend."

"Ensign Blanco—"

"Call me Javier. You're Rear Admiral Snider's niece, aren't you? The one that night at the club?"

"Yes, I am. I've been briefed and updated on your case, the one investigating Lieutenant Carlton's murder. Tell me, what's a honey trap?"

"It's a sting operation, when we use sweet bait like sex or a sex object to lure in the mark. We wanted to run one with that Chinese girl, Sheila, at The Lido nightclub. The evidence, all circumstantial right now, is pointing in her direction. Her and her bodyguard."

Meg hesitated for a split second, then plunged in.

"Yes, I figured that out from Jake's remarks. Remember that night of the nightclub fire? I ran into Sheila in the ladies' room and told her off the cuff I'd just been assigned to the USS Dixie. Honest to God, I don't know why I did that. I suppose I was trying to play a part, like you and Jake and..."

"Mary Lou—Ensign Taylor. Yeah, I remember, Sheila hit on you and got your phone number."

"Thing is, she's been calling me every day all week. She wants to meet me at the club."

The line went silent, then Meg heard Javier speaking to someone in the background.

"Does Jake know about this?"

"Well, yes and no. I told him she'd called once but didn't get a chance to tell him before he left that she'd been calling me once a day ever since. I haven't called her back. We've been busy with...well, other things."

Jake. Should she tell him? No more evasions of the truth. From now on, Meg was determined to be upfront about everything, even the inconsequential. Just to be on the safe side, she'd text or phone him the next day. He was fishing, and she was certain he wouldn't want her to ruin his day by mentioning the Carlton case.

"We're going to the club tonight," Javier said. "They've done repairs and have reopened. Wickham wants us to continue surveillance of the persons of interest. Want to meet us there tonight around nine? We'll do what we did last time. Undercover as the gay Navy scene on shore leave. We'll be in civvies. If Sheila is into you, it might give us a leg up on the investigation. If you can get her to trust you and possibly get us a hair sample from her bodyguard—"

"Whoa, wait now. You think the guy would just let me yank out a strand of his hair?"

Javier harrumphed. "Not that sumo wrestler."

"Then what? How can I be of use?" Meg caught her reflection in the mirror. The lamplight from the nightstand by her bed threw a shadowy cast on her features, like a film noir movie poster. Mysterious, creepy, and exciting all at once.

"Just play the part and cozy up to her. See what you can learn. We'll be there close by. And you'll be wired." Javier added the last bit quickly.

Meg considered her two temporary bodyguards from the local FBI field office. What could be the harm? They'd be outside in their cars, keeping watch on the club. If she could help the NCIs' investigation—and Jake's—why not? It was her chance to atone for her lack of trust in Jake's judgment.

Maybe in a small way, she could atone for all of the harm her Nazi grandmother had once caused as the Third Reich's most notorious spy. The world had spun around millions of times since then and had brought her, the granddaughter of the spy code-named Hummingbird, into an espionage plot of a different sort.

Why not help out?

"What kind of Navy officer could I pose as? I'm supposed to be a lieutenant, but I know nothing about weapons or engineering. I've been on my uncle's cruiser only once as a family guest when he first received his commission."

Silence ensued. Her heart raced. Should she get involved in this case? She'd made such a mess out of the other one.

"What about a nurse?" Javier asked. "Sick bay nurse? The USS Dixie has one, an RN with almost twenty years in the Navy, a husband and two kids. Know anything about nursing?"

Meg thought a moment. Would a high school research report into nursing as a career or First-Aid training as an intern sports trainer be enough? Her college roommate had been a nursing major, and Meg had been intrigued with human anatomy and its mysteries. She'd read several of her roommate's textbooks, listened to her summaries of symptoms, treatments, and cures, and had quizzed her for hours upon hours.

"Enough to fake it, I think. For a little while." A knot of doubt coiled its way into her stomach and burrowed there. *Can I really pull this off? Can I act as a single lesbian Navy nurse?*

Javier's next words made up her mind.

"Well, it's only for an hour or so tonight, anyway. I'll run it by our boss. If Wickham okays it, I'll call and confirm."

If Gran can act a part, so can I. Who knows? Maybe it runs in our genes.

"Okay, I'll wait for your call."

"Great! If it's a go, we'll meet you. Nine o'clock, outside. Let's learn what we can, maybe bag us a killer."

As soon as she hung up, she was about to text Jake and let him know how she was going to assist the NCIs that night. However, she stopped herself. She'd call or text after his day of fishing. Let him enjoy one day away from both cases. God knows he deserved that much.

Chapter Nineteen

THE SKY WAS LIKE A pewter lid, low and wet, muffling sea sounds but not enough to muffle the caws of overhead wheeling seagulls. The overcast sky, high fog, and heavy swells made for perfect fishing weather. Despite his nylon windbreaker, Jake was drenched. Everything on him was damp and clammy, and he shivered from the cold. Still, he was having fun.

Satisfied, Jake dumped his latest catch, a plump four-pound sole, into a shared cooler. It wriggled on top of the other four that he and his father had caught. His younger brother Gabe hadn't even got up to bat, spending most of their six chartered hours in the wheelhouse, bending over a bucket. The other dozen weekend fishermen on the charter were as lucky as Jake and his father, Martin. They were fortunate to catch a day when the sea off the coast of Long Beach was flush with fish.

Martin pulled back the hood of his yellow oilcloth poncho to gaze down at the new catch, his gray hair plastered to his head due to the thick sea mist. "Not bad, Jake, though with all the chum they've been tossing in, we should've reeled in a giant squid by now. Guess the old fish are too smart to fall for it. Just like humans, with age comes wisdom."

Uh-oh, here it comes.

He knew his parents liked Meg, so much in fact that they had made their hopes clear to him. *Time to settle down and have a family. You wouldn't take the kind of chances you take if you were a married man. She's a great girl. You can't do any better...a guy making a government salary.*

The last one hurt. They made him sound like a pauper working for peanuts.

He remained silent, though he knew Martin wouldn't take the hint. Who needed a Jewish mother when he had his father?

Earlier, Jake had explained Meg's absence to his parents with a terse, "We're taking a short break from each other."

His Irish-Catholic mother had shrugged and had wisely kept quiet. Not his dad.

Even during their peaceful fishing excursion, his father had something to say. "Meg's—what? Twenty-seven? Oh, twenty-eight now. I know you, young man. You're punishing her for some mistake she made. Your mother calls it *getting your Irish up*. That's only half of you, remember that. The other half is Jewish, always looking for the narrow path of truth, justice, and righteousness. Or always looking for the worst that can happen. That's *meshuga*. Life isn't like that. It's not always the best or the worst."

Jake usually nodded, knowing the quickest way to get his father to shut up was to agree with him. Not this time.

"It's a matter of trust, Dad. You either trust a person, or you don't. If you don't, you can't call it love."

"People sure aren't like that, Jake. They're not black and white. They're all shades of gray. Mistakes? So, she made a mistake and didn't trust you completely. That's what this is about, isn't it? Look at all the mistakes you made in your twenties, my boy. How many cars did you dent because of your lead foot? Two, three? You married the wrong girl even though we told you she was wrong for you. Meg...she's just a babe in the woods...still trusts people. Not you. If someone tells you his name, you're thinking, *oh yeah, prove it.*"

"All right, enough, Dad." Jake removed the hook, baited it again, and threw it back in the ocean, returning his rod to the rod holder in the gunwale. Despite his still aching ankle, which he'd wrapped with a vinyl-cloth brace, he remained standing, his sea-worthy legs keeping him upright amid the swells.

His father had chosen relative stability on the bench. "Are you really hearing me, son?"

Martin looked a little weary. Maybe getting up at five a.m. had something to do with it. At sixty-nine, he was still teaching history at UCLA, though he'd cut back to one class per quarter. In his free time, he was working on a book about his father, Nathan Bernstein, and the other refugee Jews in the Hollywood film industry in the thirties. People like Marlene Dietrich, Billy Wilder, and Peter Lorre—the stories of these German-born Jews often peppered the dinner table conversations. His grandfather, working as a film editor in Hollywood, had known them all.

"Jake, are you hearing me?"

"Yeah, Dad, I'm hearing you. I just don't think I've got any business taking a vow for anything lasting over six months. My life's too chaotic, all this undercover work—going here and there, wherever they need me. Meg needs a dependable, nine-to-five kind of guy. I'm anything but."

Martin stood up but held onto the gunwale railing. A big swell pitched the boat, and Jake kept him from falling. The roll down the other side was just as extreme, so he sat back down.

"Excuses, excuses. What makes you think Meg needs that? She could've left you a couple of months ago after you made her fake her death—"

"I didn't make her—"

"You see? She volunteered to do that! That proves she's game for anything. Maybe she's a little like her grandmother..."

"The Nazi spy? Are you kidding?"

Martin waved a hand aside. "No, I mean, Meg's an adventuress. She likes the thrill, the adventure."

"Yeah, like a moth to the flame, she likes it. Then when she gets burned, she flips and wants the security of marriage and a steady job. A different boyfriend."

"How do you know? Did she say that?" His father unscrewed the lid off a thermos and shakily poured some black coffee into a Styrofoam cup, splashing coffee all over.

Jake took the thermos and poured a cup for his father. "No, Dad, but I know her better than you."

"You've been together off and on for eight months. Mostly off from all your separations. I knew your mother for two years and dated her every week before I got the nerve to ask her to marry me. Although I knew from our first date that she was for me, I was scared, just like you."

"Scared? Of what? Commitment?"

"No, scared of disappointing her. I could bear anything but your mother's disappointment in me."

Jake smiled and clapped his father's shoulder. "Mom's not disappointed in you. Well, maybe a little. Maybe it took too long for you to clean out those gutters."

"Ha!" His father's upturned look of sarcasm made Jake laugh.

"None of us are disappointed in you, Dad. Gabe, Isaac, me. I mean, you put up with our squabbles, our jealousies, our little spats at one-upmanship. We were competitive little brats. But hey, you put us through college. What's not to love? We couldn't ask for a better Dad. I mean it."

Martin looked away and wiped his face. "That damn fog, it feels like rain." He put up the hood of his poncho but couldn't hide the hint of a smile.

"Good thing you and I have cast iron stomachs. Poor Gabriel, he's upchucked his whole breakfast," Martin said.

Just then, the skipper's voice came through the wheelhouse's overhead speaker. A pod of humpback whales was spotted swimming nearby on their northward migration up the coast of California for their long journey back to Alaska. This was an early bunch, among the first wave to leave the Sea of Cortez. The skipper cut the engine, and the sea surrounding them grew eerily quiet even though the swells remained.

On cue, the fishermen reeled in their lines and scrambled to the sides of the boat. Even Gabe ventured out to watch, though he stayed close to the portside gunwale. The curved backs and occasional tail flukes broke the water as the humpbacks dove gracefully, then breached the surface and spewed plumes of water and air through their blowholes. One smaller whale, perhaps a baby or juvenile, glided close to the boat and rolled over. Its eye, as big as a dinner plate, stared up at the humans staring back.

The men on board murmured in awe, their voices suffused with elation at the close-and-personal experience.

Gabe, his face bloodless from vomiting, looked over at Jake. "Wow, man," he breathed, "is this a trip or what?"

"I wonder what he thinks of us," Martin said.

Gabe managed to chuckle. "Maybe he's thinking, *I'm going to ram this boat if you guys steal any more of my food.*"

Jake laughed with his brother and father. Suddenly, the whale did a complete roll and dove, its fluke slapping the water hard and splattering a ten-foot-high spray over the men. They loved it. The creature seemed to be teasing them with its size and power as if saying, *Look what I can do, you puny humans.* Everyone was awed by the display.

Oh, yeah.

And maybe his father was right. Perhaps he was afraid, not of commitment but of disappointing Meg and racking up another failed marriage. Meg wasn't one to stick around if she wasn't satisfied.

Just as suddenly, Jake realized something else. He'd give anything to share a day like this with a son of his own.

The thought gave him pause.

ONCE AGAIN, MEG AND the NCIs approached Lisa and her bouncer. The big woman, Meg estimated at six-foot-one and at least two-hundred-and-fifty pounds, greeted her Navy customers with customary enthusiasm. Her smile faltered, however, when she recognized Javier and Mary Lou. She didn't seem sure about Meg but let her pass when the NCIs included her in their group. Neither Navy investigator had warned the club's manager that they were coming that night, but they'd gotten permission from SAC Alabastro, and by extension, Meg's security detail. The two security men were now sharing a nondescript sedan on the other side of Harbor Boulevard.

Hands stamped and aliases given, Meg and the young NCIs entered the club and began to circulate. Everything seemed the same as before. The blaring music played by a female DJ on stage and the gyrating men and women on the dance floor, some skimpily dressed and showing a lot of bare midriffs, cleavage, and legs.

Meg grew aware, as she had the first time in the club, of the prevalence of booze and the hidden but implied presence of drugs. She assumed X, or Ecstasy, and Special K would be floating around, but she hadn't yet witnessed any. She stared at the red-inked stamp on her hand after seeing several girls near her with green stamps on their hands. Funny, she hadn't noticed the difference before.

Meg and Mary Lou grabbed a table and glanced around The Lido's main floor. The club had been cleaned, painted, and reconstructed where necessary. The mirrored disco ball was back and spun over the dance floor as the multi-colored strobe lights lasered across the room in helter-skelter patterns. The once black walls were now purple and mauve but naked. Gone were the colorful Toulouse-Lautrec posters of the Folies Bergere and Moulin Rouge. The décor now was edgy and austere, almost Goth.

A cocktail waitress dressed like an extra from a Michael Jackson Thriller video approached them with a tray of drinks. The first drink to celebrate the re-opening was obviously on the house. Tonight's theme? A mystery, although Mary Lou suggested a sexy vampire or zombie fantasy. The featured drink of the night, Black Hole, according to their hand stamps. Meg didn't even want to guess the contents.

While Mary Lou and Javier idled over by the railing to watch the dancers, Meg glanced around the room. Sure enough, Sheila and her bodyguard held court in the upper tier of banquettes. Two men—one Asian, the other Caucasian—shared the seat with Sheila. Her hulking bodyguard stood ramrod straight just outside their recessed nook. He had no drink in his hand as his dark gaze roamed the place relentlessly.

Meg had been brought up to date on the murder case and couldn't help but wonder if the bodyguard was capable of killing Lieutenant Carlton. Oh, yes, she decided, and the back of her neck shivered at the thought. When he spied Meg, he turned slightly and spoke to Sheila.

Meg caught Javier's attention as Mary Lou pranced onto the dance floor, her hips pumping and her mini skirt swaying to the music. Meg had dressed in tight, low-slung jeans, a bright yellow tank top, and three-inch stiletto sandals, she even sported a Navy tattoo on one bicep—the insignia of the Navy anchor done in henna, not ink—which she'd stopped to get to add to her persona. She'd noticed the last time that all the Navy personnel in the club appeared to wear their tats with pride, so why not? She'd captured her long blond hair in a low, one-shouldered ponytail. Large gold hoops, lots of dark eye makeup, and glossy red lipstick finished the illusion of a young Navy officer looking to let her hair down and party out.

The small, round bistro tables and chairs on all three tiers of the club were filled. In the uppermost tier, where Sheila and her friends sat, every alcove was also filled.

"Meg?" Javier pulled her attention back. "Name and rank."

"Lieutenant Meghan Snider," she replied, automatically standing at attention, making Javier smile.

Javier and Mary Lou had briefed her in their car while parked in the same parking garage they'd used the last time. They'd spent thirty minutes bringing her up to speed with the salient facts of her new cover alias. A combination of lies and truth to lure Sheila and her hulking pal into their trap. Sweetening the bait, so to speak. Or so they hoped.

"Okay, play this as we discussed earlier and see what shakes loose. Remember, don't drink anything unless you take it directly from the waitress's tray. Get Sheila to loosen up and talk, but don't ask too many questions. Mention Samantha Carlton, but you're new to the ship and didn't really know her, but you heard rumors. We'll be keeping an eye on you inside the club, and remember not to cover that mike." He indicated one of the many studs on her wide, gold-plated cuff bracelet that held a hidden wireless mike and transmitter. "Your exit code word is *Amazons*. Like The Amazons café."

Javier wore wireless earbuds and a small iPod hooked to his studded armless t-shirt that concealed a short-range, wireless receiver. Add in his tight black jeans, Navy tats, and spiked hair and the cute, somewhat nerdy Hispanic investigator had transformed into one cool-looking dude.

He leaned close and whispered, "Here comes one of Sheila's fan base."

The young, tall Asian man approached her. "You Meg?" When she nodded and smiled, the man pointed up. "Sheila wants to invite you to join her upstairs. Can I grab you a drink? What'll you have?" He spoke perfect American English with no accent.

She glanced at Javier and slid around the table, grabbing her nearly full rum and Coke. "I'm doing fine with this one, thanks. See you later, Ja—" Suddenly overcome with a flare-up of nerves, she forgot Javier's undercover name.

Javier quickly covered the slip and cooed, "Cool, Meg. Have a blast. See ya later." He pursed his lips and blew her an air kiss.

As Javier wandered off, he shot her a wink of encouragement.

Keep a cool head, she admonished herself. *Calm down. You can do this. For an hour or two... You can do this.*

The Asian guy left her to head for the bar, leaving her no choice. *Too late to back out now.* She turned to the carpeted stairs that bisected the upper tiers and paused to look up at Sheila and her muscular bodyguard.

She started climbing into the serpents' pit of her own free will. And her insides suddenly quivered with pant-wetting terror.

DONNA DEL ORO

What the hell am I doing?

Chapter Twenty

MEG WAS SURPRISED TO find Sheila was as gracious as she was beautiful. She invited Meg to sit next to her, between her and the handsome young Caucasian man she introduced as Neil. The man nodded but kept silent, steadily drinking from his martini glass, while Sheila immediately started plying Meg with questions.

"Who are the two good-looking people you came with?" she asked, then crossed her long, slim legs. Each time she did so—and she did it often—the short, clinging skirt of her sheath rose up her legs an enticing inch or two at a time.

Meg held back a chuckle. Had Jake sat down beside Sheila instead of her, his pulse would probably be hammering in his chest.

Sheila's glossy black hair, straight and long, flowed down her back like dark silk. The black dress she wore had deep cleavage, slits up the sides, and fit her like a second skin. The woman was going for the full sex appeal angle.

Meg imagined it would be too easy for her undercover character—a Navy nurse and supposed lesbian—to fall for the act. Yet how could a sensible Navy officer like Samantha Carlton have fallen for it? Sheila was so blatant with her sexual appeal. Why didn't red flags go up? Samantha was no ingénue. She'd been in her forties, for crying out loud. Was she blinded by passion and then opened her eyes too late? Was she about to expose them? Or had she gone along and passed military secrets to the Chinese, as the NCIs now suspected?

"Uh, my friends? Sherisa and Chico?"

"Are they Navy like you, Meg?"

"Yes, they're assigned to other ships. We met at the commissary's coffee shop on base. Right now, we all happen to be in home port."

She continued to sip gingerly from her rum and Coke, never letting it out of her sight. Neil was sneaking little white pills out of his pocket and gulping them down. He offered her one, but she declined. She noticed that his hand stamp was green and Sheila's blue. Hers and the two NCIs' were red.

Sheila dominated the conversation with rapid fired questions concerning the Navy, barely giving Meg a chance to reply. *On which ship are you assigned? The USS Dixie? I see. I think you mentioned that before. How long? A nurse on the guided missile cruiser, how interesting! The commander of your ship is he in town?—oh, I see, classified information. Did you know Samantha, the lieutenant who was tragically killed? Not well? She came here often.*

At this point, Meg jumped in. "Sheila, did you know the lieutenant well?"

Sheila played with the gold and silver bangles on her arm a moment before gathering her long, straight hair in a bundle and draping it over one shoulder.

"We had a few drinks together. Poor woman, she was past her prime and very lonely. Looking for love in all the wrong places, as you Americans say. I didn't want to babysit her, so after the third or fourth time, I discouraged her from joining my table."

Meg considered Sheila's mixture of lies and truth. Jake and the NCIs had apparently arrived at a far different conclusion.

Sheila ran a hand up her creamy leg to the juncture of thigh and skirt, causing Meg to suppress a smile. She'd used the same ploy as a seductive move with Jake. For the life of her, she just couldn't manage a salacious pose with this woman. Not even in pretense. The woman was like a black widow spider, waiting in her web for the right prey to come along. Meg most definitely needed another angle as a lure.

"You're very pretty," Sheila murmured, placing her red lacquer-nailed fingers on Meg's knee.

"Thanks, so are you."

The woman's dark, almond-shaped eyes half closed in a fake pose of modesty. Meg studied her eyelashes, which were obviously as false as the rest of her. Mink? Maybe. Whatever they were, the lashes were incredibly thick and smoky black. She asked her where she got them.

"Oh, Neiman Marcus on Rodeo Drive," Sheila said, a trace of surprise and irritation tingeing her voice. "You, my dear Meg, couldn't afford them."

Thank you, you just gave me my in.

132

"No," Meg agreed, "probably not. Navy nurses aren't paid much. We travel around the world, granted, but it's in a tin can and filled with sweaty men. Hours are long, and the pay is terrible." She shrugged her bare shoulders. "I'm always broke, it seems."

"So you come here to, how do you say, blow off steam?"

"And maybe find a sugar daddy or momma." Meg shook out her thick, blond mane and gazed, half-lidded, around the crowd below their tier.

Sheila gave a short laugh that tinkled like ice cubes. Meg knew it was a turning point in their conversation. The woman would either kick her to the curb or...

"You don't strike me, Meg, as a—forgive my American slang if it's wrong—but someone told me it's called a *die-hard lez*. No, you don't strike me that way."

Meg leaned close to the woman, noting that the hulk in black made a sudden but subtle move to intervene. Just as subtly, with the flick of a bangled wrist, Sheila signaled him off.

"I'm not, Sheila. I'm bi. Sometimes I like men, sometimes women. Right now, I'm going through an alpha-male phase. There's a guy on the ship... He's an engineer and *so* smokin' hot. He finds any excuse to come to the sick bay, it's too funny. We get it on like rabbits, you know what I mean. But he's as broke as I am, so..."

Meg thought of Jake. If Sheila gave her a return command performance, Jake could play the alpha-male role. A half-minute passed. Sheila spoke in Mandarin to her bodyguard, then switched to English a moment later. The bodyguard left per Sheila's direction, returning carrying two drinks—refills for Sheila and himself—and insinuated himself firmly on Sheila's other side.

"Sorry, I was asking my bodyguard what time we should leave. You see, poor man, he tires of the loud music, the lights. I love it, and... Well, I am a much-beloved daughter and much indulged."

"Who is your father? A rich and important man?" Meg asked, finishing her rum and Coke.

"Very definitely, in my country, he is. I am from Taiwan, you see. My father encourages my education in the United States." Again, Sheila issued a rapid stream of Mandarin at her bodyguard's back, an obvious insult, for the man stiffened even more at his post.

Meg had heard Mandarin spoken many times and understood but a few words. But she knew Sheila lied. According to the two NCIs, Sheila was a PRC national.

Sheila's Asian American friend took her drink and held it to her bright red, prettily pouting lips. Sheila indulged him, then asked Meg, "Do you know Neil's friend, Kurt? He's Navy, also."

Shit! Was he assigned to the USS Dixie?

Meg smiled seductively, playing up her bisexual persona. "What ship?"

"The Glendale." His gaze never left Sheila's legs. "You?"

"The Dixie. Sick bay nurse. I've been there only a month. Did you know Lieutenant Carlton from the Dixie?"

Kurt finally took his attention off Sheila and looked at Meg. "No, saw her here a couple of times. Totally insane what happened to her. Newspapers say it was a hate crime. Bigoted assholes. Lisa said The Lido has been getting threats for months. Who would've thought some goons would up the ante to murder?"

Meg nodded. "That's why everyone said to come here with friends. Never alone. The club's become a target for homophobes."

Sheila glanced between her and Kurt, then smoothly cut in. "So, Meg, what kind of engineer is your...alpha male? The one you're currently with?"

"He used to be on another cruiser, but he got transferred to take Lieutenant Carlton's place on the missile system. It's all Greek to me, but he's an expert."

"Why isn't he here tonight?"

Meg signaled to the passing waitress. When the Goth-costumed girl stopped, she ordered another rum and Coke. Then she answered Sheila's question as though it was a trifling thing.

"He's on duty. Someone has to guard that weapons room around the clock. Guard it with their lives, whether in port or not. That's the Navy for you. All commitment and sacrifice, not many greenbacks." She wondered uneasily if her complaints weren't a bit heavy-handed, so she backed off. "But, hey, we do it for our country."

Sheila grinned, her gaze slyly running over Meg—undoubtedly assessing her and evaluating her words and nonverbal cues. Sheila was hard to read, but Meg had planted a seed. Didn't Javier tell her that if sex didn't work, money always did? The most notorious American traitors weren't ideologues, they were just plain garden-variety greedy bastards.

Meg leaned back and nursed her second drink for the next half-hour and listened to Kurt and Neil circuitously broach a possible threesome later that night. Sheila played them, tossing out the bait, luring them in, and then easing back and letting out some slack while citing a slew of excuses. Always on the brink of saying yes, then no, then yes again. She finally ended with, maybe next time.

The woman was a master of seduction. One moment coy, the next moment hot with desire, banking off to cool uncertainty, then heating up again as Kurt nuzzled her temple and kept his roving hand in play.

After Meg got up to visit the restroom, she returned to the cozy threesome wrapped around each other on the bench. They were five minutes from needing a hotel room.

The hulk's stance hadn't changed one iota, but his clenched jaw muscles and fists betrayed an emotion that Meg easily discerned. She would have bet her Gucci hobo bag that the bodyguard disapproved of Sheila's method of making friends. Even if it was all for Mother China and the PRC's Communist Party.

She announced to Sheila that her friends were leaving, and so was she. That got the woman's attention...briefly.

"Meg, I'll call you next week. I'd like to take you and your engineer friend out to dinner. I may have a lucrative proposition for you, one that you will find interesting. Okay with you?"

Full of delight that this beautiful, obviously rich woman should shower such attentions on her, the flat-broke nurse, she effusively accepted. "Yes, of course! I'd love that!"

As Meg and the two NCIs made their way back to the parking garage—her security detail slowly tracking their progress in their car—she felt overcome with doubt. Javier had heard everything, of course, and he'd already capsulized the gist of the encounter with Mary Lou.

"So what do you think? Did I strike out?" Meg asked.

"Hard to tell," Javier said. "If she doesn't call, you did. If she calls and sets up a meet, you didn't. At least, not entirely. You put out the bait. Whether she takes it or not, we'll soon know."

"We'll beef up your Navy nurse identity with Commander Wickham, so he and Admiral Snider are prepared," Mary Lou said. "All in all, not bad for a civie."

Meg grinned. Relief flooded her. "Good, then you're saying it could've gone worse."

"Oh, yeah. Hella worse."

"IT COULDN'T HAVE GONE worse. I think I blew it."

Meg, in her new spirit of sharing all, had just summarized her undercover night with the NCIs at the club on Saturday. Her efforts to restore transparency between them had apparently left Jake so stupefied he'd been speechless. It had taken him until Sunday to text her back, and even then, he was noncommittal. Then he'd brought home one of his fish as a peace offering, which he was now pan-frying in olive oil, garlic, and Italian spices.

"Doesn't sound like it, Meg," Jake said. "You did what Javier wanted you to, set out the bait."

It was late Monday afternoon, and Jake had returned to San Diego an hour before in his new rental vehicle—a testosterone-pumping Ford Expedition. Like his SUV in DC, he said. The larger vehicle, he'd reminded her, would carry all of his stuff back to his Alexandria condo in two weeks and might come in handy again if he had to make any more ram-and-run getaways.

"I just couldn't come on to her," she continued. "I just couldn't touch her or act, y'know, like I was into her. So I used another tactic. But I think I blew it. She hasn't called."

With his broad back to her at the stove, he grew silent. She'd just spent the past ten minutes explaining the who, what, where, when, and why of that evening. So far, the only response was the sizzling and crackling inside the pan.

"Are you angry? Pissed off? Disappointed?"

His head shook from side to side. His wavy dark brown hair caught the light of the overhead kitchen lamp and fairly gleamed. He wore faded jeans and a long-sleeve jersey instead of his usual khakis and polo shirt. The fisherman cum warrior had returned in triumph with his booty, but she hadn't let him talk about his weekend yet. Biting her bottom lip helped to remind herself that she had to shut up soon. She'd missed him so much but had to get it all out first.

"None of those, Meg." He shot her a speculative look over his shoulder. "Not too surprised, either. I've already heard Javier's version. Yours is more entertaining. Several good things, you established your undercover ID and opened the way to further contact with the targets. A money trap instead of a honey trap. Good, off-the-cuff thinking. And you avoided getting drugged and killed."

She gave a short laugh at his last dry comment. "Ha, well, guess that's a point in my favor. So you're not angry?"

He smiled. "No." He squeezed a lemon over the slab of sole. The gray skin began to flake off as the meat whitened in the heat.

Delicious aromas drifted up, and Meg leaned over to inhale a whiff. His reply encouraged her to sidle up close to him and stroke his back. "Mmm, smells good. That's the largest sole fillet I've ever seen."

Jake had used her biggest fry pan to fry the fish, and she'd already prepared a flavored dish of couscous, mango, and raisins to go with it.

"Another thing, Jake." She recalled the disturbing detail she observed at The Lido, something she hadn't noticed their first time at the club. Probably a foregone conclusion, but she felt it merited a mention. "Did you know there's drug activity going on at the club? Not unusual for a nightclub, of course. I just wondered if you noticed it the night of the fire."

Jake stilled and asked Meg to fill him in on what she'd observed. She did, noting the pills taken by both men at Sheila's booth but eschewed by both Sheila and her bodyguard.

"This is probably nothing, but my hand stamp, and Javier's and Mary Lou's, were colored red. Other people, especially those on the upper tiers, had different colors. Blue, green, and purple, but not red." She shrugged. "I just thought it kind of strange. Maybe a color code of some kind?"

He glanced over at her. "I hadn't noticed that before. The night of the fire, I was focusing on other things. So you witnessed Navy personnel taking drugs. What kind of drugs?"

"I don't know," she admitted. "I didn't ask, and they didn't tell. When they saw my stamp, it was like a signal or a code. To, y'know, stuff it or be discreet."

Jake nodded. "I see."

Happy that her unofficial briefing had gone so well, and that Jake wasn't angry with her, she ran her hand down his muscular back to his narrow waist and let her palm rest there. The magic, the strong attraction she felt for Jake, hadn't diminished at all. If anything, the pull felt more intense than it had before. She chastised herself for almost losing him, thanks to a lapse in judgment. She'd be careful not to let that happen again.

"Tell me all about your weekend. Did you have a good time fishing with Martin and Gabe? How's your mother doing? Did you see Isaac and his family?"

Over the next hour, they ate at her little kitchen table and talked. Each tidbit they shared was like the conversation of a first date. They had each other's total attention and acute interest. The Pinot Grigio she'd uncorked represented a kind of celebration for their surmounting one of their first serious fights. Her relief at finding each other again was profound and heartfelt. Meg thought Jake felt it, too.

Meg was cuddled in Jake's lap before they'd finished the bottle of wine. Dirty dishes and the stove were forgotten as they kissed each other long and deeply. They embraced tightly and whispered apologies between fervent kisses.

"No, no, you're bored with your classes," Jake murmured against her lips. "I'm not such a tightass that I don't get that you want to help. It just took me a while to process it. I just don't want to see you hurt."

"I shouldn't have doubted you." She nibbled his earlobe and slid her hand down to his crotch. Her pulse skittered and tripped, and deep inside, liquid heat pooled.

"Meg, you have the right to question anything I do or say." His breath heated her face. "I'm not perfect. I make mistakes like anybody does. I'm just a crazy-ass fool who's in love with you. If we proceed with this money trap, we proceed with extreme caution. You have good instincts, but this is real life, and people get hurt."

"I know. We'll be careful, I promise. I just want to help."

"I know, and I love that about you." With that admission, he smiled and buried his face into the curve of her throat.

She stood up, gently taking his hand, and led him into the bedroom.

Chapter Twenty-one

WITH THEIR INTIMACY restored, Jake sent Meg off to her classes with one of the security men in tow. The second man kept watch from his sedan in front of her apartment building. He approached the vehicle, keeping an eye on the area until he reached the driver's side window.

"Watch who enters the carport lot," he told the man. "These assholes are prone to making bombs."

The man, going by John Smith, nodded, unsmiling and clearly ex-military. Jake knew this security detail was among the best the private company had to offer, according to Alabastro.

"Got it," Smith said. "What about you? You need extra coverage?"

Jake patted his leather jacket, feeling the bulge of his shoulder holster. "Nope. I've got it right next to my heart." *From here on...* He was determined to not get caught again with his pants down or his pistol in the glove compartment.

A block away, he entered his rented Expedition—a big black one with chrome rims. He sat in the driver's seat for the next thirty minutes, reviewing the NCIs' transcript of their interviews again. Something caught his attention more fully than the first time he'd read the reports. After a few more minutes of thought, he knew what he had to do.

With determination thrumming through his body, Jake fired up the big V-8 engine. It roared to life, making him smile. A moment later, just as he approached a side street, his smile morphed into a scowl. A dark green sedan sat parked by the corner. He pretended not to notice, his aviator sunglasses concealing his eyes, but his gaze absorbed every detail. Khaled Daoud himself sat behind the steering wheel, and he was alone. Well, that took balls—coming alone. What did he have in mind? A tête-á-tête over the pros and cons of Sharia Law?

Bring it on, you asshole.

Alabastro had called Jake the day before, saying he'd gotten a warrant and had sent in his agents to search and seize all electronics, suspicious tools and materials, and yes, all baseball bats found on the Daoud premises. Agents had closed down the Daouds' restaurant for the day and searched it thoroughly. The search gave up nothing suspicious, but the electronics were in the lab, being taken apart—hard drives scrutinized and all communications analyzed. Alabastro mentioned it might take another week to analyze all the data but felt confident they would uncover solid evidence of sedition.

Thank goodness fanatics loved their electronics, leaving their e-footprints everywhere. With NSA's satellites eavesdropping in all corners of the planet, sooner or later, the tiny footprints popped out like Big Foot's.

Out of professional courtesy, SAC Alabastro kept Jake in the loop. Now in police custody, the owner of the sedan had clammed up and hired an attorney who was protesting FBI harassment despite the evidence to the contrary. The Escondido bunch had undoubtedly begun to feel the dragnet tightening around them. It was just a matter of time before the San Diego FBI field office slapped them all with charges of conspiracy, assault and battery, and God knew what else.

The forensic lab had discovered blood traces on the bat Jake had turned over to the SD field office. The blood, however, proved to be animal blood, indicating that one of Daoud's buddies, identified by the local field office as Hussein al-Nyad, liked practicing on cars and defenseless animals while honing his craft. Evidently, if al-Nyad was one of Mrs. Daoud's two attackers, he'd used another bat on her, which he'd since discarded.

Thanks to Jake's incriminating photos of his car bashing, the agents had already arrested al-Nyad for vandalism and aggravated assault. They'd searched the man's home and found his unregistered pistol, a .45 caliber Colt, in his bedroom closet. Ballistics matched it to the bullets Jake had pried out of his last rented Explorer.

The Fatimah Daoud investigation was ongoing, and while her husband, Khaled Daoud, appeared clean for the present, his computer and cell phone communications might prove otherwise.

The FBI would know in another week who and what they were dealing with. Was this a limited case of a failed honor killing? If so, how could they prove it if the only eyewitness refused to implicate her father and his friends? Were other attacks being plotted by Daoud and his pals? Attacks having nothing to do with a radical Muslim's version of *honor*?

In addition to keeping their IT guys busy, the San Diego FBI field office had heightened surveillance in place. Regardless of the local cops' opinion, SAC Alabastro and his team had swung their spotlight on a group of apparently radical Muslim men in Escondido.

All in all, Daoud had to be one pissed-off man.

Jake had a plan in mind for his day and a few stops to make. Along the way, he hoped to lead Daoud to the end of his rope. Tempt the man to show his true colors and maybe, just maybe, lose his cool enough to attack a federal officer. How Jake would love to take the prick down. With the security teams as witnesses, it would be enough to get the man off the streets and maybe give the daughter a little breathing room. *Who knows what she might give up then?*

Would she have the courage to face her father and recognize him for what he'd become? Another extremist who believed Sharia Law superseded American laws?

In Iraq, Pakistan, Libya, Lebanon, Syria, Iran, Nigeria, and even Indonesia and Egypt, Christians, Hindus, Buddhists, and other *infidels* often faced religious genocide by fundamentalists who invoked core Islamic texts and teachings to justify their actions. In Saudi Arabia, the very existence of Christian churches and Jewish synagogues was prohibited, along with the Bible itself. No Christian or Jew could enter Mecca lest their mere footsteps desecrate Islam's holiest sites.

In Pakistan, Afghanistan, and elsewhere in the Muslim world, conversion from Islam to Christianity was punishable by death. The ISIS terrorist organizations in Syria and Iraq were beheading non-Muslim people who would not convert to Islam. Even children did not escape their barbarism. Under Sharia Law, women and children were chattel, completely ruled by the men in their lives. Fathers, husbands, and even brothers could call for an honor killing and feel justified, and under Islamic theocracies, never be punished.

The appalling examples went on and on.

Outrage churned inside Jake as he drove to downtown La Jolla. He stopped outside a jewelry store, pretending not to notice Daoud's sedan pulling to the curb a block away. Daoud didn't know Jake was FBI. Jake wondered if the jerk would've been so bold if he'd known he was following a federal officer. Maybe the man was too pissed off to care.

INSIDE THE STORE, JAKE perused engagement rings and wedding sets. He found one he thought Meg would like—and which he could afford—but couldn't bring himself to buy it. Something held him back, and he was pretty sure he knew what it was. His fear of the one thing that terrified him more than Islamic fanatics. Marriage.

Go figure.

Two more jewelry store stops and more of the same. Jake found a slew of sparkly, expensive rings, but every time he thought of what such a ring symbolized, he froze.

Commitment. Vows. Forever.

Maybe he was committed to only serving his country, not a woman. Perhaps *that* was his destiny. The Gabriels and Isaacs of the world would marry and have sons to fish with. Not him.

Glumly, he drove on. His fourth stop...The Amazons on Harbor Boulevard. For the past two weeks, a thought churned in the back of his mind like a clump of undigested food, giving him occasional mental heartburn.

Something about the place. Why would the killer risk overpowering Samantha in the back alley? Why not wait until she pulled into her driveway on Coronado Island? Wouldn't there be fewer possible witnesses? It seemed strange there weren't any witnesses when the café was open for business that night. If it was a crime of passion or opportunity, why there? Was Samantha just in the wrong place at the wrong time? But why all the other details? Her shoes were taken but not her money or jewelry. What was the motive? Was she about to expose this ring of Chinese spies and had to be silenced?

The location of a homicide was usually a vital piece of evidence. Was *this* location meant to divert suspicion to homophobes? The threats, according to Lonnie, one of the owners, had come in during the two months leading up to

Samantha's murder. If the homicide was premeditated, then those threats would logically lead the police to jump to conclusions.

Or was the location meant to send another kind of message? A more personal one? Were Lisa and Lonnie somehow complicit in the murder? That seemed farfetched, however. What would be their motive? Samantha was one of their steady customers. Lonnie had admired her, so she said, had regarded Samantha as a friend.

Lisa... Well, he still had to interview her. The NCIs' interview with Lisa Chance hadn't shed much light. Lisa had known Samantha, of course, since Samantha had frequented The Lido, but that seemed to be the extent of their association. A dead-end? He wondered.

Jake's dark thoughts persisted as he parked in the back alleyway next to four other cars. The vehicles were parked diagonally along the back fence, leaving enough space between them and the building to allow other cars to drive through. He assumed one of the cars belonged to Lonnie Pezzerella and the others to her employees.

He'd learned from the NCIs that Lonnie and Lisa had once lived together but no longer. Lonnie lived in La Jolla, while Lisa had an apartment near Little Italy, a northern downtown neighborhood. They'd gone their separate ways but had remained friends and business partners.

Just then, he noticed Lisa Chance exiting a black Chevy Tahoe. Naturally, she'd parked behind the club about half a block away. Good, because he needed to speak to both women.

Jake entered The Amazons through the front entrance. As he did, Daoud's car drove by on Harbor Boulevard.

Keep it up, bud. I'm shaking in my boots.

He sat down at the counter, asked the tall, thin waitress for a cup of coffee, and then asked for Lonnie.

The gray-haired, middle-aged woman appeared before the first drop hit the cup. She wiped her hands on a white baker's apron and held one out.

"I thought I recognized your voice. Agent Bernstein, right?" Lonnie grinned at him.

"Call me Jake." He smiled back. There was something open and honest about the woman that he liked. Her partner, Lisa, was a different story. More guarded and reticent. "Hope you have time to talk."

She waved her arm in a semi-circle. The place had three customers, an older woman down the counter from Jake and two younger women at one of the six tables, having a late breakfast.

"Sure do. Good thing, too. You caught me between the breakfast and lunch crowd. This about the Lieutenant Carlton murder investigation?"

Jake nodded.

With a tilt of her head, Lonnie invited him to join her in the back conference room. "Bring your coffee. I'm baking some biscuits to go with the lunch stew. We're expecting rain today. Stew is always a hit at lunchtime when the weather turns. Dinner should be brisk, also. Tonight's the usual county counseling session for women at risk."

Jake looked around at the walls of the small conference room, covered as they were two weeks ago with posters and notices of the county's myriad services for women with problems. This time, the notices made an impression. "Women at risk? You mean what, exactly?"

She sat down and surveyed the wall. "Oh, single mothers who need financial help. Or help to escape a violent relationship. Several county-run shelters provide short-term and long-term relief and money grants. Married women with abusive husbands, uncontrollable kids, or both. Transgender women who need help with identity issues. Drug addicts and prostitutes who want to leave the life. You name it, we address it here on Tuesday nights. We provide free counseling and referrals. We even have guest speakers."

Jake grew very still. Maybe the two cases were crossing and blurring in his mind, but he still had to ask. "Muslim women with abusive husbands?"

She sighed heavily and dropped her eyes. "Ah, yes, we've gotten a few. When I read about that Escondido story in the papers, I thought of her. Fatimah Daoud. I should've called you, but..." She shrugged but went on, "I didn't think—no, I didn't want to call attention to our service here at the café. I didn't want those bigots to come after us again."

"Again?"

"Those bikers the cops arrested. The ones the newspaper story said were the ones who tried to kill Mrs. Daoud, the ones the cops believe sent all those threatening notes to us. Those bikers have friends, don't they? Aren't they part of a motorcycle club of white supremacists? They hate gays and lesbians. Anybody who's different. That's all we need after the fire and Sam's murder.

Another attack and our customers will take off for good. We'd have to close down." Her blue gaze lifted and locked with his. "I still should've called you. I apologize."

He nodded, tacitly accepting her apology. Internally, his heart was racing. "How often did Mrs. Daoud come to these counseling sessions on Tuesday nights?"

"Just the one time. The same Tuesday night that Sam was killed. I remember because she was the only Muslim woman in the group that night. She had that head scarf around her neck and her clothes were, y'know, loose, baggy. I remember giving her copies of the flyers I passed out that night. One of the AFDC—Aid to Families with Dependent Children—counselors was here that night. She had picked up Mrs. Daoud and brought her here. I think Mrs. Daoud was planning to leave her husband, but she needed a plan and a way to support her children. The AFDC counselor gave her a card, and I know they talked about meeting again." Lonnie took a business card from the holder attached to the poster. "Here's her card. I talked to her last week. We thought the cops had caught the right guys, but Paula, the AFDC counselor, was not so sure."

"Why not?"

"She said Fatimah was very frightened. For herself and her children. She told Paula that her husband was a dangerous man."

Jake's thoughts were tumbling over themselves like rocks on a landslide. He focused, read the card, the counselor's name, and pocketed it. The social worker was no one he'd ever heard of. Alabastro would add this contact to his office's investigation of Fatimah Daoud's attempted murder and find out if she'd been threatened by her husband or any of his cronies. It would help build his case against Khaled Daoud and his bat-wielding buddies. Regardless, the social worker would make a good witness if Daoud and his buddies ever went to trial.

This created a new wrinkle in both cases, a coincidence of monumental proportions. Was this place just an unlucky location? The intersection of Fatimah Daoud and Lieutenant Carlton that Tuesday night—the only night Mrs. Daoud had attended The Amazons' counseling session on the very night Carlton was murdered. Although staggering, was it nothing more than a monumental coincidence? But damn it, what was he not seeing?

"So you think Mrs. Daoud was planning to divorce her husband?"

"Oh, yes. She kept saying, *He's a dangerous man, but I can't live with him anymore.* I suggested that she go to the police, but she shook her head and kept saying, *No, no, he'd kill me.*"

"I'm afraid she meant it," Jake said. "Have you ever heard of Islamic honor killings?"

Lonnie hung her head and covered her face with her hands. "Oh, God..." It took several minutes before she composed herself.

"Why do this?" Jake asked, waving at the posters on the wall.

Lonnie wiped her cheeks with the edge of her apron. "Why help women at risk? Because I was one. I was trapped in a horrible marriage with three children, an abusive husband, and bills that drove us both crazy. I was thirty before I could admit to myself that I liked women, such was the kind of upbringing I had. Lisa was a nurse who treated me at the medical clinic. She opened my eyes to a whole new world and gave me the courage to leave the creep, take my kids, and start a new life. They're grown now and doing well, thank God, all thanks to Lisa. She's more than a business partner, Agent Bernstein. She's a friend. A lifesaver." She held up her hands and fanned them out. "This is my way of giving back to the social agencies that helped me start a new life."

Jake nodded and smiled. "I understand. Speaking of whom, is Lisa here? I'd like to speak to her, too."

"Sure, she's in our back office. You know, don't you, that I manage the café—everything related to it—and she does the same for the nightclub. We have a division of labor that suits us just fine."

Jake nodded, smiling, then zeroed in on the main purpose of this meeting.

"Before I see her, I want to ask you a few more questions about that night. We know that Lieutenant Carlton was waiting in the café for someone, then suddenly finished her coffee and left around nine o'clock. You said that your partner, Lisa, wasn't here that night, that she was home sick with a bad cold. Is that true?"

"Yes." Lonnie narrowed her eyes.

"Okay, so who signed off on the electrical repairs that were done that evening in the club?"

The woman frowned. "I assumed one of her people. The head bartender, maybe?"

"We have Lisa's signature on the work order and invoice," he pointed out mildly. "She must've been here that night, at the club. The electrician said that he and his apprentice left the club the same time the owner, meaning Miss Chance, did. Around eight-thirty."

Lonnie shrugged. "Yes, I think she told me that later. We were extra busy that night with the counseling session."

Jake shot her a sympathetic look. "That's fine. She signed off on the work, and they all left at the same time, according to everyone the NCIs interviewed."

"Okay," Lonnie said, "but I don't understand your nitpicking this detail—" Her eyes grew big, and her mouth dropped open.

Jake quickly held up a hand. "I haven't drawn any conclusions, Lonnie. It's still an ongoing investigation. One more question, however. When you and your staff left later that night, you saw Samantha's Cadillac in the alleyway. She'd left about nine, but her car remained in your back parking lot. What did you think was going on? Why would she leave her car here?"

Lonnie glanced over at one of her cooks, who'd appeared suddenly in the doorway. The woman looked anxious.

"I'll be there in a sec, Joanie," she said before turning back to Jake. "Why would she leave her car in our alleyway? That's what you want to know? Because, Agent Bernstein, she'd done it before. When she'd disappear with one of her girlfriends into the Radisson Hotel one block over. For discretion's sake, I guess. Sam would park here, walk over to the hotel to check in, then she'd call her friend with the room number. So when I saw her car parked there, I thought she'd finally connected with whoever she was waiting to meet that night."

Surprised by Lonnie's explanation, Jake thanked the woman for her cooperation, then followed her down a hallway to the back office. He briefly wondered if one of the beefy cooks, maybe in a jealous rage, had attacked Samantha. But no, that didn't make much sense. Armed with a hypodermic needle filled with a deadly dose of ketamine, Samantha's killer had come prepared. *Another theory shot down.*

This was clearly not a crime of impulse. It was premeditated, pure and simple, and carefully executed.

The furnishings in the fifteen-by-fifteen-foot office were Spartan. Two desks with executive-style chairs, four file cabinets, and two straight-backed chairs crowded the room. Along the wall on Lisa's side of the room was a small window behind her desk that overlooked the back alley and parking area. The blinds were opened so Jake could see the vertical rods of the wrought-iron railing outside of the window. Someone could see out, but no one could break in.

Lisa was at her computer, deep in concentration. Jake was about to greet her when Lonnie announced him.

"Leese, you remember Agent Bernstein? The one who came with the two Navy investigators after Sam was killed?"

Lisa straightened her glasses with a forefinger as she looked up. She didn't smile. "Oh, yes, the FBI agent. Have a seat. Let me close this, then you'll get my full attention."

Jake thanked Lonnie for her help, and the woman went back to her kitchen. He sat in the straight-backed chair in front of Lisa's desk and waited. He observed the woman and noticed how she filled out her nylon running suit. Her arms were long and muscular, her shoulders as heavy as a fullback's. Lisa wore her short, dark, curly hair combed back at the forehead and behind her ears. Her face was devoid of makeup, and fine lines were etched around her eyes. There were gold studs in her ears and a watch on her wrist, but no rings on her fingers. In her late forties, she was showing her age, although she still bore handsome features. All in all, she was a big, capable woman who'd done her share of physical work—the kind that some men couldn't do.

Next to him, standing against the wall, were two rows of thick cardboard boxes stacked about four feet high, bearing liquor brands. A metal dolly rested against one row. He assumed the liquor bottles were waiting to be transported to the club since the café didn't serve booze. Briefly, he wondered why they hadn't been delivered to the club directly. Instead, it appeared that Lisa would be transporting them herself. Not a big feat for a woman her size.

His cell phone buzzed. Two recent texts had come through while he'd been driving all over town. One was from Meg, the other one from Javier.

He thumbed a quick reply to Meg.

See you at 5. Alert, Daoud is on the loose.

To the NC investigator he replied.

Check the background of Lisa Chance, manager of The Lido. Education, marriage, employment, financial... Used to be a nurse.

Jake would've added more to his instructions to Javier but would do so later. Strange, but he wasn't even sure why he wanted them to take a closer look at the woman. Maybe one reason was the navy blue running suit that she was wearing. The nylon fabric was the same kind of synthetic fabric they'd found traces of under Samantha's fingernails. Whoever attacked Samantha was wearing a similar outfit, only black. Why were they looking only at big men? Couldn't a big, muscular woman have overpowered Samantha, at least long enough to incapacitate her with an injection of ketamine? Maybe he was just speculating, thinking out of the box. He had a gut feeling that he could no longer ignore.

When he looked back up, Lisa was scowling at him.

"I was wondering how long it'd take you clowns to figure it out."

Chapter Twenty-two

"'SCUSE ME?" JAKE POCKETED his cell phone.

"You heard me." She rocked back in her executive chair and laced her fingers across her midriff. Jake noticed how veiny and muscular her hands were, and how her biceps filled out the running suit's jacket sleeves. Lisa Chance was a large woman who personified the café's name, The Amazons. Yes...he'd bet this woman could bench-press close to three hundred pounds.

At least six-foot-one, Lisa easily outweighed him by twenty to forty pounds. Although Lisa was at least five years older than Samantha, she was much more fit and muscular than the Navy officer. Still, overwhelming Samantha would have required Herculean strength, the surprise element notwithstanding.

"How are we clowns, Miss Chance? And who're you including in your unflattering assessment?"

"Hmm, an educated, articulate cop? Well, that's a change."

"You don't have a high opinion of law enforcement officers? Why is that?"

The hostility rolled off her in waves, which immediately set him on alert. Instinctively, he leaned forward on the balls of his feet.

Lisa began to rock in her chair tauntingly. "It took you investigators two weeks to finally figure out that those Chinese spies had something to do with Sam's murder. I contacted the Navy base nearly a year ago and warned them. Nothing was done, absolutely nothing."

"You told the Navy that Chinese nationals were conducting espionage at your nightclub? When was this? And why didn't you share your suspicions with the NCIs?"

She steepled her long fingers and tapped the tips together. With an apparent ax to grind, she was gloating over their denseness and enjoying it.

"Those kids, those NCIs as you call them, need to earn their keep, just like everybody else. Why make it too easy for them? With the FBI involved, I figured the investigation would eventually speed up and get some results. When they showed up again Saturday night, trying so hard to fit in and pretend they belonged, I said to myself, *Well, finally! You guys finally zeroed in on Sheila and her menacing bodyguard.* I warned Sam about them."

Lisa looked down at her hands and shook her head. Sorrow clouded her features, and for a moment, Jake thought the tough woman might actually break down and cry. Rather than interrupt and ask some of the questions that now flooded his mind, he hung back. The woman obviously had something to get off her chest, so he remained silent and watched her closely. Micro expressions might give her away if she was lying, but he couldn't detect any. If she was playing him, she was an expert liar and actress.

"I warned Sam." She straightened in her seat. "Don't trust that woman, that Sheila. She's a *femme fatale.* She will do whatever it takes to steal whatever military secrets she wants. I've watched her go after the Navy boys and girls who frequent my club—Lonnie's and my club. It's the kids' home away from home. They tell me that. It's a place where they feel safe, where they can be themselves. The Navy expects them to hide a part of themselves—their sexuality—and they know that. They accept that, so when they come here, they relax and let loose. Lonnie and I wanted to provide this safe haven for those kids."

Lisa seemed to wind down temporarily, breathing deeply, evidently trying to get her emotions under control. He gave her half a minute before continuing.

"Miss Chance, you said you notified the Navy, and they did nothing? Or they found nothing?"

Her penetrating gaze raised to meet his. "I spoke to someone on the base, a...a liaison officer of some kind. I told her about my business—Lonnie and I had just opened the café and nightclub a month or two earlier. Lonnie has nothing to do with the club, as you probably know, so it fell on my shoulders to keep track of things. And keep it afloat financially, too."

She smiled. "The clientele we served was special. I welcomed the Navy kids, the local gays and lesbians, the bis, the trans, the whole LGBT crowd. Their straight friends were welcome, too. Business picked up, and I thought we'd finally be in the black. Then the county came in, and I had to renovate the restrooms and bar area. Had to bring all the electricity up to code, too. The extra costs nearly crushed us."

Jake wondered about this new financial tangent Lisa was taking. He had no idea where this was leading.

"Unexpected costs are always part of opening a new business," he said with a tinge of sympathy. "So the club struggled? How did the café do?"

Lisa slapped her hands on the desk, which seemed to refocus her train of thought. "Of course, we struggled, but I had to fulfill my side of the bargain. Lonnie and I promised each other that we would make each business self-sustaining by the sixth month of doing business or close down the section that failed. I'm telling you this because that's why I tolerated those two."

"Which two?" Jake asked, knowing full-well who she was referring to.

Lisa shot him a fulminating look. "Sheila and her bodyguard, that's who. I suspected they were spies, and that's what I told that Navy officer. Nothing was done. I thought maybe I was wrong, I was just imagining things. So that's why I took their loan. Just a bridge loan so I could get those renovations things done. Bring the club up to code and all."

"You took a private loan from Sheila Lee...Xing Lee Peong, a PRC national?" Jake's gut was right when he felt something about The Lido wasn't quite right.

"Just a six-month bridge loan. I planned to pay them back as fast as I could. And I did. I didn't feel right about taking money from someone I felt was using my club as her...her—"

"Her headquarters for espionage operations?"

The woman nodded, her short, curly brown hair stiff as a helmet around her head.

"It sounds so horrible, the way you put it, but it's true. I expected the Navy to at least alert their people, which they did. One of the kids told me about the alert, but the club was never put on their *Off-Limits* list. Good for us, but bad for gullible, socially backward types like Sam."

Jake shifted in his chair. "Are you saying Lieutenant Carlton didn't believe Sheila was a spy?"

Lisa leaned back, guffawed loudly, and slapped her leg, nearly startling him. When her mirthless laughter subsided, she smiled crookedly. But the smile fixed on her face like a grimace.

"Sam, Sam... She was a piece of work. A real Pollyanna. She thought Sheila really, truly loved her and wanted to spend the rest of her life with her. Sam was head over heels in love with love, crazy about Sheila, and couldn't see the truth. Her total faith in that woman was ridiculous. She was so blind. I felt embarrassed for her. The kids, the regulars, they all laughed behind her back. What Sheila wanted from Sam was apparent to everyone but Sam."

Jake decided to be as upfront with Lisa since she was finally open with him. "Information about the advanced weapons system on that guided missile cruiser?"

"At long last, someone gets it." Lisa blew out a noisy sigh of resignation and threw up her hands. "It was only a matter of time before Sam betrayed her country. She was—what's the word? Besotted."

"Do you think Samantha gave up any secrets?"

One brawny shoulder rose and fell as Lisa exaggerated a shrug. "Who knows? She certainly wouldn't have told me if she had."

Outside in the rear alley, a car gunned its engine. The sound registered in Jake's consciousness but just barely. He found Lisa's information riveting.

"Miss Chance, why didn't you just deny admittance to Sheila and her bodyguard? I've noticed that you screen out people who look too young, kids with fake IDs, partiers strung out on drugs, who don't fit the look. Whatever."

The woman propped her elbows on her desk and leaned toward him. "Frankly, I was afraid."

Popping sounds drew their attention. Hard, loud thuds against the rear exterior of the building had Lisa lurching to her feet.

"Get down!" Jake yelled.

Lisa quickly ducked behind her chair. A second later, the window above Lisa's head shattered as a barrage of bullets whizzed through. Shards of glass showered her as the woman shrieked and disappeared underneath her desk. Jake crouched with his back against the interior wall and pulled his Glock out of its shoulder holster.

"Are you hit?" he called out.

"No," came the strangled reply.

"Stay down." He inched over to the office door, rose to his full height, and opened it. Once in the narrow hallway, he heard women's screams emanating from the kitchen and café. "Everyone, on the floor! Stay down and call 911!"

"Is Lisa okay?" Lonnie called from the kitchen.

Jake sidled toward the rear steel door and readied himself to fling it open. "Yeah. Stay there, Lonnie! On the floor, everyone!"

A couple of metallic pings against the steel door warned him that the assailant was right outside, waiting to ambush whoever came through.

Shit! Daoud's not only pissed off, but he's also well-armed!

He heard a car rev up, then its brakes squealed. He counted to five, then whipped the door open.

To his right, Daoud's car receded down the alley. Ten yards, twenty yards... Jake fired two rounds, aiming for the rear tires. From the sparks that flared on the asphalt, he knew he'd missed both times.

In broad daylight, Daoud acted like the cornered rat he was, but firing at him and the café showed the man was desperate for revenge.

Jake punched in Alabastro's direct cell phone number, and the SAC instantly picked up. "What happened to Daoud's surveillance?"

"Jake? God, what happened? I just got the word from the team. They lost him downtown. Where's your security team?"

"Out in front, I guess, or along the side street. Daoud just drilled some serious slag into The Amazons' building." He stared over at his rental, his brand-new Ford Expedition, noting three bullet holes in the cargo door. "Damn it! He emptied several rounds into my car and just missed the club owner's head. That son of a bitch. I'm going after him!"

"Where are you?"

He was already climbing into the Expedition's driver's seat. He looked around. All three bullets had penetrated the rear seats, and one had gone through and buried its head into the front passenger seat.

Jake switched the call to the car's Bluetooth. "The alley behind The Amazons café. Daoud just stormed through. I think he's headed south on Harbor Boulevard. Relay to your surveillance team. I see my security coming into the alley."

He revved the engine, relieved it wasn't damaged, and put it into reverse, backing out of his parking space. Turning onto Harbor Boulevard, he spied Daoud's dark green sedan as it turned left and headed up J Street past Petco Park, the San Diego Padres' home ballpark. His pulse racing, he placed his

Glock on his lap and kept pace with the sedan, trailing him by no more than sixty or seventy yards.

"Are you tracking us?" he asked Alabastro.

"Roger that. Security is behind you. Daoud's surveillance is right behind them in an unmarked maroon Lincoln MRX. You're in the black Expedition?"

"The one with the three bullet holes in the rear? Yeah." He broke off to concentrate on the sedan's movements. The Lincoln suddenly passed him, their sirens blaring and light-globe flashing. He followed the maroon Lincoln and Daoud's car as they all barreled through two red lights, honking his horn in warning. The ramp onto Highway Five approached, and just as he expected, Daoud veered off to take it.

The high arch of the Coronado Bridge arose in Jake's windshield. Coronado Island? Where the fuck was this lunatic going? And why?

Cold realization swept Jake's confusion aside. His experience with Islamic fanatics prompted him to face the awful truth. He felt sick to his stomach. No...no...not again.

Alabastro had stayed on the line, fielding and relaying radio sitreps—situation reports—from his surveillance team.

"Tom, Tom, he's headed for the Navy base on North Island. I think he's planning an attack. Maybe a bomb in his car." Jake disconnected the call.

Alabastro knew what to do. He'd call the base and warn them what was headed their way. He'd also warn the surveillance team to hang back so they wouldn't be taken out by the explosion that was bound to happen. So what could Jake do if Daoud was hell-bent on becoming a martyr for Jihad?

Not much at this point.

He descended from the bridge's extreme incline, continuing to closely track the surveillance Lincoln, and had to brake when it became apparent they'd received word.

Jake punched in Rear Admiral Snider's direct line. John would never forgive him if Jake didn't at least make the effort to give him a heads-up. "John, this is Jake. We believe a Muslim radical is on his way to the base with a car bomb. If you can, alert the Marines at the gates. Put up barriers."

"Jake? You're telling me NBC's a target?"

"ETA, about five or six minutes. Or less. He's coming in fast down Fourth Street in a green sedan. I'll try to head him off, but don't know if—" He swerved around a biker wearing earphones and not paying attention. He peeled off at Orange and made a left on Third Street, which ran parallel to Fourth, the straight shot to the Naval Base's main gates.

John had dropped the line, and no doubt was busy giving orders. The base's Marines would be scrambling about now, grabbing MP 17 automatic rifles and RPGs and heading for the gates. He hoped they'd have time to line up some concrete barriers, at the very least.

He pressed the accelerator and raced up Third like a maniac, praying that some slow-moving vehicle didn't get in his way. He thumbed the safety off his Glock and used his knees to steer as he racked a bullet into the chamber. The intersection just before the lead-in to the base's gates was along Rogers Road. He braked hard and rocked the Expedition to a stop between Third and Fourth streets. He jumped down and ran to the intersection but remained in the middle of the side street. Seconds later, he spotted Daoud's car, barreling toward the gates like an Indy car racing to the finish line.

A glance back at the gates reminded Jake to show his badge, when several Marines inside the gates leveled their automatic rifles in his direction. He held up his badge until he saw one of them bark at the others to stand down. As one, they trained their rifles on the car bearing down on them.

Daoud kept a steady track for the double iron gates at the end of Fourth Street. Jake would have maybe two seconds to get a head shot, a near impossibility but he had to try.

The Marines behind the gates backed up as eight steel bollards rose like stalwart robotic sentinels from their subterranean tracks in front of the entrance. Good, he'd forgotten about the steel bollards.

Jake took a deep breath and let it out as he raised his Glock in his right hand, using his left hand to hold it steady. He squeezed off two rapid shots, aiming for the blur that was Daoud's head and upper torso inside the dark green car.

Jake's mind went blank when a concussion blast hit his body and lifted him into the air. He landed on his ass on top of a low-slung hedge. A moment later, he rolled off and hit the ground. Total silence ensued as he lay prone, staring up at the blue sky. A billowing cloud of smoke and fire blotted out the blue, turning the sky orange, yellow, and black. The air turned putrid with the acrid scent of burning tires.

He lay there for a long time, slowly counting and assessing his body parts. He took a moment to thank God for his continued good luck and wondered if God would eventually grow tired of him and let Fate take over. Why was he working overtime to use up his nine lives or whatever allotted time he had left on this planet? It was a question his mother often asked him, and if he married Meg, she would probably ask as well. *Why you?*

Why me? What could he tell them? *Somebody has to do it. Why not me?*

He wondered about that. What was he trying to prove?

Was his mother right? Did he have a hero complex?

Gradually, some of his hearing returned. High-pitched sirens rent the air, and heavy boots pounded the pavement. The ground still seemed to be moving, but maybe that was just his head spinning. His ears rang with a thousand bells. Too dizzy to sit up, Jake continued to lie still, examining his motives.

Wondering, wondering...

Chapter Twenty-three

THE EVENTS THAT TRANSPIRED afterward became jumbled in Jake's mind as the pounding in his head developed into a throbbing headache. His body felt like one big wet noodle, and his hearing kept fading in and out. When he tried to talk, he couldn't hear his own voice.

He vaguely recalled being carried and driven by two men to the hospital. A male orderly had cut off his pants and shirt and then put him to bed in his underwear and hospital gown. All the while, he felt like an old man who'd suddenly developed dementia—confused and disoriented.

For the life of him, he couldn't remember what had happened that landed him in the hospital. His mind wandered aimlessly like Grandpa Nate's in his last six months. He might've even muttered something aloud, as though he were talking to Gramps—*See, I told you I'd get those sons-a-bitches. They can't treat us Jews like dirt...*

Then he'd imagined spouting German to the male orderly like Grandpa Nate had scolded some unseen enemy during his delirium the last day of his life—spewing his pent-up rage at all those Nazis some sixty-odd years later.

At some point, Jake crashed on his hospital bed and slept when the muscle relaxers and painkillers finally eased the aches of his body. When he woke hours later, Meg was there with water and hot chicken soup. Managing a few spoonfuls, he thanked her in German—still in his Grandpa Nate persona thanking Grandma Rachel for all her years of devotion. Somehow Meg knew what had happened at the Navy base gates and told him what he had tried to do to stop Daoud from detonating his bomb.

How did that work for you, Bernstein? You got a concussion for nothing.

Meg seemed to understand why he was speaking German, how muddled his mind was, and how his whole body ached. She soothed him when the nausea hit, and he began vomiting buckets, and she ensured that newly washed-out pans appeared at the side of the bed after each upheaval. He had visions of Meg, her blond hair flowing over one shoulder, sitting on the edge of the bed, bathing his face, neck, chest, and arms with a cold cloth, speaking to him with a soft, soothing voice.

Gradually, bits and pieces of the car chase and resulting explosion flashed back, but the entire sequence still eluded him. Both Meg and the nurse assured him his memories would return as soon as the swelling in his brain went down. He remembered telling Meg at one point not to call his parents. He was fine and just needed a few days to recover. She promised him she wouldn't, and he believed her. She told him about her uncle John calling, concerned about him and grateful for what he'd tried to do to stop the attack.

Which was what, exactly?

Then, satisfied by Meg's promise not to stress out his parents and warmed by her compassionate presence, Jake slept more calmly, as the doctors had recommended. Mild concussion, hell, this was his second concussion in a matter of three months.

Better watch it, pal, or you'll end up like those punch-drunk boxers.

He wondered if he wasn't paying too high a price for trying to be righteous. Was he trying to undo all the evil in the world in his own small way to appease Grandpa Nate's guilt over losing his entire German family? A Jewish survival-guilt type of thing? Or was it some big, out-of-control ego thing?

BY THURSDAY, JAKE MANAGED to stay awake more often during the day. His self-recriminations had abated, along with his memory loss and hearing loss. Hunger pangs had him turning over in the bed, only to face two men standing by his bedside dressed in natty suits and ties, looking greatly relieved.

"How do you feel, Jake?" Alabastro greeted him, overflowing with good spirits.

The Assistant SAC, a gray-haired man at least ten years older than Alabastro, held up a hand. "Oh, don't worry, Jake, we're not taking your statement right now. We'll give you a couple more days to recover. My surveillance team sends its regrets about Daoud. Daoud turned out to be cleverer at evading them than they thought. Anyway, we were happy to learn that no one at The Amazons was hit."

Jake nodded and turned to Alabastro. "What caliber?"

"A .45 semi-automatic." Alabastro held his palms in the air. "Free country, y'know. Even radicals who've just returned from a jihadist training camp in Lebanon can buy guns."

The Assistant SAC added, "We've learned more about this Khaled Daoud character since he blew himself up. He spent a month abroad in Lebanon at a Hezbollah camp. Daoud and his pals were planning something big. Thanks to you, their plot's exposed. And thanks to you, he didn't make it to the NBC gate. We believe one of your bullets slowed him down, and the steel bollards stopped the car, but not before he set off the bomb."

"Too bad," Jake muttered. "The Marines at the gate?"

"They're fine, got out of the way in time. The base'll need a new gate, though. Anyway, what we learned about Daoud," Alabastro said, "will put away his whole cell. We also learned who attacked Fatimah Daoud, The daughter has come forward with the truth and ID'd two of her father's pals as the real perps. Two more were recent recruits from their mosque. Naturally, they're all lawyered up."

"Poor girl. Poor mother. How're they doing?" Jake asked.

Alabastro grinned. "You can ask Sarah, yourself, Jake. She's waiting in the hall. She wants to talk to you. Meg's with her. We'll give her a few minutes...if you're up to it."

"Sure," Jake said, although his head hurt like hell, and his stomach felt like he hadn't eaten in days.

A minute later, Meg's arms encircled him. "How do you feel?"

"Better. Hungry as a tiger...or horse. No, I could eat a horse. I think that's how it goes. Mainly, it hurts to think."

Meg stepped aside and motioned for Sarah to join her beside Jake's bed. The girl's hair was hidden by her *hijab*, but her dark eyes glowed brightly. Pretty and so very young, the fifteen-year-old had seen more in her short life than many Americans see in a lifetime. She shyly approached.

"Tell him about your mother and her family in Detroit." Meg put her hand on the girl's shoulder.

Sarah spoke softly. "My mother is better. She came out of her coma and is talking and eating. They told her about Papa—" She broke off, gulped, and somehow found the strength to go on. "We—my mother, brother, and I—are so sorry for all the terrible things he did. He was planning on doing even more terrible things. My mother found out and told me. I didn't believe her at first, but when those friends of my father attacked her, I knew my mother was telling the truth. They tried to kill her...to stop her from going to the police. I was so afraid..."

"We know, Sarah." Meg squeezed the girl's shoulder. "We don't blame you." Her beautiful but concerned face swung his way. "Jake, Sarah's aunt has arrived from Detroit. The FBI offered to set Sarah's family up with the Witness Security Program through the US Marshals Service, but they declined. Instead, they're going to move to Detroit and live with Mrs. Daoud's family. They'll do their best to protect Sarah and her mother, and Deputy Marshals will be assigned to them until the trials of the other conspirators are over."

Knowing not to touch the Muslim girl, Jake seized Meg's free hand instead. "Thanks for letting me know." He smiled at Sarah even though the effort shot a stab of pain through his head. "Thanks, Sarah. I'm glad this nightmare is nearly over for you and your family."

He wanted to say more but his thoughts scattered as his eyelids grew heavy.

THE NEXT THING JAKE knew, people were moving him out of the hospital on a gurney, then carried him up a flight of stairs into Meg's apartment. He tried to get up, but his bones felt like rubber. His world shrank to the size of Meg's bedroom, where he mostly slept.

When he finally managed to stay awake more often, he began moving around the bedroom and taking strolls to the bathroom.

One afternoon, Meg appeared and offered him her hands. "If you feel up to it, come to the kitchen with me. I'll warm up the pizza I got last night."

Like a grateful child, he let her lead him into the kitchen. For once, his head didn't hurt, and though his body still ached, he was no longer stiff and in pain.

"What time is it? What day is it?" He peered through the blinds at the gray sky.

"Five p.m. It's Thursday. Sit down, Jake." She pointed to one of the kitchen chairs and smiled.

A little dazed by how ravenous he felt, he eyed the box of crackers on the table and dove in. Half the box had disappeared before two steaming hot wedges of pizza appeared on a plate in front of him, followed by a tall glass of cold milk. Memories surfaced as he blew on the melted cheese and gingerly took a bite. Including the sickening smell of burnt tires...

"Did the Expedition make it?"

"Your rental car? Yes, it did. Except for the three bullet holes in the back, it's in good shape. The FBI agents said it was far enough down the street. You, on the other hand, got a little too close for comfort. They said the blast was mostly contained inside a big metal cooler in the back of the sedan and that it was a good thing the man hadn't used more explosives in his makeshift bomb. Tom Alabastro asked that when you're ready, come to the office to give them a statement, but not to hurry, they have plenty of eyewitnesses to fill in the gaps."

The sequence of events rushed back in a burst of clarity. The back alley fusillade of bullets by an enraged Khaled Daoud, the car chase, and his ultimate plan to blow up as many members of the military as he could. First, though, he'd tried to take out Jake. Daoud's plot most likely began to unravel with Jake's hospital visit and his recording of that hallway conversation.

"Another foot soldier for the Islamist cause," he grumbled, stuffing the second piece of pizza into his mouth and washing it down with milk.

Meg continued, her dark blue eyes glistening with emotion. "The two men who beat up Sarah's mother and tried to kill her threatened to kill Sarah, too. Mrs. Daoud was going to leave her husband and report him and his jihad pals to the cops. Sarah wanted to tell the truth but was too afraid. With her father gone and her mother recovered, she found the courage to come forward."

Jake nodded. It all made sense now, Fatimah Daoud's meeting with the social workers that night at The Amazons. Her husband had found out, somehow, and probably followed her there.

"And Mrs. Daoud? Will she fully recover?"

Meg beamed. "Sarah said the doctors expect so, but it'll take time. Sarah's sad, of course, about her father and what he did. But now, she's mostly happy and relieved."

"Good." Jake took another bite, this time smaller, as his hunger faded. There was something else he wanted to ask, but it eluded him. Then the name popped up suddenly, as clear as day. "Basheera. What about him? He gave your address to Daoud. That's how they followed you and me."

"It's so strange you ask that. He wasn't in class all week, not since Monday. It's all over the Foreign Language department that Professor Basheera left the country out of the blue. He just left his position and went back to Egypt, and according to a few people, he plans to lead a faction of the Muslim Brotherhood. That could just be a rumor. However, Alabastro said his field office has recommended that the State Department revoke Basheera's visa. Professor Heinz has taken over the European History classes for the remainder of the quarter."

Damn, that meant ol' *Scheisse-Gesicht, aka Shit-face,* would be seeing more of Meg...every day.

The news about Basheera didn't surprise him. "Thanks to you, all this came to a head sooner rather than later."

"Why thanks to me?" Meg asked.

"By going to Basheera with that recording, you let him and Daoud know we were on to them. Meg, you didn't intend it, but maybe you sensed something."

That earned him a broad smile, though she immediately lowered her eyes in a gesture of genuine humility. "I don't know about that. Mostly, I was stupid. I almost got us both killed."

Jake tossed the rest of the pizza on his plate, suddenly not so hungry. He grabbed her hand and lifted it to his lips. As he gazed into her eyes, his thoughts flowed in German. *I don't know if I want to get married again, Meg. But we can compromise and maybe...*

"*...sich verloben?*" Get engaged? When her eyes widened, he realized he had actually spoken the words aloud.

The look she fixed upon him was pure bafflement. "What did you just say?"

"Uh, I was just thinking out loud."

"In German?"

"Yeah, sometimes I do that. An old habit, thanks to Grandpa Nate."

She gave him an odd look but nodded and changed the subject. "Javier called and wants to know if we'll be up to pulling off the money-trap operation this weekend."

"When?"

"Tomorrow night. Sheila called...wants to meet us. By *us*, I mean my Navy nurse persona and her alpha male—the weapons engineer boyfriend. Both are so desperate for money that they're ripe to be bought off for the right price."

Jake barely heard what she said, shocked by his own spoken words, albeit phrased in German. The moment of...weakness—impulsive weakness, that's all it was—passed.

Was he *Verruckt*...crazy or what? Had the concussion scrambled his brain? Zapped a few neurons?

Damn, he hoped not. He needed every brain cell just to keep up with Meg.

"No, forget it," Meg said. "It's too soon. You're not well enough yet."

He kissed her knuckles gently, grateful for her endless compassion. She was his lover but also a good friend. A better woman than he probably deserved, but was he ready for a lifetime of gratitude?

"Sure, tomorrow night, I'll be ready." He paused to think. Something else bothered him, something he told Javier to look into. But for the life of him, he couldn't recall what it was.

He turned his head and suddenly got a whiff of his armpits. "Right now, I need a shower." He stood up and stretched his back. His entire body was still so sore that he felt ten years older. "Okay, Meg, we'll set the money trap and see what we catch."

She pressed his hand, still entwined with hers, against her cheek. She looked more resolved than he felt. As long as they didn't catch a bullet in the process, he was willing to try to trap a couple of spies.

Chapter Twenty-four

JAKE AND MEG SAT IN a small booth inside Sevilla's, watching Javier approach their table. He had just arrived for their pre-briefing, excitement flushing his face and neck, breathing heavily like he'd run all the way from his car. Mary Lou was holding a parking space at the Fish Market restaurant on Harbor Boulevard, where Meg had agreed to meet Sheila. The darkness of Sevilla's interior seemed to match the cloak-and-dagger tone of their meeting.

"Here's what we've learned," Javier stared but paused when a waitress stopped by to take his order.

Jake felt his pulse skip with excitement but waited until Javier settled and ordered a beer. Although on duty, he and Meg encouraged him to have one to take the edge off.

"Go on." Jake eyed the file that Javier opened.

"Sheila's not just a low-level operative. She's the daughter of a high-ranking official of the Communist Party, the Politburo. Xi Leung is a Minister of Culture."

"Is she really a student at San Diego State U?" Meg wanted to know.

"Yeah, electrical engineering, but she already has a degree from Beijing's National Defense University."

"One of the best science and tech institutes in the PRC." Jake had already begun to wonder whether they'd miscalculated Sheila and her bodyguard.

"She's obviously very smart," Meg interjected. "Much smarter than we thought." She shook her head with a look of disgust. "She's doing this, prostituting herself to Navy officers, for the sake of gathering our military information?"

Jake looked at the woman he'd fallen in love with. Meg was way out of her depth here. Having her at that dinner meeting wasn't sitting well with him.

Thankfully, he would be with her. "Meg, that's what spies do. Whatever it takes."

Javier shot them both a wry smile. "There's more. Sheila, or Xing Lee Peong, is actually Colonel Lee of the PLA."

"PLA?" Meg queried.

Jake jumped in. "People's Liberation Army. Of the People's Republic of China."

Meg gulped and glanced at Javier. "She's no slouch, is she?"

"Not just a pretty face. Hell no, she's one tough *chica*." Javier nodded. "I suggest we cancel this meeting, Meg. Mary Lou agrees with me. This is too dangerous."

Jake sighed and swore under his breath. He already wore a hidden mike, prepared to at least fake his way through this preliminary meet-and-greet. With Admiral Snider's permission, he'd spoken with one of the Aegis Weapons Systems engineers at length that morning, had taken copious notes, and memorized key phrases related to the Aegis's system operations and protocols meant to be teasers and nothing more. He wouldn't be giving away anything secret or classified, but he could give Sheila the impression he knew what he was talking about. He now doubted the woman would be so gullible. Not with her science and engineering background.

Anger made him clench his jaw and grit his teeth. He said nothing, however. It was Meg's contact, but the NCIs' call. They seemed to have confidence in Meg, that maybe Meg had sensed a desperation in the Chinese woman that would make her careless.

"There's more," Javier added.

"Of course, there is," Jake muttered.

"With Alabastro's help, we accessed Homeland Security's databases and learned that China now has at least one hundred more Navy ships than the US. They're building their naval presence and flexing their muscles in the Pacific. Their guided missile destroyers are new, and their defense spending has more than doubled since 2006, so they have the money to spend. What they don't have is the latest and greatest weapons systems. That's what they're trying to steal here. The Aegis is globally the best, and the Chinese don't just want a peek, they want to duplicate its power and precision capabilities. Commander Wickham believes it's their top priority."

"Anything else?" Jake asked, eager to either call it a day or move ahead. Manpower had been assigned, so it was time to work the op or close up shop.

Javier took long swallows from his beer bottle, holding it by its neck.

"Time is a factor here, too. They know the fleet's pulling out in two weeks. They have to act now. Their main source was Lieutenant Carlton. Whether Sam was an informant or not, we may never know. If she was, why would they kill the golden goose? Y'know? That doesn't make sense. Mary Lou and I think Carlton didn't give Sheila any dirt. Maybe a little lovin', but no military secrets. We'd like to be able to prove it and clear any suspicion tainting her name."

Javier closed the file. "As far as we know, Meg and especially her weapons-engineer boyfriend are Sheila's last-ditch hope to develop a reliable asset in the naval weapons field. Sheila, or Colonel Lee, is highly competitive, it's safe to say, and Wickham thinks she's bucking for a PLA promotion." He wiped his mouth on the sleeve of his shirt. "Oh, and though she looks twenty-five, she's actually thirty-four."

"Older and wiser." Jake downed the last of his drink. "Okay, we get it. Let's call it off."

Meg looked shocked. "Jake, we can't!"

Javier's expression became frantic. "Look, I know I suggested canceling the meeting, but let's give it a shot. I told you all this so you'd go into the meeting with a degree of...uh, y'know—"

"Circumspection? What about resignation? Or acceptance that we're barking up the wrong tree?" Jake picked up his leather jacket and Meg's quilted one. The weather had turned wintry cool, and the radio had forecasted rain later that night. He wouldn't mind going home and calling it a day. Occasional headaches from his concussion continued to plague him, as well as general fatigue and malaise.

And something else. A nagging sense they'd arrived at the wrong conclusion about Sam's murder.

Meg placed a hand on his arm. "Jake, I know you're not feeling that well, and maybe we should call this off. But if we're protected and surrounded by Alabastro's agents, what's the harm in trying to get Sheila to show her hand? If she doesn't, then we go home and have some hot chocolate by the fire." She smiled impishly and snapped her fingers. "Oh, that's right. I don't have a fireplace here, but my Dallas house does."

She then tugged his sleeve and held up her wrist with the cuff bracelet that contained a wireless transmitter. She was wired, so to speak, and so was he. She wanted to do this. Jake marveled at her spirit but still hesitated. This was an adventure—a game—to her. However, her professional reputation was not at stake.

Javier had a hungry look in his eyes, and Jake commiserated with him. The NCIs wanted to snare the clever Chinese spy because, sooner or later, Sheila would get what she wanted. And the country would ultimately suffer for it.

"Backups?" he asked Javier. Knowing that NCI Commander Wickham had their backs and supported this operation provided a modicum of comfort. Admiral Snider had given his consent, albeit with a proviso that plenty of support personnel would be on the scene.

"Visual and auditory communication at all times. Mary Lou will be at the bar, part of a watch team inside the restaurant. A surveillance team, on loan from Alabastro's field office, is tracking Sheila and her bodyguard driver as we speak and will remain in the parking lot. A squad of Marines is on call on the aircraft carrier next door. Two more NCIs in constant radio contact will be in plain clothes by the Bob Hope statue."

Meg had specifically requested the Fish Market for its location along the wharf. Tourists and locals meandered up and down Harbor Boulevard, crowding the area adjacent to the decommissioned USS Midway, the renowned aircraft carrier turned naval museum. In tribute to the famous comedian who spent every Christmas making US servicemen laugh, the bronze Bob Hope statue, fixed with motion sensors, emitted sporadic and humorous commentary. Both tourist sites, so close to the Fish Market, would ensure them a modicum of safety in numbers, at least.

Jake helped Meg don her jacket, then shrugged on his, making sure the iPod clipped to his pocket stayed in place to transmit every word spoken that night. "All right, let's give it a try."

Javier rubbed his hands together, obviously relieved.

"Oh, another thing. Don't take a drink from Sheila's hands or her bodyguard's. And watch any plate that's served to you. Our dear colonel has a record of leaving poisoned victims behind."

That grabbed Jake's attention. "What kind of poison? Ketamine?"

"No." Javier led the way out of the restaurant. "Her favorite is mushrooms. In particular, the death cap. So don't order anything with mushrooms, just in case." He gave a short laugh a moment before noticing their quelling frowns. "Anyway, our file suggests that she might've caused her first husband's death. She was never prosecuted, of course. Her daddy intervened and sent her abroad. Aren't we lucky? Bet the State Department never checked out that one."

Jake harrumphed and nodded. In his line of work, he was never surprised, but the passing remark startled Meg.

She spun around outside the restaurant's front doors, facing Javier. "First husband? You mean, Sheila's married?"

"Yeah. According to the latest intel, Xu-wen Ton's her husband, her bodyguard, and head of the security team at the PRC's consulate in Los Angeles."

Jake wondered if Mr. Ton had access to ketamine. The drug had been injected into Samantha Carlton in a massive overdose that had caused her heart to stop, according to the NCI forensics team's official cause of death.

His next thought, one that had eluded him for days, rushed through his brain like a freight train. He halted in place, causing Javier and Meg to stop and throw him questioning looks.

"Remind me to get that file from you, the one on Lisa Chance."

"Sure. When?"

"Tomorrow. Let's get through tonight first."

Chapter Twenty-five

ALL THREE LEVELS OF the restaurant's dining room boasted picture-window views of the bay. Meg and Jake found Sheila and her bodyguard seated at a table on the lowest level next to one of the windows facing the ocean. Surprised to see Sheila's bodyguard—no, make that *husband*—sitting next to her, Meg approached them, trying hard not to let her smile slip. She, too, had an uneasy feeling about this meeting.

The restaurant was packed with people and bustling servers, which is why Meg had chosen The Fish Market for the meeting. The noisy, public place would allow Sheila to check out Jake—Meg's alpha male slash Navy weapons engineer—while curtailing any chance of attack. Yet Meg's gut told her something wasn't right.

Jake's arm squeeze indicated he sensed the same. Something was wrong but it was too late to call off the meeting.

They took their seats facing the bay. Sheila's bodyguard sat with his back to the window, neither smiling nor acknowledging them, his gaze constantly scanning the place. His massive bulk nearly blocked their view of the ocean, and Meg suddenly wondered if he wore a weapon under his sports jacket.

Sheila, on the other hand, was all smiles and air-kisses with Meg. She dressed conservatively in a scoop-necked shift and matching jacket. She'd pulled her long black hair up into a knot at the crown of her head. Despite her more severe look, she personified beauty, capturing the attention of every male in the room and not a few envious glances from the women.

Meg cast a sidelong glance at Jake's reaction. He blinked rapidly a couple of times as if blinded by Sheila's beauty. Irritated, Meg tossed her long mane over her shoulders and introduced Jake, giving his arm a squeeze. A hard squeeze.

Sheila enthusiastically shook Jake's hand and introduced him to her *bodyguard and driver, Mr. Ton*. In keeping with their cover, Meg and Jake nodded their greeting and ordered cocktails. No sooner had they taken their first sips than the other shoe dropped.

Sheila smirked. "While I'd be amused to see your little act, Jake the Navy engineer, I lack the time and inclination to continue this charade...Mister FBI agent. I highly doubt you know an algorithm from a logarithm. However, my sources tell me you are a talented counter-terrorism specialist." She paused for his reaction and appeared disappointed when all he gave back was a bland poker face.

Meg, meanwhile, had sucked in a loud gasp.

Well, so much for their undercover roles.

Sheila resumed her supercilious smile. "So we are going to save time tonight, and you are not going to insult my intelligence. Also, we want you to call off your—what's the phrase?—government goons. I love that alliteration. English is so full of them." She sat back and tapped her long, red nails on her martini glass.

Meg and Jake exchanged looks, his meant to persuade her to remain silent.

"Oh, please. Meg, while I think you're a very attractive woman, you are no undercover agent. As soon as you walked in with those two Navy investigators, I knew you were the honeypot of the team."

Meg touched Jake's arm in alarm. "Jake..."

"No, it's okay, Meg." He patted her hand. "Let's hear what Sheila Lee, aka Communist Party official Xing Lee Peong, aka Peoples Liberation Army Colonel Lee, has to say. We've been made. I want to know how."

Sheila's round face split into a wide smile, showing off two rows of even, white teeth. "That's the spirit, Agent Bernstein. You remind me of that American actor, Ben Affleck, so I hope you don't mind if I call you Agent Ben." She chuckled at her little joke. "We have excellent resources and informants, of course, Agent Ben, and spy satellites just as sweeping as yours Another giveaway was the photo of you both entering the FBI's field office on Aero Drive. Not just once but twice. Our watch team, which Mr. Ton arranged, took high-resolution photos of your visits, which naturally made us curious, especially when we noticed Meg with you. The visits occurred shortly after the Navy officer's death, and while we were tracking the police investigation, we were more than a little curious about a parallel one conducted by the Navy investigators and the local FBI."

Meg, dumbfounded and panicky, began to breathe in short pants.

Jake took her hand to calm her down. "Well, Colonel Lee, it's nice to know your intel teams are working overtime. And, of course, they're all cultural attaches connected to the consulate."

Sheila smiled slyly at Mr. Ton, who, for the first time, returned a stony half-grin.

"Diplomatic immunity is such a wonderful safeguard," Sheila purred. "Don't pretend your CIA isn't doing the same in my country."

"Go on," Jake said, conceding nothing. "I'm sure there's more gloating you'd like to do."

"First, make sure your agents don't become trigger-happy cowboys and make a scene. We don't want that, do we?"

Jake spoke into the mic attached to his fake iPod. "Stand down, Javier. Everyone, stay in place but stand down." His tone was icy, and his expression immutable.

Sheila's and Mr. Ton's gazes flew to his pocket and the clipped iPod. Meg glanced down at her cuff bracelet, unintentionally giving away her transmitter.

"Oh, how clever! I must have one," Sheila exclaimed to her bodyguard.

Much to Meg's amazement, Mr. Ton nodded, his expression as matter-of-fact as if they were shopping for a trinket or bauble.

"Go on," Jake repeated evenly. His face betrayed no emotion, but he was clearly unhappy. His posture tensed, and his right hand disappeared under the table. Was he expecting violence from the two Chinese spies?

Meg had never experienced anything like this before and didn't know what to do or how to behave. Silence was her only alternative.

Sheila sipped her martini and grimaced. "This vodka is horrible, must be Russian"—she turned to Mr. Ton—"but don't tell them I said so." She turned back and leveled a steady gaze on Jake and Meg. "I specifically requested Grey Goose. Anyway, to continue this table-turning conversation, if I'm using that idiom correctly."

Meg heard Jake expel breath through his teeth and knew he was beginning to lose his temper. Even Sheila noticed his reaction and leaned back, gazing at

Jake with slitted eyes. Mr. Ton straightened up and puffed out his chest, his dark gaze settling on Jake's arm.

"Maybe we all should place our hands on the table," Jake suggested. "Too many civilians around."

"Which is why we agreed to such a public place," Sheila said, enjoying her brag-fest. "We needed to control this meeting. Americans are such cowboys. What's the expression? Shoot first and ask questions later? Because of the Navy officer's sudden death and the suspicions directed our way, we have decided to end our operation here. We wanted you to know that and to know we had nothing to do with that woman's murder."

"Really?" Coming from Jake, it was a sarcastic statement, not a question. "Can you prove that? Didn't you have an affair with Samantha Carlton? Didn't you attempt to coerce the Navy officer into stealing military secrets for you?"

"Well, I won't deny that I misled the woman into thinking I found her attractive, even desirable," Sheila said. "Beyond that, I deny everything. When that woman—"

"Lieutenant Samantha Carlton," Jake snapped.

"When I realized that Lieutenant Carlton became, shall we say, a lost cause, I stopped returning her phone calls."

"What about her shoes?"

"Shoes? I don't know what you're talking about." Sheila's thin, black eyebrows furrowed prettily.

The woman was quite an actress, Meg thought sourly, but that was clearly the kind of spy Sheila was. A honeypot who convinced innocents to fall in love or lust with her and do her favors. Even if that meant betraying their country.

Did American spies do the same thing in other countries? She supposed she already knew the answer to that.

Jake sat stock-still, then brought both hands up to the table, assuring the two spies that he wasn't going to turn *cowboy* on them.

When the server showed up to take dinner orders, Sheila sent him away. "Sorry we can't stay for dinner, but we're leaving tomorrow. Another assignment."

Meg noted that Sheila instantly underwent a shocking transformation of attitude and demeanor, even her appearance seemed to change. A deadly serious woman emerged, and her voice carried a razor's edge to it.

"Don't bother with warrants or searches, Agent Ben. We are exercising diplomatic immunity from this moment on. Our further cooperation is conditional upon your acceptance of our position."

Jake brought both hands to his chin, supporting it with two angry fists. He nodded slowly. "What else do you have?"

"I will give you something for your time and trouble, Agent Ben. Perhaps someday our paths will cross again, and you can do me a favor."

Jake shrugged noncommittally.

"You should know that The Lido is a hotbed of drug activity including bags of X, as those American kids call it, and Special K or K-hole as it is known to the club regulars. LSD, Rohypnol, GHB, and Ecstasy or E, I think it's called, are also sold to the club's regulars."

She looked at Meg, a look that sent chills down her back.

"You noticed Kurt with one of those bags last week. Your investigation has spotlighted us due to my unfortunate friendship with Lieutenant Carlton. Throw your spotlight somewhere else. That is if you truly intend to solve that woman's murder."

Sheila paused to finish her martini, and Mr. Ton downed the last of his glass of beer. A look passed between them as though to say it was time to go.

Jake slipped the iPod out of his pocket and said, "Teams One and Two, stand down. Suzie and the Big Bad Wolf are leaving. Do not follow. The operation is a bust."

The pre-arranged code names Jake had given to Javier in Team One and Alabastro's agents in Team Two made Sheila snicker. Meanwhile, Mr. Ton stood behind Sheila and protectively placed beefy hands on her shoulders.

"Suzie and the Big Bad Wolf," Sheila chortled, "I like those names."

Jake sat forward. "One last question for you. You had many occasions to speak to Lieutenant Carlton about the drug activity at the club. What did she think about it? Did she know where the drugs came from and who was behind the trafficking?"

Mr. Ton edged back her chair and Sheila stood, her hand resting briefly on her bodyguard's muscular arm.

"That's two questions, so I will answer only the first one. Lieutenant Carlton despised the drugs that the club made available to the regulars—all those young people, the Navy men and women, too. The system was a bit clever, I have to admit. If clubbers were cleared by Lisa and her bouncer, they got a special-colored stamp on their hands. The bartenders knew who the safe, discreet buyers were by that stamp. Red was no...other colors were yes. The bartenders dispensed the drugs with the drinks accordingly, and money changed hands. Simple and effective. I'm surprised your Navy investigators didn't know this." Mr. Ton slipped a hand under Sheila's arm. "Or maybe they did, but they didn't want to get their Navy friends into trouble. As I said, the lieutenant wanted to stop it. So, as I said, throw your spotlight elsewhere, Agent Ben."

Meg watched the two Chinese spies vanish into the restaurant crowd before she looked back at Jake. Spots of red flushed his cheeks, and muscles twitched in his jaw. He inhaled audibly, clenching and unclenching his fists as if he wanted to punch something or someone. Other than that subtle movement, he bore a full rictus of distress.

Meg wasn't certain why their money trap had blown up in their faces, but she'd just watched two Chinese spies call their bluff, get up, and walk out. Their plan had not only been one-upped by the foreigners, but Jake obviously also felt humiliated. What she didn't have to guess was his reaction a minute later. When he stood and stormed out of the restaurant, Meg silently followed.

She broke into a run when she realized what he was about to do.

Chapter Twenty-six

JAKE GRABBED JAVIER'S jacket lapels and shook the young man so hard his head snapped back and forth. He slammed the NC investigator against the side of his car and got in his face. Mary Lou, her mouth agape, staggered back.

"Hey, man—" Javier managed.

"Don't *hey man* me! Do you realize what you and Ensign Taylor have done? By withholding vital information from me, you've obstructed your own murder investigation. We should've been looking at Lisa Chance all along. She had means and opportunity, and a PRC spy has just filled in the motive. You heard what was said. That woman has now had nearly three weeks to cover up and destroy the evidence. Do you realize what you two have done?" Jake's face grew hot, his breathing hard, so furious he could barely get the words out. He glared at Mary Lou. *If you weren't a woman...*

When Meg tried to intervene, his temper rose another notch—she could have been killed. He turned to the two FBI agents standing nearby. "Take her home! Now! I've got to make these two understand how they fucked up this investigation."

Jake let go of Javier's jacket, stepped back, and watched Meg fall into step with Alabastro's men as they headed across the parking lot to their car. She stared back at him, her gaze pleading with him to let her stay, but he *needed* her safe. He clenched his fists at his sides, feeling like he could kill someone. Still, he knew Meg sympathized with him at this meeting's outcome, he'd sensed her anger. This wasn't her fault. She simply wanted to help their investigation. Helping the NCIs...

A HEADACHE BEGAN TO form in the back of Jake's head—its inner drumbeat building in intensity. He held his head as he leaned over the car's front fender, forcing himself to calm down. Ensigns Blanco and Taylor remained quiet for all of ten seconds.

Then they erupted.

"We're sorry, Jake," Javier said. "But we have Navy friends who're regulars at The Lido. We couldn't rat them out by reporting the drugs."

"We didn't believe Lisa could've killed Sam," Mary Lou added. "And we still don't! Those Chinese spies are just yanking our chain."

"The drug scene—every club has one!" Javier continued. "We knew someone in the club was peddling... And yes, we were told Lisa was most likely working the system."

"We figured Sam got mad at the drug scene and at Lisa for peddling, but hey, we're not even sure about that. Maybe she's just..." Mary Lou ground to a stop, clearly lacking further rationale for withholding vital information in a murder investigation.

Jake straightened, folded his arms across his chest, and stared at the ground, couching his fists under his arms to avoid hitting something or someone. What a fool he'd been. The evidence was right there last Tuesday in Lisa's office. Yet he'd ignored what was hiding in plain sight—the stack of boxes along the wall in front of Lisa's desk.

He had been sitting right next to them as he spoke with Lisa before the shooting started, and he got distracted by Daoud and the subsequent car chase to Coronado Island.

"I saw four boxes in Lisa's office." He shook with anger at his own stupidity. "Big liquor bottle boxes, the kind you see in The Lido storage room. The boxes were closed and taped, but all four had initials marked in felt pen. One had an R on the side, another G. The other two X and K. I assumed at the time, R stood for rum, G for gin. Had no clue about X and K. Now I know. X for Ecstasy, K for Ketamine or Special K. R was probably Rohypnol, the date-rape drug. I presume the G was for the hallucinogenic GHB."

Jake gauged their reaction. The two NCIs looked at each other. If Jake had affronted Javier's manhood by grabbing him, the young man didn't show it. It was almost as though he'd expected Jake's blowup and knew he deserved it.

"No one we've spoken to has ever seen Lisa's supplier," Mary Lou said. "Could be from across the Mexican border. There are lots of drug cartel tunnels between here and Tijuana. Somehow, the bartenders would get the drugs and use Lisa's hand-stamp system to dispense them. We just didn't think any of that was relevant to Sam's murder."

Javier nodded vehemently. "The drugs are never in big quantities—just small baggies of pills. There's never been an overdose in the club, so we thought it was contained and fairly harmless. Little thrills and bits of pleasure. Y'know?"

The two NCIs shrugged collectively as if their decision to remain mum about the drug situation at the nightclub was perfectly reasonable.

Jake scowled at them. Were they just naïve, corrupt, or in collusion? He couldn't decide. Probably just young fucking fools who'd grown up in a culture that too readily tolerated drug use.

"It's still illegal," he snapped. "Drugs are part of the club scene? What a crock of shit! Drugs are always a criminal activity. Whoever killed Samantha played you *and* me. Lisa left enough breadcrumbs to throw us off track. She knew we'd sniff out those Chinese spies and assume the worst."

It began to rain—small droplets at first before the deluge hit. Mary Lou pulled up the hood of her parka while Javier turned up his jacket collar.

Javier glanced at Jake. "You think Lisa's supplying her own stuff? Making it herself? But why put those boxes in her office where Lonnie works, too? Do you think Lonnie knows?"

"I don't know," Jake confessed. "The café is closed on Sunday and Monday. It was Tuesday morning when I saw the boxes in their office and a dolly nearby. It's possible she baked the powder into tablets in the café's ovens while Lonnie and her staff were gone and then put the pills into empty liquor bottles, which were placed into delivery boxes. It would be a clever ploy. Maybe clever enough to even fool Lonnie. Maybe she didn't have a chance to move the boxes to the club's storeroom before Tuesday morning. With the dolly standing there, it looked like she might have been getting ready to do that. Then I showed up, and that fanatic started shooting."

"So, you don't think Lonnie knows?" Mary Lou asked.

"Is Lonnie complicit? Doubtful. She's a do-gooder. I can't see her approving any drug activity. It sounds like it disturbed Samantha enough for her to threaten Lisa. Maybe that was her mistake. She should've gone directly to the police. Or Navy."

Mary Lou looked down at the ground. "Sam did mention to me once that she thought the nightclub wasn't a good influence on the Navy kids—that's what she called us: Navy kids. But I just thought it was because of her age. She was a lot older than us. But I know for a fact that Sam didn't want the club closed down, either."

"Because of the social contacts she and the others in the GLBT crowd made there," Javier supplied.

Jake buttonholed Mary Lou with a piercing stare. "You knew Samantha well. Were she and Lisa Chance once involved romantically?"

Mary Lou raised her dark eyes and nodded. "It ended before she met Sheila. Maybe it ended over the drug issue, I don't know. Sam never told me why they ended it."

Jake mashed his lips together, furious that another important detail had been withheld from him. He took another deep breath and hissed it out slowly. *Un-fucking-believable!*

He steeled himself, fighting to remain rational. "So it's possible Chance knew about the boots with the secret heel. and that we'd assume the worst about Samantha if they went missing, that we'd presume she was spying for the Chinese and hiding thumb drives in the heel of her shoes. That Asian hair found at the crime scene might've been planted. Although I spent an hour with one of Captain Snider's weapons engineers—an Asian American male whom Samantha worked next to all day. Very likely the strand of hair was just workplace transfer."

"But the cleanup and staging of Sam's apartment?" Mary Lou reminded them. "How can we explain that, and Sam's missing laptop?"

Javier muttered something before speaking aloud, "Could be that Lisa was afraid Sam had written stuff about the club's drugs. Or they'd exchanged emails with Sam threatening to expose what was going on. Lisa may have spent some time at Sam's, trying to persuade her to go along, and had to clean the evidence."

"We'll never know," Jake admitted. The worst scenario loomed in his head. "The evidence is long gone, you can bet on that. All we have is circumstantial evidence—no physical evidence, no confession, no eyewitnesses. Hence, no prosecution. Find powder residue in the café ovens and you'd have the tablet baking source, but I'd bet that's long gone, too. With Lisa's nursing background, she knew the basics of chemistry and must've learned the rest of the recipes somewhere."

The steady patter of rain drenched them, but Jake ignored it. The NCIs appeared to accept the fact that Jake was deep into working through the details of his new theory about Samantha's murder. Just a theory. No proof.

The hard truth of their failure seemed to be slowly sinking in, their expressions growing more morose by the minute. Especially Javier, who looked crushed.

Jake shook his head. "Murder, the window's closed on that one...unless you find some physical evidence. Right now, we—no, *you* have a flimsy, circumstantial case at best. And you'll have to live with that. If you're lucky and her bartenders talk, you can get Lisa Chance on drug trafficking...if you act quickly."

Rivulets of water ran down Javier's face, making him look young and vulnerable, as if he were weeping non-stop.

"You mean, arrest her tonight?"

There was no getting around it. Jake was going to have to spell it out.

"Take her into custody. Tonight," he said, "Get her to talk. If she doesn't lawyer up first, you might get her to reveal something you can take to the DA. Otherwise, you turn it over to the SDPD narc squad and get her on drug violations."

Mary Lou approached him cautiously, her face hidden under her hood.

"That's it? We don't get Sam's murderer?"

Jake looked at the two young officers. He was ten years their senior, yet he felt a generation apart. They just didn't get it.

"Probably not. You guys blew it. Big time. By withholding vital information, you gave the murderer time to clear all the evidence. Hindering a murder investigation is a felony, you know. If either of you tip off Lisa Chance before the arrest and she runs, I'll make sure you both face court-martials. Do you understand me? I'll be reporting you two if you fuck this up."

Jake pointed a forefinger at Javier, then at Mary Lou. Feeling like an angry parent, he was nevertheless deadly serious.

Javier's stricken face crumpled. He'd finally gotten it. Mary Lou was clearly still in denial, biting her nails and staring at the ground.

"Go do your job! The right way," Jake commanded.

"Where're you going?" Javier asked.

"Officially, I'm on medical leave. I'm done here."

With that, Jake took the walkway in the direction of Harbor Boulevard. He needed to walk and think to deal with this monumental failure. The cool rain pelted him steadily as if the heavens were also making their displeasure known.

Guilt and self-blame weighed him down. Like lead weights, he put one foot in front of the other and walked. His mind churned relentlessly over the details of Samantha's case. What could he have done differently? How could he have saved this investigation?

An hour later, his body soaked to the bone, he still had no answers.

Chapter Twenty-seven

WHEN JAKE ARRIVED AT Meg's apartment two hours later, he let himself in with her extra key. What he saw made him stop in his tracks.

Meg and Chuck, the scuba diving agent from the SD field office, were sitting on her sofa, one on either end, drinking from mugs and chatting in subdued tones. Jake couldn't tell how long they'd been sitting like that, but they looked like a cozy twosome—two handsome blonds with California tans. Like Mother Nature had created them for each other.

Meg turned to face him and smiled. "Jake, what happened?"

He peeled off his sodden leather jacket, probably ruined beyond repair, and hung it over one of the kitchen chairs. He'd hailed a taxi after aimlessly wandering the length of Harbor Boulevard in the pouring rain. Maybe getting thoroughly soaked and chilled was a kind of self-castigation for letting the two NCI neophytes blow the case.

"Nothing. I gave the two ensigns one last piece of advice and left them. Lisa Chance is our perp, but they'll never prove it. She's had too much time to eliminate the evidence. So much for working with Navy rookies... They're on their way to take her into custody. She'll probably be out in a couple of hours with an attorney batting the reporters out of her way. A search warrant might turn up something, but I doubt it. It'll take some of her staff to testify before she can be indicted for drug trafficking."

"That's it? Drug trafficking charges? What about Sam's murder?" Meg stared at him strangely, as though she expected the case to roll up neatly, just like crime dramas on TV.

"A bust." He sat down in the kitchen, dripping on the vinyl floor, not the living room carpet.

As Meg went to the bathroom for a towel, Chuck stood up to leave. He offered Jake his commiserations—he'd been there, too, at the cusp of solving a case but lacking the hard evidence. The agent offered his hand, which Jake shook, appreciating his words.

The man's blue gaze studied Jake like a rival sized up the quarterback on the opposing team—with respect and caution. Meg could always say one day that Jake had brought the two of them together. Her dream fulfilled... Staying in San Diego and meeting Mr. Sexy Scuba Diver.

Way to go, Bernstein!

Chuck called out a goodbye to Meg and then left. When she reappeared, she handed Jake the towel and helped him shed his sodden shirt.

He felt compelled to ask, "You and Chuckie have a lot to talk about?"

"Oh, yeah, mostly about you and how I met you. I told him about Gran and how you saved us from those neo-Nazis. And how Gran confessed everything to you in her native German about her years posing as an Irish girl, Mary McCoy, working for Churchill's War Office and stealing secrets for the Third Reich." She shook her head. "Sixty years of lies, and yet, I loved her with all my heart. Go figure."

Meg stood still, holding a huge body towel in her arms, watching him remove his shoes and pants.

She continued, "People are strange, aren't they? I guess I still don't understand how that's possible, but there it is. I suppose we can't help but love the people who're good to us and love us when we're children."

Jake nodded. What she said was probably true, since humans were sentient creatures, not logically driven.

He was down to his wet briefs when she wrapped the body towel around his middle. It was the size of two beach towels and hung on him from shoulders to knees. Then she went to a credenza and poured some whiskey into two shot glasses. She handed him one and pointed to his briefs.

"Take those off," she ordered. "I'll hang up your clothes over the shower and dry them tomorrow in the laundry downstairs. Your jacket, I don't know. It'll need a dry cleaner."

He stripped off the briefs, dropped them on the kitchen floor, and held up his glass. "You guys were drinking this stuff in mugs?"

"No." She returned to the sofa. "We were having coffee. He's on duty until midnight. Poor guy. He had to relieve one of my security guys so I invited him for coffee."

Jake noticed the empty cardboard boxes stacked along one wall of the small living room. Confused, he asked, "You going somewhere?" He joined her on the sofa after wrapping the giant body towel around his shoulders and hips.

"You said because of Basheera and those Escondido radicals, I wasn't safe here. So I'm moving in with Aunt Pat while Uncle John's out on deployment. His fleet leaves in one week to who-knows-where, it's top-secret stuff, but Pat says it's the Red Sea. He'll be gone six months."

"You're staying in San Diego?" His gut clenched in anticipation of her response. She was staying, and he was going. Could be worse...but not much. His headache had diminished, however, thanks to the whiskey. His heartache was another story.

"Yes. I've got four more months of coursework to finish my teaching minor in German. Then I'll be applying for a teaching job somewhere here in the San Diego area."

Throwing her head back, she killed her shot in one gulp. He grew very still, bracing himself for more bad news. *This is going to be the fuck-all end to a really fucking bad day.*

"Well, Jacob Bernstein, here's the deal. If we don't at least become engaged... Yes, I know what *sich verloben* means. If we don't at least get engaged, I'll be staying here. Move in with Aunt Pat and the boys, finish my classes this quarter, and begin dating...who knows, maybe Chuck."

He moved way beyond confused to total befuddlement.

"So you're breaking up with me? You're ditching me for pretty-boy Chuckie? Barbie and Ken, huh?"

Her dark blue gaze lasered through him like electric spears.

"For a big, bad G-man, you don't pick up on my cues very well. Or my words. I said *if* we don't become engaged. And because of my track record with men, I want a long engagement. Not too long, but long enough to learn about a man. With my first fiancé, it took me six months of living with him before I discovered he was a closet binge drinker."

Her voice softened, but determination glinted in her dark blue eyes.

"Jake, we've known each other just seven months, and lived together for two of those. Aside from your occasional jealousy, I haven't detected any serious character flaws. Well, tonight showed me you've got a temper, though you might've been a little bit justified."

Little bit justified?

He said nothing but emptied his shot glass. Too many tables were turning on him. He couldn't keep up with them all. It was like riding a carousel that never stopped and the horse he rode bobbed up and down at hyped-up speed. Even if he wanted to get off, how could he?

"Shall I speak in plain English? I want to be with you—live with you—but only if we're engaged. I'm not turning my life upside down for a man who can't commit. You either commit or don't."

Momentarily speechless, he finally realized what this was—an honestly and bluntly delivered ultimatum.

Fish or cut bait, Bernstein.

Yet, despite everything, he froze again, like he had in the jewelry stores.

After a minute, he'd said nothing but sat, huddled in his big towel, staring into space and feeling miserable.

Finally, Meg quietly got up and went to bed.

Chapter Twenty-eight

JAKE WOKE THE NEXT morning to a pleading call from Javier. Jake had slept in his birthday suit on the sofa, wrapped in two thick blankets and a pillow provided during the night by a silent Meg. Half awake, he listened to the NCI, then clicked off his cell phone and swore.

He found clean clothes—jeans, a polo shirt, and sneakers—in Meg's bedroom closet and dressed in the darkness, trying not to wake her up. After shrugging on his navy-blue wool peacoat-style jacket, he leaned over and kissed her forehead. She moaned and rolled away.

For a long moment, he stared down at her. Meg Larsen was the kind of woman who could make his life a living hell. Or heaven. She'd never be dull or let him get away with crap. She'd offer him a dry towel and a shot of whiskey instead of blame. *Just like she did last night.*

He'd blamed himself enough for the fiasco the night before, but Meg hadn't. That kind of love didn't grow on trees.

On his way to the SDPD's holding facility downtown—due to Lisa Chance's civilian status and it being a criminal case—he drove through a Starbucks and zapped his brain with caffeine. Thirty minutes later, he faced two gruff-looking homicide detectives and two very nervous NCIs.

"So the feds have arrived," Dave MacDonald, one of the SDPD detectives, said.

"Just one." Jake remain stoic, in no mood for ribbing. "Where's the collar?"

MacDonald, beefy, red-haired, and red-faced, jerked a thumb to his right. His eyes narrowed to slits, letting Jake know the local cops were pissed off as hell at the NCIs.

"Room four. She's as tight-lipped as a clam at low tide. Her lawyer's there, and neither's saying jack-shit. Based on the flimsy evidence these two pantywaists are showing us, we'll be charging her with drug possession, but even that's wafer-thin. Their search warrant got them boxes with drug residue but that was all. If you can't get her to talk, we're cutting her loose with an arraignment date."

The other dickhead, with a toothpick clenched between his teeth, raked his hooded gaze over Jake. "You got ten minutes. She don't talk, you and these weenies can clear out. Don't waste our time."

Holding his temper, Jake glanced at the two NCIs, dressed in their fatigues and looking close to tears. He motioned them to follow him. When they entered Interrogation Room Four, he found an angry attorney—a dark-haired woman in her thirties, clean and professional in her black pantsuit and white Oxford shirt. Sitting next to her, dressed in a black nylon-and-white-striped running suit, Lisa Chance smirked.

No sooner had he introduced himself than the criminal defense attorney made her position clear. "You can ask all you want, but I've advised her to say nothing."

While Jake and the two NCIs took seats across the metal table from Lisa and her attorney, Lisa's pale blue gaze fixed upon all three of them, each in turn. Then she smirked again. Her dismissive gaze—calm and full of contempt—came back to rest on Jake, but she said nothing.

"Miss Chance," Jake began, "I'm sorry it's come to this. I had questions that I never got to ask you the other day before we were so rudely interrupted."

That got a smile out of her. A thin, lopsided one.

"I'll get to the point if you don't mind," he continued, "and even if you do, I'm giving you my theory of what happened that Tuesday night, the third of January. I believe you lured Lieutenant Samantha Carlton to The Amazons with a text from a disposable cell phone, the kind of phone you'd learned Sheila Lee had used to contact Lieutenant Carlton. Samantha thought it was her lover setting up a rendezvous, and when Sheila didn't show, you knew Sam would leave. You'd been there at The Lido, overseeing the electrical work, and when you left at eight-thirty, I believe you doubled back and parked around the block."

Jake paused, staring at Lisa to gauge her reaction, micro-expressions that might show his words were triggering a reaction. He saw nothing. No tell. No emotional tic. Then and there, he knew he'd get nothing from her. Still, he had to lay out the whole scene, step by step, so one day, these two rookie NCIs might overcome their immature biases and do the same to another perp.

"You knew Samantha would eventually return to her car, which you'd seen parked in the back alley. You probably hid behind some other car, knowing Lonnie and the other coffee shop workers would be occupied for another hour at least. You waited with a hypodermic syringe in your pocket, filled with enough liquid ketamine to stop a horse's heart. When Samantha got to her car, you ambushed her, overpowered her with your superior strength, crushing her larynx so she couldn't cry out. Then with cold precision, you injected the ketamine into her carotid artery. Having worked as an RN, you had the skills to do this."

He paused when he detected a slight widening of Lisa's pale eyes. She straightened and shifted in her chair, a sign that could be interpreted in several ways. But the woman was no longer smirking. She clearly didn't yet know that the NCIs had nothing on her except drug powder residue in a couple of liquor boxes.

They basically had nothing but Jake's imagination and the re-creation of a possible crime scenario.

"Why ketamine? You know its properties in low doses and heavy ones. You knew its potential to be fatal, and you had access. Once we get the DEA involved, you'll probably find your supply lines drying up. Pity, huh? All those young Navy kids doping up on Special K? All those profits disappearing? That's what it was all about, wasn't it? Not just keeping the club afloat but making *real* money for a change."

The woman gave little reaction, but her nostrils flared. She sniffed loudly as if with great disdain.

"You put her in the trunk of her car," Jake went on, "so a little time would pass before her body would be found. Maybe for a kind of payback for all the times Samantha had left her car there while she'd met other lovers at the nearby hotel. Like a slap in your face? Maybe because you heard noises and had to make it quick. Maybe you were improvising a bit that night. But you didn't forget to grab her shoes and cell phone. That was a clever move because you knew it would lead the NCIs to begin looking at Sheila, especially after discovering from Mr. Carlton that her work shoes had a secret compartment.

What better way to sneak out a thumb drive full of classified Aegis Weapons data? Old school, but old school spycraft is often effective in today's world."

Jake paused to take a deep breath. Maybe he was just spinning his wheels, but he had to give the NCIs what he could.

"I figure you left the diamond earrings because of that note to Sheila, pointing us her way. Your strategy worked...for a while. It bought you time to dispose of whatever you needed to dispose of. And you were banking on the NCIs' Navy pals and what might happen to them if your club's drug scene was exposed. You were counting on the NCIs' callow youth and their foolish need to protect their pals."

Jake heard Mary Lou make a strangled sound. He glanced over as Javier hung his head briefly before raising it stoically again.

He turned back to Lisa and continued his scenario.

"The running suit that Samantha clawed at as she fought for her life is very similar to the suit you're now wearing. Black nylon. You probably burned or disposed of the one you were wearing that night. If you had scratches on your head and neck, the fleece hat and turtleneck you wore at their"—he indicated the two NCIs—"first interview with you would have concealed all that. The only slip-up was last Tuesday morning when I showed up unexpectedly. For some reason, you hadn't had time to move the boxes with used liquor bottles full of pills over to the nightclub. But thanks to a crazy Islamic fanatic bent on suicide, you were saved. I think you thanked your lucky stars and cleared everything out that very day."

The dark-haired attorney leaned forward and smiled drily.

"Special Agent Bernstein, do you have any physical evidence to back up these patently absurd allegations?"

"Not yet," Jake admitted, turning to the NCIs, "but these two investigators will make it their life's quest to find some. Isn't that right?" he asked the two ensigns.

Mary Lou and Javier nodded curtly, but Jake could see the defeat in their eyes. They'd bungled badly and a killer would go free.

The lawyer harrumphed. "Circumstantial evidence won't even get you a return phone call from JAG or the Attorney General's office."

The attorney was correct.

Jake smiled crookedly and stood up. "Maybe not, but a suspect with means, motive, and opportunity will swing the spotlight her way. And there's no statute of limitations on murder."

He was done. He'd painted the picture for the two NCIs. It was now their job to find the evidence they'd allowed to disappear. He said nothing to them as they left the precinct.

AN HOUR LATER, AFTER making two stops, Jake returned to Meg's apartment. Only to find her gone. One of the men in her security detail looked at the items he was carrying in his hands and told him she'd gone jogging around the UCSD campus with the other bodyguard in tow.

Jake knew what he had to do. To balance his life and to convince Meg that, despite his being a dickhead and asshole, she would enrich his life. And God knew...his life needed it.

But what could he do for her? Was hooking up with him going to enrich *her* life?

Glad he wore his sneakers, for his sore ankle was bothering him again, he limped to the spot where Meg always stopped to stretch on her way back from her loop around the campus. A patch of lawn by the Foreign Language building. Since it was Saturday, he hoped that few people would be milling around. Still, the rain had passed, and the sky gleamed brightly in the sunlight.

He found her there and approached with a bouquet of yellow roses and a black velvet jewelry box in his hands. She and the security guy saw him coming from thirty yards away and both froze in place. With her hands fixed on her waist, her expression dared him to come closer.

He smiled. It was time for him to eat humble pie.

"Okay," he said when he arrived at the patch of grass.

The security guy backed away a few feet but kept his alert stance. A knowing smile crept onto the man's face. Jake looked around. A few students, lounging nearby on the concrete steps, were elbowing each other, taking in the show. When Jake finally knelt, the wetness of the grass soaked his jeans. Some girls nearby giggled. But he ignored everything except Meg's shiny, expectant face as he held up the bouquet, which she took happily.

"I'm a jerk, a dickhead—"

Meg winced. "I don't want to hear that, Jake, because you're not."

He stopped to regroup. "I know I don't deserve you," he said, "but you're the best thing in my life. I-I..."

She smiled warmly. "Go on."

Man up, Bernstein, and spit it out.

"I love you, Meg Larsen." His voice cracked. He paused to swallow back tears so he could start again. "I know a good jewelry store." He opened the velvet box and showed her the diamond engagement ring.

She said nothing, but her smile grew wider.

Shit! Why is this so difficult?

His mind abruptly conjured up a visual of Meg and Chuck, the scuba-diving FBI agent, snuggled together on her couch in nothing but one big body towel. Suddenly, he found the courage to take the leap.

"*Können wir uns verloben?*" He shook his head and switched to English. "Can we get engaged? Will you give me a try? See how it works out?"

"Now you're talking, Jake Bernstein. Yes, I'd love to give you a try."

He stood up and heaved a sigh. "Thank God!"

Then he forgot the audience around them, pulled her into his arms, and kissed her soundly.

The End

About the Author

DONNA DEL ORO'S DREAM since childhood, when she used to create her own comic books and share them with her friends, has been to write fiction and escape the humdrum of ordinary life. As soon as she retired from teaching high school, which was a suspenseful adventure in itself, Donna turned to fiction writing. Becoming a member of Sisters in Crime—and its local chapter, Capitol Crimes—has helped her to learn the craft and share her knowledge of fiction writing.

Donna Del Oro writes romantic suspense and mystery-crime thrillers.

Her two latest romantic suspense books are part of *The Jake Bernstein FBI Thriller* series: *Undercover Lies* (Book One) and *Undercover in Silicon Valley* (Book Two). *Undercover in San Diego* is Book Three in this series.

Her paranormal thriller series, *The Delphi Bloodline* involves a young, clairvoyant artist and her consultations with homicide detectives. This series includes: *Athena's Secrets*, *Athena's Fears*, and *Athena's Dilemma*.

Her comedic romantic-suspense novel *Saving La Familia*, reflects the author's Hispanic heritage and won the Silver Falchion Award for Best Comedy-Suspense in 2022 and the Bronze Medal by the International Latino Book Awards Organization. The sequel to this award-winning novel, *Saving the Fool*, is also now available.

Find her books at: www.DonnaDelOroBooks.com

And www.Amazon.com/Books by Donna Del Oro

www.ingramcontent.com/pod-product-compliance
Lightning Source LLC
Chambersburg PA
CBHW060049260626
47160CB00005B/1635